AFIYA CLARKE

Chaos At The Throne

The selection begins

This book is dedicated to a little girl who's greatest dream was to become an author one day. May this be a reminder to you that all things are possible

Contents

Preface

These characters have a mind of their own and I just write what they tell me to

Acknowledgments

Firstly, I'd like to thank my mom (editor) for supporting my goals of becoming an author since the age of twelve. Chaos at The Throne never would've existed without her support.

I'd like to thank Tyra, a friend I made on tiktok who was kind enough to guide me every step of the way through my publishing process. @tyradotcom

Beta readers! Thank you for your honest feedback and encouraging words.

Last and certainly not least, my book cover artist TV, thank you so much for your amazing work. You can reach out to her with this link. https://www.behance.net/tvdidit

CHAPTER 1: New Beginnings

My brain was at war with my heart. The right decision was as clear as day but pride remained the dominant influence of my mind. Jason clenched his jaw with a sharpened glare, finally granting him that split second to intimidate me, the moment he tightened his fists.

"What? Why are you looking at me like that?" My anger intertwined with every vibration in my vocal cords.

"We have no choice. If we resist we'll be dragged into the kingdom by force. The outcome remains the same whether you like it or not. We're going." He tried to sound calm but the irritation in his voice was evident. I didn't care and I certainly did not want to go.

"Well I guess they're taking me by force because I'm not going," petulance chained to every word that peeled off my lips. It was as if the sky was blue and I argued that it was a shade of purple.

"Look around!" He raised his voice. I refused. I already knew what he was going to touch on next. We both slept on a couch, living in a shack without a bedroom. Just a room, a kitchen and the toilet. "We've been given an opportunity to live in the kingdom for three years, to live as nobles. Why do you have a problem with that?" He looked at me keenly, searching for the sign that would lead him to believe that I agreed with him.

"So what? You think this is a grand gesture of kindness?" I retaliated. I wasn't done. "It's not an opportunity if we're forced to do it. Why don't you understand that?" Jason's face was fuming, the temperature in the room dropped significantly. He didn't respond to me, he was concentrating on retaining his composure. At times like this I would apologise but I just couldn't throw in the towel this time. "What? Say something." I kept talking but fear was hidden in my words, I just hoped he didn't sense it. He looked at me then stammered. I could sense the anger but I yearned to hear what he was saying. "I can't hear a word you're saying." His chin tilted, he glanced at me this time and turned around.

"What, so you're walking off on me now?" I spluttered. He stopped but didn't turn around to face me. With his chin still tilted, he glanced at me from the corner of his eyes but still said nothing. "Well I guess this conversation is over and I'm not going anywhere…." I stopped talking as his body turned and he approached me boldly with heavy steps. He stood about three inches from me, invading my personal space; his chest, literally in my face. I always envied his height when he did shit like this. I tried to speak but this time he cut me off.

"So…."

"Go pack your things." His calm demeanor only amplified the intensity of his command. I raised my head and stared. His eyes were sharper than mine no doubt, but I couldn't care less. I tried to say no, but this time he didn't allow me to speak the full word into existence.

"NOW!" My chest squeezed and the hairs on my skin stood at attention. His voice, face, body-language, everything changed. The last time I saw him like this, he killed someone. That was two weeks ago. I diverted my eyes from his to remain calm. Seeing that I didn't move, his anger and frustration increased.

"We've finally gotten a chance to leave this dump, live in a castle for three years, but you want to stay because we have no choice but to go? You want to miss out on a life of living comfortably, not worrying about what our next meal will be for once, or if we'll have enough money to pay our land lord in time. Sometimes we go days without eating just to afford a place to stay. I'm not going to let your pride spoil this opportunity that we've been given." He bent his head towards me and raised my chin, forcing me to look into his eyes. "Go pack your things and let's go. Don't make me repeat myself."

The temperature of my skin rose rapidly, my body was burning. I pushed hard against his chest to get him away from me but he only flinched. "My problem is not living in the castle, Jason. My problem is fighting among a bunch of girls over a MAN!" I screamed. He arched his brow and bit his bottom lip. I was uncertain whether that was a gesture of guilt or if he was holding back from saying something. "I don't know the guy Jason. I'M NOT interested."

"I'm being forced to compete for a woman that I don't know either, but I'm not complaining," He responded, trying to make my point seem invalid. He said his words with no remorse, I was disgusted.

"That's because you're a typical guy. Of course it doesn't bother you." I rolled my eyes. "You're probably interested in her and that's dumb because you don't know her." He stumbled a bit, I guess my words finally got to him, but then a smirk escaped his lips.

"I'm a typical guy? Now that's funny," he grinned. "I'm not interested in her either, I'm looking at the bigger picture. We'd be fools to turn down this opportunity, but you're right, this isn't an opportunity, we're forced to go, but aren't you happy to leave this place?"

"Yes, but…." I muttered feeling a bit defeated. I looked around the room. I couldn't believe we called this dump a house. The yellow paint was definitely past its expiration date and was already peeling off the walls. The wooden boards that tiled the floor showed the consequences of countless relationships it had with the millions of termites that roamed our place. Our only furniture were two ancient brown couches, a termite infested center table and a worn out closet.

"Yes we're forced to be in this competition, but who said we had to compete?" Jason continued. "Participants are sent home periodically when the prince is no longer interested in what they have to offer. And, most importantly we're given a reward every month based on how well we impress or interest …."

"I know how it works," I interrupted. What he said made sense. I guessed it was worth a try. "So basically we can compete but not try to win."

"Exactly." Jason nodded, satisfied that we finally came to an agreement. "We need to play smart, we want to lose but not be hated. So instead of making them dislike us, we should be irrelevant."

I grinned slightly. I was definitely satisfied with his plan. "So basically anything that we're required to do, once we don't do it to the best of our abilities we're good," I stated. I observed his reaction, trying to figure out where his head was at. But all I got was a gentle smile of relief. It wasn't much to work with. I figured it was best to ask what his true intentions were and get rid of my curiosity. "So, earlier you mentioned that we've been given the opportunity to live a better life for three years." He arched his brow again but I wasn't finished. "Does that mean that you're going to try to last that long?"

His face didn't change much, just a guilty smile that he tried to hide. He grinned and walked away, planting himself comfortably on the couch. "Pack your things Amaris." His words were bland, leading me to believe that he was hiding something.

"I want to know what your intentions are," I demanded. All I wanted was honesty, but something as simple as that was rare between us. He let out a loud sigh and rolled his eyes. He always told the truth when he rolled his eyes.

"I just want a chance of living a better life. If we can, I'm going to look for a job over there, probably be a soldier or something. If we get knocked out in a year it's cool. The rewards we'll get monthly should be enough for us to start over." His words were grave so I believed him.

"So just to be clear, you don't care about winning right?" I questioned again. I could tell that he was irritated, but I just had to be sure. This time when he looked at me his eyes were cold and the loud sigh he made had me regretting that I asked.

"Amaris, I do not know the woman. Why would I, fight to win the heart of someone that I don't love?" He bent his head and waited on a response.

"I guess I'll go pack my bags," I stammered, a little upset even though I had no reason to be. We didn't have a room so our clothes were packed in two boxes that were stacked against the wall. One box would've been enough to fit both our clothes, but for the sake of privacy, we separated them. I packed everything I owned, which wasn't much anyway so storage wasn't an issue. I stared at my clothes and laughed, I couldn't help it. The whole situation was just comical to me.

"What's all the laughing about?" Jason asked, intrigued.

"Our life's a joke Jason. My best dress and your best suit isn't even something the servants in the kingdom would wear." Doubts ran through my mind, I had no intentions of embarrassing myself among a bunch of rich people.

"And so what?" Jason shrugged his shoulders and rotated his neck. The cracking sounds stemming from this gesture made me cringe. "We're not going there to impress anyway. We're basically going to lose," he continued. Clearly he did not understand what my true issue was.

"Jason we're going to draw a lot of attention to ourselves if we go to the palace dressed in filthy rags. It'd be even worse when we enter the castle claiming that we're a selected pair. We can't just…."

"What do you suggest we do buy something nice?" he interrupted. "We can't afford to. And these aren't rags these are just old clothes."

"They're going to see it as rags Jason." The thought of negatively being the centre of attention troubled me. But there's nothing that could've been done about it so I had to accept reality and move on. "I don't care what they see me as, I will…"

"Good, so stop complaining," Jason nagged. Choosing to keep my mouth shut, I bit my tongue, recognizing that sometimes silence was the most effective way to handle him. "Are you finished packing?" he asked, his tone still laced with an undertone of impatience. In the corner of the box beneath my clothes, a smaller box remained hidden. Seeing that box caused an instant shift in my emotions.

"No," I muttered, suddenly finding it difficult to breathe. I opened the box which contained the last gift my mother had given me before the incident happened; a simple leather necklace with a ring for a pendant and a plastic bottle which contained a perfume that smelt like a splash of berries. I held it against my chest and muttered "I miss you."

"You said something?" Jason asked. I rolled my eyes and said no. And just like that, I was breathing comfortably again. "We need to leave now Amaris." He stressed on my name, it irritated me; clearly he was anxious to leave but a part of me still wanted to stay. "The castle is three hours away, we need to be there for six and its three o'clock," he continued. "Are you going with your hair like that?"

My hair rebelled in a frizzy mess, exposing the fact that it wasn't naturally straight. I passed a flat iron through it a week earlier but by the second day it was already a mess. "I'll deal with that after I put on my clothes," I assured him. I took my outfit of choice and left to change. Claustrophobic people won't survive a minute in there. There were no tiles, just a concrete dusty floor. Cracks were all over the walls from the few earthquakes that the building survived. The glass of the mirror was shattered with some pieces still holding on. I stared at myself for a minute, a pep talk was definitely needed.

"You're only going there for a year, so just relax. Time will fly quickly like it always does." My words weren't convincing enough but it was worth the try. I changed into a short flared blue dress. It was very simple; no patterns, just a round neck and short sleeves. I passed the flat iron through my hair four times on each section until it was bone straight again. I hid behind the straightened hair to look acceptable in Mandora. I never saw another person that looked like me other than my deceased mother.

I slammed the door and left with my things in hand. Jason turned to say something, but then he froze and stared. "You look just like mom..."

"I know," I interrupted. I didn't want to talk about it. "Let's go."

CHAPTER 2: Do You Care Now?

We used our rent money for a ride to the kingdom's capital on two horses. Initially, we requested a ride straight to the castle but that wasn't allowed. The journey lasted a little more than two hours, which meant that we had less than an hour to reach our destination. The change was drastic. Back home was just withering trees or small plants suffocated by malicious weeds, coarse dirt and wooden rotten houses that were falling apart.

On our journey, we saw the surrounding houses steadily grow in size, durability and attractiveness. I paid attention to the people dressed in identical clothing while landlords gave orders for work they'd never do themselves. I witnessed one of the workers being beaten and based on the shouts coming from the one inflicting the punishment, it seemed that the issue was something about a lady's hair pin being stolen. When we reached the Kingdom's capital, everything was just…. Different. We looked different. I looked different.

The riders dropped us off at the copper gates that stood tall and shone with elegance. A display of fire and mist surrounding what seemed to be a sword was carved into it. It was the kingdom's crest. I didn't quite get it but I didn't care much for it either. There were two sentinels that stood guarding the gate, fully dressed in copper coated armour. It looked weird but I paid no mind. They watched us keenly as we passed by and then finally one of them said something.

"Who are you? You're not from here." He gripped my arm and pulled me away from Jason. Puzzled by his actions, I pulled back and escaped his grip. I then felt another thug on my arm. It was Jason; he grabbed me closely and whispered in my ear. "Look above you, to the right and to the left." I raised my head and looked at the corner of my eyes. Guards in silver armour stood on the copper coloured walls of the kingdom, each one looking closely at us ready to make a move. But no weapons were seen on them. I was confused, how could they attack with no weapons?

"We're here to see the royal family," I explained. I dug into my bag and showed them the letter. A stamp with the kingdom's crest was on it so they had to believe me. The second guard stood behind us. He pressed the grip of the sword harshly in my brother's back but hid his provoking actions while standing behind him. Jason hid his emotions by keeping a calm composure but I could feel him breathing heavily down the side of my face since he stood right beside me. My personal space was invaded, but he did this to protect me. The guard stared at us harshly after reading the letter.

"You two are a selected pair? Nonsense..." he stammered. The guard behind us grinned. "They'll never make it." As I raised my head the letter was thrown at me, unfortunately I missed it. I picked it up quickly and placed it in my bag. "You may go now," he said.

"Aren't you going to apologize?" Jason goaded. I slapped my hand against my forehead loudly. The last thing I wanted was Jason speaking his mind. We both had self-control issues but he had it worse and it had resulted in him killing some people, but he did it to protect me. I grabbed his arm and ran through the gates and into the kingdom's capital. Pulling his weight while running took a strain on me so it wasn't long before I stopped to take deep breaths.

"I was wondering when you were going to stop," Jason teased. "Why did you do that? Have you no pride?"

"I would've lasted longer if we had eaten something last night or this morning," I snapped. "We don't have time to spend babbling with guards, we're late." He didn't say anything he just stared at me with an arched brow. It was disturbing. "What? Why aren't you saying anything?" I panted, swerving side to side a bit.

"You're starving aren't you? Your face is turning pale again. On our way here you had problems focusing as well. We should stop to get something to eat," he insisted. He was right, I was incredibly hungry. The kingdom's capital was basically a market, where items and food were sold at almost every corner. The structures around us were huge and detailed, nothing like what we had at home. The materials used to build were much stronger, more expensive and certainly much more pleasing to the eyes than what we've ever encountered. I looked down and something about the floor's appearance just caught my attention.

"Jason look at the ground, there's a copper tile path," I explained. He looked at me then grinned. I guess he thought that because I was amazed by something so simple that it was funny.

"You're only now noticing that?" he laughed. "So when are you going to notice that everyone is staring at us, especially you."

I looked around again. It was as though everyone stopped what they were doing to look at us. Some even tried to listen to our conversation. We looked homeless compared to them; my best dress wasn't enough to fit in, I stood out, but in a bad way.

"I knew that our clothes would........"

"It's not the clothes," Jason interrupted. "Do you see anyone else that looks like you? Don't forget, people like you are rare in Mandora." Everything finally made sense, I felt less insecure about my outfit. To be honest, it wasn't that bad. I dug into my purse to see what we could afford.

"We have seven pieces of silver remaining," I said.

"At home that's enough money to last us three days, but we're in the kingdom's capital so it's expensive here. We're going to live in the castle anyway so we'll be treated well. Let's see what we can afford for the both of us," Jason suggested. Food was sold at almost every corner but the prices were too high and the lines were too long. We couldn't risk being late. We kept walking until we encountered a fruit vendor. A senior lady that took charge, but her area was tight, very small. The line wasn't long, just five people ahead of us. She was our best option.

"I'll stand in line and buy us two apples. It's three pieces of silver for one," I said. Jason didn't object, he stood beside me and nodded his head in agreement. The lady attending to the customers appeared to be weak and frail so service was slow. Finally after five minutes of waiting, I was next in line. Suddenly, someone grazed my shoulder and skipped passed me. The person smelled expensive but he did not dress expensive.

He wore a black cloak with a hoodie on. My guess was that he didn't want his identity to be known. Jason tilted his head with his left brow arched to his hairline. He took a step or two forward but I kicked him. He stepped back and allowed me to me handle it. The person was engaged in conversation with the old lady. Judging from the voice, I could tell that it was a young man. All I wanted was two apples for my brother and I, why couldn't he pass by later, why now?

"Good day miss Maple, I just came to check up on you." He said. It surprised me that a guy who displayed such poor etiquette as he pushed past the line of customers showed care and concern toward the vendor. The old lady looked happy to see him but her reaction was confusing. She tilted her head a bit but he stopped her. "No don't do that, not here."

"Why are you here my..."

"Don't call me that either. Shhh," he interrupted. "Like I said I'm just here to see you."

"You shouldn't be here right now!" she scolded. "You should be in the castle right now. You're going to be late. You have about twenty more minutes remaining. Where is your sister?!"

"She's already there Ms. Maple. Relax, I'll be there in 5 minutes if I travel by horse. I won't be late.

"You better behave over there young man." Her words were stern but she said it kindly. I couldn't take it anymore I had to say something.

"What do you mean, I'm ....."

"Excuse me, I've been standing in line here for too long," I interrupted. "I did not come here just for this guy to skip me and engage in conversation. I'm hungry." Irritated by my complaint, the old lady slammed the table and glared at me.

"How dare you!" she screamed. "Do you know who's in front

13

of you right now?"

Jason stood beside me and scratched his head. He wasn't interested in petty arguments, he just wanted to eat and so did I. Her yelling made my headache worsen. I just wanted to lay down somewhere and get a head massage. Her response aggravated me, I couldn't think clearly, I just spoke my mind.

"No. I don't know who he is and I don't care." I stammered. The tall figure before me turned around and took off his hoodie. He looked at me and smirked, but his smirking didn't last long when his mischievous eyes laid eyes on me.

"There's another one?" he muttered. His eyes were a malicious green colour, I noticed it first. His jawline was sharp and his blonde hair had a nice smooth wavy texture with some light brown hues that he styled into a messy bun.

"Do you care now?" he grinned. Everyone around us bowed, but I was too light-headed to think or act right. Eating something was the only thing on my mind. Jason hissed at me but I paid him no mind. This guy in front of me was too bold, he looked like he was accustomed to getting whatever he wanted. His stupid statement 'Do you care now' upset me.

"What is there to care about? Please move," I requested. Although I was upset and even though I shouted, I still had to end my words with some manners because my mother taught me well. Murmuring began, everyone was talking but I couldn't quite hear what they were saying.

"HOW DARE YOU!" someone shouted behind me. The man standing before me said nothing, he looked just as confused as I was, but his attention was focused on me. I turned around to address the person that yelled at me, but everyone including my brother was bowing on the floor. I couldn't think right, I was too weak to process everything. I just stood there and stared.

"BOW! You insolent fool!" the vendor shouted. "You think that because you're a rare gem in Mandora you can do as you please?"

"No, there's no need. Everyone rise," the man said. He said his words with authority, by then I knew that he was a noble. I could still sense his presence behind me, his scent became much stronger. I looked at Jason for help but he laughed gently and looked away. "Don't look at me, you got yourself into this mess, so get yourself out," he grinned. I just insulted a noble and all he could think about was acting petty because I kicked him.

I felt a heavy tap on my shoulder behind me. I was hoping that it was Jason but Jason stood before me and his laughter increased. My heart squeezed as I turned around.

"Do you care now?" he asked again with a sickening smirk on his face. It triggered me. I wanted him gone, out of my sight, but he continued. "I'd like to continue my conversation with Ms. Maple." He stared at me waiting for my response. That disgusting smirk remained on his face.

"Look I don't know who you are but I just want....." I was unable to finish my statement. My stomach gave out on me, I felt as though my innards were being replaced by a black hole. The nausea crept from my abdomen to my head and my world went black. With one step forward I crumbled into his arms. The last thing I heard was Jason shouting my name.

CHAPTER 3: No

I wasn't unconscious, just weak and unbalanced. "Put me down I'm fine," I mumbled. My words weren't as deceiving as I wanted them to be.

"Is that your way of saying thank you?" the guy asked. I sensed frustration and annoyance in his voice, but in my opinion he had no right to be upset. He should've waited in line to talk to his friend; then I would've gotten something to eat and last two hours well on feet.

"To people like you, of course," I said my words with no hesitation. People like him upset me the most.

"Is that so?" he responded. His arms loosened and I fell, ass first to the ground. I gasped for air as the pain struck me. I turned around to curse him but his back was already faced towards me. He was engaged in another conversation with the old lady. I dug into the dirt and pulled myself up with the little bit of strength I had remaining. After maintaining my balance Jason brushed passed my shoulder causing me to be unstable on my feet once more

16

"Stay right there and don't cause any more trouble," he said softly. His words escaped through clenched teeth which made it barely audible for me to understand. But after his eyes sharpened when he looked at me I interpreted the message clearly. I kept my mouth shut and watched everything unfold as Jason took over. Things didn't go so well when I dealt with it. To be fair, I didn't know who he was, if I knew I would've acted differently to begin with. Secondly, the impression I had of the stranger's personality, caused me to feel disgusted and was no small contribution to my handling of the matter. I concurred that it was for the best that Jason should now take charge of the situation.

After taking a few steps forward to approach the guy, Jason stood two feet away from him and tapped his shoulder, trying to engage in a conversation with him. "Excuse me sir but….." The guy barely turned his neck, it was a very slight movement, almost as if he didn't do anything at all. His green iris moved swiftly to the corner of his eyes staring sharply at Jason. Those eyes looked familiar. Death always followed the look of those eyes every time I've seen it. Jason returned the favour and gave him the same stare. The stare of Blood lust. The young man carried his left hand across his shoulder and vigorously grabbed on to Jason's arm, flipping him over his back without hesitation. Jason landed on his feet gracefully, but his arm was still trapped in the guy's hand. The man used his right hand and gripped the upper part of Jason's arm. The tension between them increased and a crowd appeared.

"Leave now! All of you!" the man demanded. Everyone scattered. Jason stared at his arm as the guy tightened his grip, almost feeling his bones being squeezed.

"Break my arm, or dislocate it and I will kill you today," Jason

17

threatened. His eyes got colder and his face lost all signs of emotions. The guy leaned back, still holding on to Jason and grinned.

"What's my name?" he asked.

Jason stared at him harder, confused by his question. "I don't know, why do you ask?"

"My name's Joel," he said. Jason's expression didn't change. He shrugged his shoulder and rotated his neck.

"Ok," Jason replied. There was no interest in his voice whatsoever. Joel slowly loosened his grip. Jason took that opportunity and pulled himself free. The temperature dropped significantly low again, a gust of cold wind surrounded Jason. "I don't care what your name is, I won't hesitate to kill you if you….."

"If I what? You're mad that I dropped your girlfriend on the floor so you want to fight?" Joel interrupted. Jason flinched slightly, a slight grin escaped his lips.

"Girlfriend….." he laughed. "That's my sister. I don't care about you dropping her, you can do it again if you like. You flipped me over basically asking for a fight when I approached you."

"Sister….." Joel mumbled. He turned his attention to me and then stared at Jason. "You two don't look alike." He continued. "You really don't know who I am….." he laughed

"Is it that we don't look alike, or are you just shocked that she's black and I'm white?" Jason stated. "But that doesn't matter," he continued. "We'd just like to buy two apples and we'd be on our way. We're running la…."

"I'm sorry but I bought the last two," Joel interrupted. The temperature around us went back to normal.

I got tired of waiting, tired of listening, and it was all in vain.

"Let's go Jason," I interrupted.

"I'm not leaving till we get you something to eat," he insisted.

I sighed deeply. We had less than half an hour to get to the castle with all the time we wasted. "I'm not buying anything here. This woman's customer's service is terrible let's go," I protested. We weren't dressed in accordance with the expected standard of the castle therefore, it occurred to me that reaching last or even late will automatically call unwanted, negative attention to us. "We're running terribly late Jason let's go," I demanded. "Look at your watch and tell me the time. I'm pretty sure they'd serve us food at the castle anyway. We...."

"It's fifteen minutes to six. You're right, let's go," he interrupted. His tone was harsh, I could tell that he just wanted me to shut up. I was too physically weak to continue arguing with him. It wasn't worth it. We were about to leave but the guy I disliked just had to barge in.

"So you two are siblings and you're expected to be at the castle for six pm. Are you participants for the event this evening?" Joel asked.

"Yes we are," Jason responded. "If you don't mind can you....."

Joel let out a scandalous laugh. He paused then looked at us and laughed again. I didn't get it but I knew that we were a joke to him. "I'm one of the prince's closest friends, I may actually be his right hand man soon. The prince isn't used to bold girls like you with no manners. I don't think you're his type. He's more used to young ladies that carry about themselves properly and have respect," he babbled.

"Blah blah blah all this crap you talk," I snapped. "It won't be a problem if he doesn't like me, especially if he's someone like you....."

"Someone like me?" he retaliated. "Would you care to

explain?"

"Gladly," I said with my head held high and folded arms. "You're just a noble asshole that takes advantage of his title to get what he wants, no matter how it affects others. A typical noble actually,"

"I'm not just any typical noble, but I'll be a part of this competition. The information you've given me is quite valuable, thank you for that," he admitted. His ending statement was sarcastic and followed by a shy smirk on his lips. I thought the conversation was over, but he continued. "We have approximately thirteen minutes to reach our main destination. I'm a noble, I should be there already. Its five minutes away on horse and twenty minutes if you walk. You're late because of me so I'll offer you a ride."

The world froze for a split second and my eyes widened. Clearly he'd know that my answer would be......

"Thank you for your generosity, we gladly accept," Jason answered. "You saved us big time. We owe you one.

"You don't owe me anything, it's the least I can do for holding back you two. Now let's go, like I said we're running late, especially me," he laughed. "I'm a noble after all, I should be there already."

No.... my answer would've been no.

CHAPTER 4: Change of Plans

If he truly regretted holding us back he could've just given us some money. He's a noble, soon to be the prince's right hand man, at least that's what he claimed. Surely he's used to throwing his money around, isn't that what nobles did? Following him all over the place wasn't something I would ever have looked forward to, and doing so was a pain on my soul. We followed him like stray dogs looking for a new owner, while he walked around boldly with a proud smile painted on his face. I was almost certain that it was just for show.

Everywhere we went eyes followed along with the footsteps of nosey people. All eyes were on him but I got the feeling that they were looking at me too. I didn't quite get it when everyone said that I'm rare, but now I've noticed that I'm the only person with darker skin. I hadn't realised it before as there weren't many people back at the village. Not a single person that I've seen in Mandora thus far was like me, except for my mother. I had made up my mind to keep my hair straightened to fit in at least a little, even though I didn't fit in at all, but if my true hair texture was obvious, the attention I received would've been much more intense.

I never knew how stupid women could be until I walked with a noble womanizer. Cries of "We love you sir!" and "Would you marry me?" echoed through the crowd of women, desperately trying to get Joel's attention. I was surprised to see him actually responding to them, but then again, what was there to be surprised about? A grin peeled across his lips as he prepared to speak, he made no effort to hide how much he was enjoying it.

"I'm sorry, but you know I can't do that given the circumstances that I'm in." His smile grew even larger. Pride. He probably had more of it in his veins than blood. As we passed by everyone bowed at us, and not wanting to stand out any more than I already did, I bowed back. I thought it was a fair enough reason to do so, I never had to go through anything like that in the village. It's not like I was a noble or that I deserved praise, I was just a poor commoner girl. Joel caught my movements from the corner of his eye and locked eyes with me. His chin was tilted slightly as he kept in connection with me, but his stare didn't last long as he turned his head and kept walking. There it was, that stupid smirk of his again, I just met him and already didn't like him, seeing him grin at me made my blood boil.

His pace suddenly slowed and before I knew it, I crashed face first into his back. Many inappropriate words came to mind, but with all those people around I knew better than to say what was on my mind. Instead, I squeezed his fluffy black cloak to suppress my anger and let out a loud sigh.

"Damn it..." I muttered. My nose burned, it had suffered the most from the collision. I could almost hear Jason grinning behind me. I had always felt the urge to laugh when he laughed. His small, simple actions always made me feel somewhat better at times, because he was an asshole. A slight grin managed to slip unto my face, but it wasn't allowed to last very long.

"What do you think you're doing?" Joel groaned, "Stop, you're embarrassing me. You're accompanying me, you shouldn't be bowing to those that are bowing to me, and now you look even more stupid bumping into me!" His words were stern and harsh, and he, making a scene was an embarrassment that I could have done without. Then, without another word, his stupid smile appeared once more as he turned his head and resumed walking.

I can tolerate harsh words to an extent, but I couldn't handle someone shouting at me. It only took a split second for the crowd around us to burst into laughter. Stupid remarks swept through the air for my ears to hear. "She may be a rare and pretty, but she sure is dumb."

I kept my head down and continued walking. The manner in which Joel spoke to me struck at my very core. My heart sunk, I hated the fact that a scumbag like him could get to me, but it was beyond my control. Harsh words and their loud delivery always had an effect on me, so I remained timid with my face down. Not only was I embarrassed, but I was somewhat hurt as well.

Just when I thought things couldn't possibly get any worse, I collided with him once more. He turned to face me, his fists clenched tightly, and let out a loud sigh. His warm breath swatted against my face as he breathed heavily through his nose. A bitten apple soared out of the crowd, and if the intended target was my head, then the thrower's aim was impeccable. A slight sound escaped Joel's lips, but before he could say a word I brushed past his shoulder and skipped ahead of him. The very moment my body made contact with his, the entire crowd turned silent. I stopped and turned to face him, disbelief was all over his face, I couldn't tell if he was upset, but he definitely was not happy. He spoke softly but sternly. "What do you think you're doing?"

Jason hissed at me, seeking my attention. His arms were folded so I guess he was chill. He nodded his neck slightly to the left with his eyes wide open. It was basically him indicating that I should undo whatever it was I did.

"I'm leaving, I'll go to the castle on my own." The words flew out my mouth without hesitation, without thinking. I wanted to take it back but I didn't bother. I wanted to be free anyway so why not try?

Tension emerged as Joel took a few steps towards me. He stopped and gave me a lopsided smile. It was clearly fake but unfolded into a genuine grin when he stared at me for a few seconds. "Are you really doing this right now?" he asked. He clenched his jaw and looked away for a moment. He held back from saying something.

"Yes I'm serious. I don't need your help for anything and you definitely don't need my company." My voice grew a little louder and more aggressive than it should've been. I took another step back and muttered an apology.

"I'm sorry."

His eyes turned narrow, rigid and cold. I didn't know how to respond to a look like that. It was blood curdling; my body trembled and the hair on my skin rose. "Don't look at me like that." I kept my tone down so that only he could hear me. He sighed at me and looked away. I flinched like a coward and

24

cleared my throat, as if that made anything better.

"So you really think that you're going to make it to the castle on your own in this current state?" Joel questioned.

"What's my current state!?" I blurted. Every second I spent with him annoyed me, but his bold statements couldn't be more aggravating.

"You collapsed in my arms because you haven't eaten since... ..whenever. Do you even know where you're going?"

"Yes I know where I'm going. I'm a very observant person."

"Ok fine." His words were sarcastic. I sensed frustration in his tone but he hid those emotions behind that mask he called a face. The awkward silence didn't last long. Jason had his two cents to put in, but my mind was already made up.

"Amaris are you for real right now? You can't...."

"I can and I will!" I snapped. "I know where I'm going." I really did, it wasn't hard to figure out. Jason made a few steps towards me but wasn't able to past three. Joel blocked him by stretching out his arm in his way.

"No, let her go."

"Are you dumb? Remove your hand." He removed his arm but not the way everyone expected him to. He gripped Jason by his collar and pulled him closer, to the point where his lips were centimeters away from his ear. He whispered something, it seemed a bit sinister to me. Jason never smirked when it came to my safety but he did this time.

"Go ahead. Leave." Jason's face was slowly turning red and his eyes were watery. His cheeks were bloated and there was that stupid smirk that he struggled to get rid of. This fool was trying not to laugh.

"What's so funny?" I asked. I didn't see what there was to joke about.

25

"Didn't you say that you were leaving? We're not going to beg you to stay with us. Just go."

I was triggered, but that's just an understatement. My body froze. Didn't stay frozen for long when Joel got me heated.

"How did you think this would've turned out? Me asking for an apology and begging you to stay?" Joel babbled.

"I'm leaving." I turned around and started walking. Jason yelled at me like the idiot he was.

"Byeeeeeee…."

"Let's see how long she lasts." Joel whispered. It wasn't meant for me to hear but I heard it. I kept walking and didn't turn back, the only thing that went through my head were his last words. 'Let's see how long she lasts.' I wondered what that even meant.

CHAPTER 5: Caught

My intentions were different from what they thought. I managed to stay ahead of them for a while but my main goal was to lose them. I promised my brother to try, I promised him to go, but people broke promises all the time. It wouldn't be considered a crime if I did. He talked as if we had nothing. We really did have nothing, but starting over was always an option. What I desired most was a stable location, a safe location, we always moved every three months as if we were on the run from something or someone. We were at a better place now, a richer place with potential opportunities. I observed the stores around me, silently critiquing them to determine which one would be best suited for me.

My attention was drawn to the left, with my nose leading the way. The smell of pastries enticed me, leading me to this bakery with a sign at the front which announced, 'Employees Wanted.' I froze for a moment and my pores raised. I was in denial at first but at this point I had to accept that I was being followed.

I looked over my shoulder, I tried to act like I didn't notice but they scattered into the shadows.

'If anything happens I'll just scream or cry out for help,' I thought.

I pushed the door open and entered. My heart squeezed, I didn't know why but it did. It wasn't an active store with plenty customers. It was small, a little cramped, but it was definitely going to be my best option. I was excited, a bit nervous, but very optimistic. The entire place was made of wood. The floor, walls, ceiling, chairs and tables were made from the same ash-brown coloured wood. I stood in the middle of the bakery, just staring. The seats and tables were so smooth, no termites at all. They had lights on their ceiling whilst Jason and I used candles. These elements were luxury to me although the people in the bakery seemed quite indifferent about it.

"Excuse me miss can I help you?"

I was so focused on admiring the store that I didn't notice the gentleman standing before me, nor did I notice that all eyes were on me. I probably drew attention to myself since I just stood there staring for two minutes, or maybe it was because I looked different. Judging from the young man's attire, I could tell that he was a worker. He was neat and his hair was well groomed but what gave it away was his copper coloured tag on his shirt collar. It was an identity card with his name on it. 'Ruben'. I couldn't have been happier to meet an employee, it just made things easier.

"Yes. Actually, I read the sign on the wall outside and it brought me here. Is there room available for one more worker? I'm looking for a job." After saying those words, nervousness kicked in. Doubts ran through my mind, I began to think that a peasant girl like me didn't deserve the job. His face lit up with a smile and all my doubts vanished.

"Sure. You're hired." Those words came out his mouth too easily. His smile seemed genuine but I was no fool. There's no way someone can get a job that easily. He definitely had an objective in mind, but as long as I was getting paid there was no problem. I smiled at him and played off my suspicions.

"So when do I start?"

His smile grew wider. "You can start right now if you'd like," he said. This time my face gave it away and my tongue reacted on its own.

"Huh?" I stuttered and took a step back. He looked at me and grinned. It didn't seem like he had bad intentions but his actions were showing so many red flags.

"Relax, I'm thrilled to have you here. Someone like you will bring us plenty customers." He said those words with ease. I wasn't upset I just didn't know how to feel. He clearly just wanted me to work here because of my melanin.

"I'm sorry but who are you exactly?" I questioned. It didn't make sense that I'd just walked in, talk to an employee and get hired. I didn't even meet the manager.

"Sorry, I forget to introduce myself, you're probably thinking that I'm ill-mannered. My name is Ruben and my father is the owner of this place." He folded his arms and took a step forward. Flaunting authority seemed to be a common trait among these people. He leaned a bit closer till I felt the air that escaped his nostrils in between my eyes. "Is that enough information for you or should I tell you more?" Pride.

"Pride, pride, pride, he's just another Joel," I muttered. Luckily he didn't hear; he just saw my lips moving.

"Speak up, I can't hear you pretty." I wasn't sure I heard that 'p' word right, but it sounded like he said "pretty"

"Pretty?" I stuttered.

"Yes pretty, that's your nickname. I would've said gorgeous but that would've raised your confidence a little too high." He stared at me looking for a reaction. I didn't know how to respond. My face showed no emotions. No words came to mind either but I had to break the silence.

"Okay," I responded. My vocabulary was scarce as all the words I knew seemed to have vacated my brain. It appeared that the same had happened to him. He stuttered for a moment and took a step back.

"Is that it?" His voice got deeper and his smile faded.

"What? What is it?"

"N-nothing, your shift starts now so just follow me. You'll take the customers' orders." At this point I battled between heading to the castle or staying. I felt an awkward vibe between us but I couldn't let that interfere with making a good impression on my first day. He took me to the cash register where a brunet girl with rosy red checks stood. I looked at her and smiled, she stared at me frozen for a moment with her lips trembling a little. A broad bright smile with happy teeth slipped through.

"Oh …. My……..GOD!" She stammered, then let out a screeching scream. I covered my ears then played it off with a smile. "Can I please shake your hand?" she squealed. Ruben intervened and forced himself between us.

"No need for formalities now, we have a business to run. She'll be working at the cash register for today," He stated.

"IS THAT SO!?" A dominant voice swept through the room, loud and demanding, followed by a different harsh and aggressive voice.

"WHAT DO YOU THINK YOU'RE DOING!?" the other

shouted. The voices were so familiar that it made my blood crawl. The place got silent for a moment and then instantly the sound of tables and chairs dragging on the floor, followed by the footsteps of people running out the building was heard. Judging by the men's voices I already knew who they were. My instincts urged me to run out the building like everyone else, but I stood there frozen, hesitating to make a move. The voices had come from behind me and I had no desire to turn and face them. I had no intentions of being involved.

Ruben brushed passed me and stepped forward. "H-how can I help you….."

"It's not you it's her," they both interrupted. I turned around quickly with the broadest fake smile on my face.

"O hey Jason…. And the guy I don't really like."

CHAPTER 6: *Long Ride*

For the short time that I had met Joel, he always had that annoying smirk on his face but this time he didn't, and for the first time I wished he did. Jason's tone was harsher than Joel's so I chose not to look at his face. I looked at his chest when I talked, it was easier that way.

Joel snapped but quickly caught himself trying to compose his words properly. "WHAT THE……what are you doing here?"

I fumbled with my fingers a bit trying to distract myself from looking at his face, but he wouldn't allow me to. "LOOK AT ME AND SPEAK." His tone turned harshly aggressive all of a sudden, causing my lips to tremble uncontrollably.

"I was just going to buy a cupcake and…."

"Behind the cash register? What were you planning to do to get those cupcakes?" he interrupted. He was beyond angry. I wasn't even given the opportunity to speak a proper sentence in his presence. Just when I thought things couldn't get any worse Ruben pushed through with his unwanted words.

"She came to me for a job, not cupcakes. That's why she was behind the register, there's nothing fishy going on."

"A JOB!? So you really didn't have any intentions of going to the castle did you?" Jason snapped. Now the both of them were pissed. At this point it didn't make sense for me to sugar coat anything.

"We're leaving. Now." Joel groaned. He tugged my arm and dragged me along, placing me in between them.

"But I haven't even eaten what I– "

"Here...." He stretched out his arm, offering me one of the apples he bought. "Take it."

I didn't want to take it because it was his, but I had to toss my pride aside and eat something. I wouldn't last ten more minutes without it anyway.

"I'm sorry," I stammered. Joel's green eyes stared sharply.

"What did you say?"

"I said that I'm–"

"The liar said that she's sorry. Probably ready to play the victim as usual," Jason retorted. It pained a little, having to hold back my thoughts; it wasn't my place to talk back. I gave my word and I broke it.

"I'm serious. I have no intentions of playing victim. I'm owning up to the stunt I just pulled."

"Well good for you." Jason squeezed my arm and handled me like a soldier capturing a criminal.

"Jason that's unnecessary, you're hurting me," I complained.

"No, this is how you should be treated. You lost both our trust," Joel stated. "Stop making a fuss, everyone's attention is already drawn to us, don't give them more reason to stare," he whispered harshly. His black cloak was on with the hoodie over his head and he bent his head downwards.

"What are you hiding from?" I asked. His response was plain.

"The less you know the better. At this point in time I'm a wanted person on the loose." He said those words so simple as if nothing was wrong.

"E-excuse me?" I stammered.

"It doesn't matter. I'm a wanted person in our area too," Jason commented. I was shocked to see him open up so easily as if Joel was a safe person to talk to. Joel's vibe suddenly changed. His voice got deeper and he spoke slower.

"O really? Why?" he asked.

"I killed three men two days ago because they tried to rape my – "

"That's enough!" I snapped. Jason released way too much information to someone we had just met. "We barely know him why will you tell him all that?"

"It's okay, we're both wanted people. What…. You think he's going to rat me out?" At this point I didn't know if my brother was dumb or in denial. I raised my voice at him to see if he'd come back to his senses.

"I don't want our personal information being spread to STRANGERS!"

"That was dumb of me, I apologise."

"That's not the only issue!" I snapped. "You can't trust him, he's lying."

"Excuse me?" Joel interrupted.

"How can you be hiding your face with your cloak cause you're wanted when you walked around the streets earlier praised by women. You didn't care about being caught earlier didn't you? You didn't care when you walked in the bakery either."

"As I said, I'm the prince's right hand man and they're probably looking for me right now. I'll be in trouble if they find me here."

"I had a feeling that's what you meant when you said that you were wanted." Jason admitted.

"Then why will you tell him something so personal?" I groaned.

"Because I know that I can trust him. When you were gone, we kept talking so I know."

"Well I'm glad you finally made a friend in twenty four years," I muttered, but loud enough for them to hear. The copper trail we followed came to an end leading us to a silver gate. It was slightly larger than the copper gates we saw at the entrance to the city. There were four guards at the gates dressed in silver armour, two on each side. I was beginning to see a pattern. Copper trail, copper guards, silver trail silver guards. Made sense, but I wondered if there was hidden meaning behind it. The guards looked more appealing in silver, but they weren't very welcoming.

"What do you peasants want?" they asked. It was more of an insult than a welcome, but we were used to that sought of treatment. Joel wasn't. He brushed passed their shoulders and blew at the gates. I thought he was crazy until the gate swung open in flames. The guards rushed towards him with swords in hand. My heart was pounding as I watched everything unfold. I looked at Jason taking some deep breaths and a few steps forward.

"No! Stay out of this," I pleaded. He stomped the ground and the earth trembled. A wall of ice arose from the ground, standing between Joel and the guards. He made it to shield Joel, but in the blink of an eye, the ice wall collapsed. The guards laughed and insulted him, not aware of what really happened.

"Ha-ha, this weak peasant can't even keep his wall of ice up for a second but yet he wants to join the fight."

"The ice wall didn't collapse on its own. I did it –" Joel interrupted their laughter with this information that seemed disappointing to them. He let down his hoodie and revealed his face. The guards cowered to the floor and trembled.

"W- We didn't know it was you," they mumbled.

"For your information, my acquaintance is stronger than the two of you. I just avoided the problem of you two possibly being killed. I'm taking your horses and going, we can't keep the royal family waiting now can we?"

"No sir, we can't." They bowed quickly and moved out of the way.

"Good, because the king wouldn't like that... and you know what happens when the king is upset," That sinister smile appeared on his lips again. He looked our way with an even bigger smile. "You two, come with me. We're late."

One of the guards cowered at his feet again. "M-my lord, the king will be upset if one of us doesn't accompany you. You must have at least one guard with you always."

Joel shrugged his shoulder and glared at them. His muscles were tense and he clenched his fists. Judging from his tone I could only assume that he was irritated. "I have no need for guards I can handle myself. I am the right hand man and my own guard."

"I'm sorry but I'm more afraid of the king than I am of you. If you have a problem with one of us riding with you, I'll ride with that guy and you ride with the girl," the other guard stated. He grabbed the horse's collar and pulled himself gracefully on its back. "As you said, we're late, so let's go."

Joel's eyes turned rigid and cold. His eyebrows furrowed vertically while he clenched his jaw. His lips separated to say something but held back and stayed quiet for a moment. His voice got intensely deeper. He didn't bother to face us when he spoke. "Amaris, you come with me. I just might accidentally kill someone today so let's avoid an unnecessary scandal," he said.

I followed behind him trying to keep up as he briskly walked towards the white horse. He hopped on gracefully as his cloak gently moved with the wind. He stretched out his hand towards me, somewhat avoiding eye contact. I held on to it and helped myself up. I almost slipped but I think I managed to pull it off without anyone noticing.

Joel leaned forward and gripped the reins of the horse, commanding it to move forward. "Ya!" With that word the horse was already on the move. I didn't expect the horse to react so quickly. I felt my body swaying to the side as though I was going to fall off. My heart raced while my eyes seemed connected to the ground. I felt as though I was slipping in slow motion until I felt a hand grip my waist and held me back in place. Joel's chest was pressed against my back and his lips met my ear. "Don't fall," he whispered. His whisper slowly turned into a grin and the heat of his gentle laughter tickled my ear. As I turned to face him I saw that annoying smirk on his face again.

"I don't plan to," I said, flicking my hair in his face. He flinched a little and let out a stupid remark.

"Your hair smells burnt," he stated. He smirked again, "Hopefully they'll fix that for you at the castle."

"And hopefully the prince isn't an asshole like you!" I retaliated. Joel stammered for a moment as he struggled to find the right words to respond.

"Excuse me? How am I the asshole? Is that how you thank

someone when they protected you from falling?" he expressed.

"For your information, I wasn't falling. I just leaned a bit to the side," I lied. "And stop smirking; it irritates the hell out of me. Then you make those stupid smart insults that – "

"That's because your hair does smell burnt," Joel interrupted. I could hear Jason and the guard laughing behind us as if something was funny.

"You know what, that's it," I muttered. Joel grinned again but tried to stop himself. I turned to look at him but he tilted his head away quickly with a hand covering his mouth.

"What do you mean by that's it?" he asked, trying his best to not widen the gap between his lips again. His cheeks were red and he began to bluff. "What?" That stupid smile expanded with soft giggles escaping his lips. I turned my back against him and ignored his presence.

"Usually when she says "that's it", she's giving you the silent treatment," Jason explained.

"O really?" Joel laughed. "That's petty." I faced him instantly after he made that comment. I wanted to say something but I held back and bit my bottom lip. I let out a loud steaming sigh and flicked my hair again. This time he bit on it and yanked my hair with his teeth. I fell back against his chest and screamed.

"What are you doing!"

"I thought you weren't going to speak to me?" he asked sarcastically with my hair still in his mouth. I was disgusted and on the brink of tearing up. My hair is my baby, my pride. I put so much work into keeping it healthy and decent looking.

"Are your eyes getting wet?" he asked. He sounded concerned as if he cared.

"Take my hair out of your mouth!" I screamed. I felt the grip in my hair loosen and my hair was finally free. As I ran my fingers through my hair I could feel that my ends were damp and heavy. I cringed as the wet areas pressed on my neck. Although the horse-ride was short it was one of the longest three minutes of my life.

CHAPTER 7: LATE

As we turned the corner we spotted a colossal structure of an extraordinary castle, roughly two hundred feet tall, composed of silver and gold up ahead. Mandora's crest was carved at the very front and center of the castle's walls for everyone to see. This symbol brought respect to all nations when spotted - *The never defeated Kingdom of Mandora.*

There was no turning back at this point, it was time to suck it up and stick to plan A. "Just do it for the money and you'll have a better life." I repeated those words a thousand times in my mind just to encourage myself for this new life-changing journey. The silver trail we followed took us to the palace garden. The air was so sweet, so refreshing and cool and large trees provided us with shade. The garden was like a colourful rainbow stacked with at least sixty different species of flowers.

Maids dressed in bright purple and gold attended to the plants. They bowed as they saw us passing by but I assumed their courtesies were meant for Joel, a noble among strangers.

"Good day ladies," he said, greeting them with a gentle wave. They blushed and looked away at the rare scene of a noble greeting them. It wasn't long before their attention diverted to Jason and I.

"My lord...would you like me to show the recruited servants where they'd be staying?" a maid asked.

Joel looked away and bent his head, I heard him grinning with his mouth covered. He raised his head, gazing at the sky to hide the tears that had already escaped his eyes. "No, that won't be necessary, this is the last two for the competition," he said, trying to control his amusement again but his lips just wouldn't stop trembling.

"I-I'm sorry, It's just that they look like peasants so I –"

"Well we are," I answered. It was so arrogant of her to think that the only reason peasants enter the castle is to become maids. Maybe that's how she started her journey but not everyone's the same. I didn't even want to be there. I was forced into all this and she stood there looking at my brother and I with disgust. The more I processed my thoughts, the more irritated I became.

"I can feel your tense breathing," Joel whispered.

"Cause I'm mad, I don't want to be here," with those words I tried to stay as calm as possible, but that maid just couldn't stop talking.

"Young lady, although you're a rare gem with a pretty face, it doesn't mean that the prince will choose you. Wait are you even a rare gem? Or are you just another black girl? Your attitude is unacceptable and he loves women with class not women that –"

"I'm not a rare gem or whatever it is you call it. Bold of you to assume that I want to win over the prince's heart." I laughed mockingly. She laughed back, twice as loud as I did, with more teeth showing than I've ever seen. She was sickening to look at for too long. Or maybe I was just overcome with anger, but I hated the sight of her.

"Little girl…..We all know peasants like you would love to take this as an opportunity to lay with the prince."

My jaw dropped till I gagged. I disappointed myself by taking too long to respond but I still had to say something. "What did you say to me?" My body was trembling, and my chest pounded till it ached as I continued to glower at her. My mind went blank, blinded by fury till Jason stepped in and made his stand.

"Don't you ever, talk to her like that again –"

"Or else what? Do you think I'm afraid of you?" The idiot nagged.

"THAT'S ENOUGH!" Joel snapped. "Heather you know that they're among the chosen and yet you still disrespect them. They may be peasants, but they're worth a lot more than you so have some respect."

"I-I'm sorry," She didn't look sorry to me, just embarrassed and scared. I guessed it was a common feeling to experience when a noble was noticeably angry or disappointed in you.

"Well?" Joel said almost inaudibly, as he laid eyes on me. "Is there anything you'd like to say?" The only thing I wanted to say is what I had already repeated over a hundred times. I want to go home.

"Nope," I lied. I could've told her that she was an arrogant asshole and that I didn't want anything to do with the royal family, but I was better than that.

"Fine, let's get going," he tapped the horse's side and we were on the move again. "We're already late." Jason and the guard picked up the pace as they followed behind us. A sudden burst of red fog released into the air from the very tip of the castle.

"Ahh shit," Joel mumbled. For the first time I sensed panic in his voice. A noble was panicking because some red fog got released in the air. I didn't know what was going on, but he being worried made me nervous.

"It has begun..." the guard stated. "We're late..."

"I KNOW!" Joel flared. I didn't care, Jason and I had nothing to lose, but we did have a lot to gain. The only thing that bothered me was the unnecessary attention we'd receive for arriving late. We were already noticeable peasants that'd stand out anywhere among higher classed citizens

"So much for a good first impression," Jason joked. "We're going to be late but at least we'll be two peasants with a noble companion at our side. That should lessen the blow of embarrassment."

"Ha-ha, it won't look as bad for you but what about me?" Joel grinned, locking eyes with Jason

"Just make up an excuse. We're entering together so it'll look as though we're late for the same reason," I implied. I didn't see what other choice we had.

"That would've been a great idea, but I'm not stepping in with you two. You'll be dropped off at the front and I'll...."

"Why not?" Curiosity took over me and the words just flew out my mouth without me thinking. I really just wanted to know if he felt too ashamed to be seen with us.

"I'm a noble who's already late. If I'm going to be late, I should be fashionably late." His response was reasonable so I decided not to query it.

"Ha-ha, you want to be fashionably late?" Jason chimed in. "What Amaris and I are wearing right now is the best we can offer. Fashionably late looks like this for us. On a scale of one to ten, how do we look for this....this thing that we're about to get ourselves involved in?"

There was silence for a while, no one spoke for probably eight seconds. We waited anxiously for a response, not that I cared about his opinion, but I was a very curious. I guess I cared. I looked over my shoulder to examine what his facial expressions were like, if he didn't verbally tell us I'd just jump to conclusions by reading his face. Our eyes accidentally met, but he didn't stare at me for long. There wasn't much noticeable emotions on his face either, but I saw his eyes travel downwards then upwards when looking at me. It seemed as if he was examining me too, but his objectives weren't the same as mine, he was judging my overall look.

"Do you want me to be honest?" he asked. "Because if I am, I won't hold back." I looked away immediately and avoided his question. I don't know why but for some reason I didn't want to hear it.

"Sure why not?" Jason insisted. "I don't expect anything but honesty."

"When the guards and maids saw you, their first impression of you two were peasants, and that's the best you can do. You're about to enter a castle where everyone is accustomed to riches and wealth. I don't know what the other chosen are like, so I can't speak on their behalf. Need I say more?"

"Ha-ha, we understand, no need to say more," Jason chuckled. "Brace yourself Amaris." I evaluated the situation in my head and unfortunately for me, an uncontrollable smile peeled across my lips.

"What are you so happy about?" Joel teased. His words instantly rubbed that smile off my face, being caught was somewhat embarrassing.

"It's just that when people look at us, we seem so low in

their eyes, so maybe we'll be irrelevant and easily forgotten. I don't like attention being drawn to me anyway. I also don't like fighting over a guy I've never met so maybe if…"

"Ha-ha…. Don't be ridiculous. The moment you step inside all eyes will be drawn to you. First of all, you look different, you look different and your brother doesn't look like you. There is some resemblance but you know what I mean. Secondly, you're late. They'll already be talking by the time you enter and your appearance will make a slight disturbance. Lastly, you look just as poor as you are. A low class citizen being granted the chance to marry the prince….how does that really look? But what has the most impact is that you're different. This is the second time in my life to lay eyes on another person with your skin tone, although I'm not surprised you're not a rare gem. The term rare gem was….."

"I KNOWWW!" I snapped. Everything he said was right, but I didn't want to hear it any longer.

"Don't interrupt me when I'm speaking to you," he said quite calmly despite the unmistakably stern undertone in his voice. I was never exposed to the authority of nobles, so I never feared them and I wasn't going to start now.

"So it's okay for you to interrupt me but I can't interrupt you?" As I made eye contact with him once more his sharp eyes caught me off guard. My tough girl act was completely disoriented, I felt a weird tingly sensation in my chest and it wasn't a good one. "What? You're staring at me but you won't say anything. I guess I left you speechless." I used my words and my face as a mask to hide any trail of nervousness that I felt. The sharpness in his eyes slowly disappeared and his lips widened slightly. He looked away with a peculiar expression and a grin that left me concerned. I wish I knew what was going on in that head of his.

"I won't say much, you'll learn eventually," he lowered his tone with words of hidden meaning and aggression. "You act like you're still living in this little world of yours where everyone is equal and treated the same. In a few minutes you'll be introduced to a new reality and the speechless one will be you." His somber tone scared me more than his words but his words still managed to strike a nerve.

"Bet," I responded, trying my best to appear unbothered. Although what he said was intimidating, it was also intriguing. As stubborn as I was, his view of me changing when I entered the castle was just absurd to me. "I'm fully aware that not everyone is equal and that some are treated with more respect than others. You're a noble, a high rank in the kingdom aren't you?"

"Yes, so what?"

"Where I'm from, we know that somewhere in the land there's a castle and a king. We had no clue that he had children and a wife. Soldiers haven't been spotted in years, we have no protection and we depend on ourselves to survive. If you were to enter our territory and say that you're the right hand man, no one would care. Where I'm from, you're irrelevant so don't think for a second….."

"That's enough," Jason interrupted. I sensed a strong feeling of annoyance in his voice. I definitely said too much but I wasn't thinking. I felt threatened so I stood my ground and barked like a dog guarding what's important to it. This guy made me disregard my logic and that rarely ever happened.

"It seems that I've over stepped…." I tried to make things better by apologising but he didn't grant me an opportunity to do so.

"In your territory I'll be irrelevant, but you're in my territory now. I'm a noble and you're just a lowly peasant stepping into rough waters with a pretty face and a unique appearance." His voice got deeper but he wasn't finished yet. "For your information, there is no such thing as your territory, every inch of this land belongs to the king, belongs to the royal family. If any noble requested to own the land that you and your people occupied, he'd get it once approved by the king. You'd be living under that noble's rule and forced to adhere to his commands. Of course you people may put up a fight, most of you might die and some thrown in prison. Where do you live? I'd like to check it out one day."

My body was fuming, everything he said bothered me and this time, being aware and choosing my words wisely was the last thing I wanted to do. The last thing I'd allow him to do was control my emotions.

"Find out your damn self," I snarled. Anybody willing to marry him was a damn fool in my eyes, I figured he'd be kicked out the competition just as soon as me. Deep down I knew that as a noble, he'd be kept longer only because of his status.

"You'll tell me eventually," he said nonchalantly. Evidently he had mastered the art of hiding his emotions, allowing people to see what he wanted them to see. I was certainly entertained by it and was fully aware of how dangerous people like him could be. I lived with my brother for twenty one years so I knew. I focused my thoughts on other things, anything that'd take my mind off the tension.

My mind left reality and drifted into my fantasy. In this dream I was finally living a better life; a life where I was comfortable, never worrying about another meal or a safe and stable place to call home. Even though this race was for the prince's heart, everyone was expected to leave happy with something. I just hoped that that something was the key to a better life for Jason and I.

Unfortunately for me, my escape from reality didn't last long. Unfamiliar voices of middle aged men rang through my ears as a rude awakening.

"He's here! He's here!" they shouted. The castle was directly in front of us. I day dreamed for so long that I didn't even notice. The only thing that stood between us and the castle were the guards. I've never seen people so excited to meet anyone, but that was probably just the life of a noble. The soldiers that guarded the front were dressed in gold armour. It was completely absurd and a little extra in my eyes.

"What in the hell," I muttered. No one heard me, so that was good. The front door of the castle was gold, real gold. Mandora was indeed a very rich land, people lived lavishly in the kingdom but where I'm from, wondering when your next meal would be was everyone's main concern. I couldn't understand why people that were so rich would neglect the poor.

"Approximately 32 guards on the first floor guarding outside," Jason stated. "Is that what you were looking at Amaris?" He knew me so well.

"Yup, but it seems like you calculated it before me again," I admitted. "I'm still a little slow when it comes to these things."

"The calculation isn't completed yet," He continued. His eyes travelled to every corner that he could possibly see.

"What do you mean?" To me his calculation seemed accurate; there were exactly thirty two guards, at least from what I saw.

"A few more are hiding in the shadows…." He explained. "If you look at the…"

"How do you know that?"

I forgot that Jason had one of the soldiers as his companion.

He caught me by surprise when he asked, he didn't even talk for almost the whole ride.

"I just know." Jason was right, he always knew. Four maids came rushing out the door towards us, but they only came for one person. They abruptly stopped when they saw me and stared. I stared back, it was awkward but I didn't know how to respond. Their hair was well kept and placed in a neat bun, there was no sign of frizz, not even one strand of hair escaped. Each of their faces had a youthful glow and they didn't seem much older than me.

"I-is she a..." one of them stuttered.

"Yes, she is," Joel answered. I yearned to know what her question was even though Joel had already answered. His gentle response fuelled their confidence to conduct what felt like a brief interview.

"Is that why you're late?"

"Why are you with her?"

"Where did you find her? Did you see anymore?" That last question struck a nerve. 'Did you see anymore?'

"She's here with her brother, they're a part of the..."

"WHAT!" One of them shouted, her excitement switched to envy in the blink of an eye. It was written all over her face by her furrowed brows. "Why was she even chosen? Is it because she's a rare gem? That's not enough, a prince should not be with a low status woman just because she's rare and pretty, there's more to it than that."

"Excuse me?" I was quiet even though all their questions revolved around me but I couldn't keep my mouth shut towards disrespect. "You know I can hear you right?"

"We know, we don't expect you to be deaf," another responded. "We saw the other women that were chosen, you're nothing like

49

them. You won't last longer than a month here." Baffled by their responses, I had nothing to say. I couldn't say out loud that I didn't want the prince, at some point I had to stop venting so I decided to start right then and there.

"Ok." I said nothing else after that. I hopped off the horse and stumbled slightly but I didn't fall. There was no reason to continue a conversation when we were already late.

"All we need to do is walk up those stairs and enter through that door right?" Jason asked.

"Yup," Joel confirmed. "I should've been there at the side of the royal family already. We'll separate for now, hopefully the guards don't give you too much trouble."

CHAPTER 8: IN IT FOR WHAT?

Minor things seemed appealing to me, like the pearl white steps before the castle's doors, the advanced architecture of buildings and even the horse rides, but the garden was my favorite. Jason and I were never able to afford something as simple as a ride. It felt good not using our feet and energy to travel, but riding with a noble gave it a slightly sour taste. I overstepped a little when I spoke my mind, but it revealed to me how nasty nobles became when upset. I stopped for a moment, gathered my thoughts and smiled uncontrollably. It was all going to be worth it, I thought.

"I'm ready," I tried to convince myself, picking up the pace as I climbed the pearly white steps. Jason was already ahead of me. I tapped his shoulder and walked past him. "Let's do this." Four men guarded the door but one was noticeably different in his attire. The others wore heavy metal gold armour but he wore a silk blue suit with a red robe attached to his back with the kingdom's crest sewed onto his collar. It was completely unnecessary, two would've been just fine, but four guards addressing us was too intimidating for me.

"I can hear your heavy breathing, calm down," Jason whispered. He leaned closer. "Remember why we're here so let's stick to the plan."

"I'm sorry but whatever your plan is, you'll have to save it for another time. Peasants can plead their cases to Lord Elzar tomorrow and get their money." Our eyes followed the sound of a squeaky voice that irked our ears. He was confusing to look at, just a pale, feeble old man in golden armour. He didn't fit my expectations for a guard stationed at the castle, but I assumed that whoever placed him there had their reasons. His statement was like music to my ears, I completely disregarded his appearance in a matter of seconds and focused on his words.

"Wait, poor people can come here and get money?" I asked, a bit too excitingly.

"Why is someone's feeble grandpa in the army?" Jason interrupted. I knew what his intentions were, I should've known better than to sound desperate moments before entering the castle. I giggled a bit to play along and finally took a proper look at the old man. He had little to no meat on his bones and his armour looked too heavy for the muscles he lacked. His hairline was receding with thin hairs and multiple bald spots. His long crooked nose stood out the most with a few boogers and hairs playing peek a-boo. I cringed till I laughed softly then pulled myself together.

"If you don't leave, we'll escort you ourselves. I heard what you said when you whispered to your sister. Whatever it is you're planning I'll deal with you personally. We won't accept anyone spoiling this day for the royal..."

"I've heard enough from this old hag, let us through." Jason demanded. Time froze, for me but not for everyone else. I remained still with trembling hands and a racing heart, thinking of ways to ease the soon coming disaster.

"O-old HAG!" The guard stammered until he shouted. "An old hag is what you call a woman..."

"I know you're a man but you nag like a woman. Now I'm politely asking you to let us through." Jason continued. It may not have seemed like a nice way of asking but it was Jason's version of being polite. I looked at the guard again and his boogers kept saying hello.

"Eww," I said lowly. His neck turned like an owl as he diverted his attention to me.

"I heard what you said young lady." I didn't respond. He just seemed crazy to me but Jason was a lunatic. The more he spoke the more I wanted him to just shut up, his pride scared me. We weren't back at home in our village. These were the castle's guards dressed in golden armour. The royal family stood behind those doors and the event had already begun, the last thing I wanted was to cause a scene with the authorities involved.

"You can't hear what she said, I'm next to her and didn't hear a thing. Is reading lips a hobby of yours or something?" Jason interrogated. People always assumed he was the quiet respectable one, but he clearly wasn't. We're the same when aggravated but different things triggered us.

The old man smirked and looked away, allowing his boogers and hairs to be seen from another angle. "These ignorant fools always think they know everything," he stammered. The unfamiliar voice of another guard grasped our attention. He was a tall lean middle aged man that stood out from the rest, noticeably stronger, confident and most of all he was the man with the red robe and blue suit.

"For your information, his ability is hearing and he's very essential to us in battle. He can hear even the slightest thing, for example, your heart beat. I believe there's no need for me to further explain how useful he is to our kingdom."

I rolled my eyes unconsciously, being around someone that hears literally everything was mentally draining. I turned slightly to my right and glanced at Jason, his brows arched in confusion with tightly clenched fists as a minor display of how irritated he felt. We didn't say a word.

"What's the problem are you two lost? Don't you know there're people with special abilities in Mandora?" He paused for a while and his eyes travelled our bodies from head to toe until he lost himself in laughter. "Judging from your appearance you're either foreigners or two peasants from a village far from here. Don't tell me in that poor village of yours, you two weren't exposed to people with different abilities...Do you guys even have powers?" he laughed till he coughed, I wished he'd choke and pass out. "Listen, my name is Hezron and I'm sure you heard about me so..."

"Nope, never heard of you," I interrupted. He gasped, almost as if he struggled to breathe for a moment.

"And YES, I have powers," Jason responded quickly, annoyed by everything Hezron spewed. Hezron's glare sharpened with his eyes fixed on Jason until his lips formed into a sinister smile.

"It's so interesting how quickly you reacted. Are you scared? It's okay if you don't have any special abilities. There really is no need to lie," Hezron teased. "Roughly twenty percent of our population are gifted with such things, we won't expect peasants like you to be gifted. If you did, it'd be such a waste. How is it that someone can have powers and still remain at such a low rank?"

I didn't know whether to be offended or just take notes, but I became restless. We were inches away from the final step and yet people remained in our way after facing so many obstacles that could've been avoided. Jason's patience was limited. I just hoped he kept his composure a little longer to avoid disaster.

"Why would I lie? To impress who...you? Don't be ridiculous." Jason laughed while I quivered. I may have been a hypocrite, but nothing was funny about disrespecting high authority stationed at the castle.

"Do you take me for a joke...BOY?" As intimidating as Hezron seemed with his tense muscles and aggravated tone, Jason couldn't help but be entertained. His facial expressions alone was an issue; all he did was smirk and talked back.

"I should ask you the same thing. Do you take me for a joke?" Jason paused, scanning him from head to toe with the same judgmental energy. The man was tall, but not taller than Jason. His muscles were defined with a lot of meat on his bones, the total opposite of my brother. He had a few grey hairs hidden in his beard but they were much more apparent in the strands on his head. "Young man," the palace guard teased, "yes you're a joke. I'll take you seriously if you tell me that power of yours with some proof," Hezron negotiated.

"My power... my power is making people like you upset easily." I discretely tugged on Jason's shirt to make him stop but he ignored me. Someone had to put an end to Jason's games for the sake of everyone's peace, but it wasn't going to be me. I knew what battles to pick and this was not one.

"Just as I thought. You're a worthless piece of trash with no outstanding abilities," Hezron concluded. It was only a matter of time before the truth was revealed.

"That's what you think." Jason teased, whatever his plan was, he needed to be stopped. I never agreed to aggravating guards dressed in golden armour, especially the ones that guarded the castle's front doors.

"THEN SHOW ME!" Hezron snapped. The door creaked open before either one of us could react, my knees buckled and my mind went blank.

"Idiot..." Jason muttered. I looked at him and he revealed the broadest smile on his face. That was his intention along. A smile peeled across my lips but disappeared just as quickly when the person behind the door appeared.

A tall male figure stepped forward, fully clothed in silver. His uniform was the same as Hezron's but silver. His ash brown hair was well polished and slicked back so I assumed he was well dressed for the same occasion. His jaw line was sharp, but not as sharp as his eyes. Any woman that denied his attractiveness, couldn't deny that he was manly. His body was bulky and properly defined in all the right areas but what stood out the most, was his deep dominant voice.

His piercing eyes fixed its attention on Jason and I, then moved towards Hezron. I gulped as he looked at me, especially as he stared at me longer than he did anyone else, but there was no expression on his face. For the first time I wished that someone had some sought of expression when they looked at me because this felt nerve wrecking. Jason maintained that smirk on his face but I couldn't tell if he was nervous or pleased.

"What's going on here?" he questioned. This time his attention was drawn to Hezron and aggression could be felt in the atmosphere.

"Lord Logan....." Hezron stammered falling to his knees. The other guards did the same. I was confused, I didn't know if they cowered in fear or bowed out of respect. The calmest person at the moment was Jason. His smile was gone but he was still noticeably amused. Just as his face was easy to read I wondered if I was noticeably nervous as well. I felt a tapping sensation on my shoulder; Jason was trying to get my attention.

"I think we should bow too, everyone is bowing," he said. His back was already slightly arched when I looked at him. I looked up and the man's eyes were sharper than before.

"You don't know who I am, do you?" he asked. The aggression in his tone left but his deep voice still made me nervous.

"No sir...sorry if we..." I stammered, and positioned my body to bow immediately.

"That won't be necessary. Everyone rise." I didn't know if he was irritated at me or at everyone. He was clearly a high ranking noble, so high that another noble cowered and bowed in his presence, but I didn't. I wondered how he felt about that. Everyone avoided eye contact with him but when I looked at Jason he was nowhere near the look of fear. His calmness eventually relaxed me. There was no reason to be scared, it's not like he was going to hurt us or anything. At least I hoped not.

"My name is Logan, and I'm guessing that you two are the final contestants that everyone's been waiting for. If I am correct, then you two are late."

"Everyone?" I stuttered. It was probably a stupid query, we were late to a royal event or whatever it was, so of course everyone was there.

"Although you're only ten minutes late, no one is ever late to events like these. Congratulations, you two just made history," Logan mentioned. As he said those words, Jason and I locked eyes with each other instantly. We communicated with each other through our eyes and I knew exactly what he was thinking.

57

It seemed to me that he was ready to play the blame game. His mouth opened slightly to say something but Logan intervened.

"Well clearly you two had your reasons but let's not keep everyone waiting much longer." He didn't even give us time to respond, he turned his back on us as he opened the door and let out a rather loud announcement.

"The final two, AMARIS AND JASON ARE HERE!"

"How do you know our names?" Jason whispered over his shoulder. He displayed a lot of guts to even invade a noble's personal space as if they shared struggle meals together over the years.

"Everyone's names except you two were ticked off when they arrived so....."

"Ooooh." I didn't know what to say in the moment, all I could do was just gasp. Everything was happening so quickly, I was not yet prepared to face our new reality but I was already there. I heard voices of people talking but as we stepped into the hall, the atmosphere was heavy. All eyes were on us, harsh stares mixed with shocked expressions. Everything I wanted to avoid was happening, but I knew from the start that I couldn't avoid it because I was noticeably different, but Logan's announcement caused everyone's attention to be drawn to us at the same time. Despite all that was happening, it was so easy to disregard curious stares when other things caught my attention.

My eyes were drawn to the beauty of the castle. The walls were overlaid with gold and the chandeliers that hung on the ceiling were also golden. The floor was made of crystal ceramic tiles which formed the Kingdom's crest in the center of the room. It was like a puzzle that had all the right pieces put together to form a beautiful picture... the kingdom's crest. It was probably the third or fourth time I saw it. They just won't give us the chance to forget it. Different fragrances; sweet, strong and mild mingled in the air, although the mixtures of the scents were still pleasing to my senses.

"Jason do you smell that?" I asked. I made sure to keep my voice low, the last thing I wanted was people hearing our conversation. "The scent of rich is in the air."

"Yup, we're basically sheep among a pack of wolves, let's see how long it takes for one of them to bite." He whispered. I wondered if the ugly old guard heard us behind the door but I didn't care, I was just curious. Although I was amazed by the design of the castle, I couldn't forget my intentions for being there in the first place.

Women wore dresses that cost a fortune; dresses that would've taken me at least five years without spending, to afford what they were wearing. Their hair were so well styled, not one strand of frizz was found, the same went for the guys. I was not at all intimidated, I actually felt relieved to see that everyone was trying so hard to make a good first impression. Even though we didn't look it, Jason and I did our best too, but our reasons were different. We were in it for the money. They were in it for the crown.

If a mosquito passed by singing, It's song would probably resonate in the room since everyone seemed to be in shocked silence. I noticed their hawk eyes evaluating us from head to toe. My plain blue dress that I thought I looked cute in, was not impressive to anyone. Their dresses over shadowed my simple, designer-less outfit. I only hoped that no one noticed the two stains and slight discoloration from the lemonade that I spilled on myself three years ago. My flat shoes were old, worn out and slightly bursting in some areas.

Jason's outfit wasn't impressive either. His black leather pants was getting old and so was his brown leather jacket that he wore over his white long sleeve shirt but that was the best he had. His hair was somewhat presentable, nothing too special about it, just his wavy hair brushed upwards with an ingrown fade. The silence in the room slowly faded as murmuring began to rise and slowly turned into an uproar.

"Everyone's watching us," I whispered. "Do you think they're talking about us too?"

"That's because they're all dressed in clothes that costs a fortune and we're poor and it shows. You're also uniquely different, I thought by now you'd get used to it at least." He sounded slightly annoyed but he was right. I experienced it all the time and yet I never seemed to get over it or at least own it. His words left an effect on me. It finally opened my eyes. I no longer gave a shit. It felt good not caring any more, almost as if a heavy burden was lifted off my shoulders. I wished I did it sooner.

"Jason well I..." He yanked part of my dress and cut me off.

"Shh..." he was very subtle. He tried his best to keep quiet when silencing me. To my surprise, the place was quiet again and I knew it could not have been a coincidence. Something happened. A loud but very familiar voice swept across the room.

"Good Evening Everyone," the voice was deep, very deep. It was certainly strong enough to get everyone's attention and shut down an entire crowd of roughly five hundred people. I raised my head and acknowledge the person that spoke above us. As I laid eyes on him I was so relieved to see a familiar face, it was Logan. But my relief was accompanied by, a trail of curiosity as everyone waited to hear his announcement.

"When did he leave our side?" I muttered. Although I was

interested in what he had to say, I was very confused as to when he disappeared without me realizing it. It seemed that all of a sudden he appeared above us on a higher floor. I should've at least seen when he was ascending the stairs.

A heavy presence rested on my shoulder with a warm soft breath resting against my ear. "He left our presence when you were amazed at the golden chandeliers on the ceiling. In those thirty seconds of you staring at them, that's when he left. You should be more aware of your surroundings," Jason whispered. He always noticed the little details of everything, nothing ever got past him.

"You shouldn't have your guard up all the time, loosen up a bit..." I pleaded. His rigid manner of constant alertness took a toll on me.

"I do loosen up but...."

"You two have been talking since you got here, just be quiet for once and listen to what he has to say!" The voice was weak, but loud enough for everyone to hear and it came from behind us. I didn't turn my head but everyone else did. I glanced at Jason from the corner of my eyes and he did the same.

"Is he talking about us?" I whispered.

"Yes I'm talking about you!" he continued, this time he raised his voice even louder. At that moment we knew exactly who it was. Everyone stood there confused so we just played along, making him look like the fool. At least that was the plan, but he kept talking and then became more specific.

"You peasants just..."

"What is your problem? Why are you still talking...just leave us alone," Jason retaliated. As he turned and faced him I did the same. It didn't make sense to act confused any more. Jason blew our cover and the man called us peasants, now everyone

61

knew he was talking to us. The pale feeble guard grinned along with Hezron and his men, after making a scene. Every time I looked at him the uglier he became. Hezron's smile grew wider as he seemed intent on dragging out the scene. The moment he opened his mouth, I surely wasn't interested in anything he had to say.

"Well if you two peasants had just…"

"THAT'S ENOUGH!" That was the strongest and most demanding voice I'd ever heard. My chest tightened, causing me to experience a shortness of breath as goose bumps rose uncontrollably. Chills ran up my spine instantly. The atmosphere got increasingly heavy as if the air was pressing heavily against us. For the first time, from the corner of my eyes, I actually witnessed Jason flinch. He never had a noticeable reaction to anything, he always played it cool, always appeared to be strong and unbothered but this time his barrier of emotions cracked, though only for a few seconds. He played it off instantly as if nothing happened and then grinned, but his smile wasn't fake because he was intrigued.

"This is interesting," Jason laughed. "I love it here already.

CHAPTER 9: FIRST IMPRESSIONS

His footsteps reverberated loudly throughout the room, becoming louder each second. I ran my fingers through my hair nervously to distract myself but it didn't work. My heart pounded so heavily that I felt a little pain in my chest, but it wasn't too much to bear. There wasn't much I could do. I let out a loud sigh in another attempt to de-stress. I was a bit naive, but I needed clarification.

"He's coming here isn't he?" I murmured with high hopes in Jason's ear that he'd at least tell me I was wrong. Unfortunately that wasn't the case.

"Yup." His response was so dry, so dull that I wondered what was going through that head of his. I didn't know if he was calm, nervous or intrigued. I just didn't know.

"I am so over this shit," I made sure to keep my voice low but I knew that ugly old man still heard me. I glanced over my shoulder to see his reaction, his legs and lips trembled, matching Hezron's body-language beside him. I looked around and realized no one seemed calm; they were all so skittish with eyes wide opened.

"Relax," Jason whispered. "The most he's going to do, whoever he is, is humiliate us in front of everyone, he won't hurt us physically. We should be used to it by now. People with money never failed to take an opportunity to embarrass us because of our lower class lifestyle"

"You're right, but even some of the nobles fear him, look at Hezron," I stated. He peeked over his shoulder and looked at him for about two seconds then grinned.

"I don't care."

I guessed that since he didn't care, there wasn't much reason for me to care either. Once Jason was calm, I was always fine.

As the steps got increasingly louder the crowd parted and made way for whoever the person was. We did the same to blend with everyone else, even though we stood out as peasants, it would've been harder to find us in a crowd. Eventually there was an empty path left in the middle of two separate crowds for him to pass through, and as he finally came near us my heart sank to my feet at the sight of the golden crown he wore boldly upon his head. His sharp piercing eyes stood out the most. I wouldn't be surprised if that feature of him intimidated everyone.

"O shit..." Jason indistinctly murmured. I didn't say anything. He was only a dozen feet away, but the smell of his perfume triggered every nerve in my body. The scent of a king. He wrapped himself with a brilliant gold cloak that bore the crest of the realm on his back. I didn't see his suit underneath, but I noticed his brilliant white shoes and golden slacks. His beard was well groomed and connected with his moustache. I looked at Jason, I wanted to see if his *'I don't care'* mind-set had changed. He didn't look nervous but his eyes were narrowed and fixed on the king. He evaluated every inch of the man before us, for a quick estimate of his strength based on his physical appearance.

"Isn't he supposed to be in his early fifties?" I asked. " He looks just as strong as Logan." I didn't get much of a reaction out of him. He shrugged his shoulders to my statement and ignored me.

"He's strong," he unconsciously muttered. My ears flickered at the sound of his words.

"He's supposed to be strong Jason, he's the king."

"No, he's strong, a different kind of strong. Someone like that is not an enemy we want, he'll be hard to deal with."

I yanked his leather jacket, to remind him of our situation. "Shhh… the old man can hear us, be careful of what you say."

"I don't care." It seemed to be his favourite phrase of the day. I was a bit hesitant at first but I looked at the feeble guard again to be sure he'd leave us alone. He shook his head and slowly opened his mouth to say something but Hezron tapped his shoulder and whispered in his ear. I crossed my fingers and prayed silently that they'd leave us alone and not scheme against us. They bothered us since we arrived and this was their perfect opportunity to torment us some more, but all that didn't matter when the king spoke. The authority in his voice was unnerving. A simple question seemed like a life or death situation if answered incorrectly or not in his favour.

"Hezron?"

"Y- yes your majesty," Hezron stuttered, falling to his knees.

"What's your reason for interrupting my gathering?"

"My Lord …. I," his arms were trembling as he tried to remain balanced on the floor.

"GET UP!" The king's tone switched like a roaring lion. The more he sensed fear the more he acted upon it.

"Yes your majesty!" Hezron panicked as he got to his feet. Seeing him vulnerable and scared was a fascinating sight to witness. He spent all that time acting strong when attempting to degrade us but he was an obvious wimp in the presence of the king. Even though it was an amusing sight to take in, another part of me felt overwrought by the king's presence. The air seemed thin, but it was probably due to my uncontrollable heavy breathing. Jason tried to keep his voice low as he chuckled incessantly, but the place was too quiet for him to not be heard. The king altered his attention to Jason with a threatening glare. Jason stared back seemingly unbothered, apparently unperturbed that the king wanted him silenced. When he looked at Jason I noticed a shift in his attention towards me, his eyes widened for a quick second, but he quickly regained his poise and looked away.

"Get that smirk off your face….BOY!" Everything seemed to not be going according to plan. The last thing we wanted to do was catch everyone's attention, especially not like this, and above all, we definitely didn't want attention from the king, definitely not this kind. Our first impressions plan had already fallen apart. Jason turned his head clockwise then anti clockwise and finally looked at me. We spoke through our eyes, there was no need for words to communicate our thoughts but I basically told him not to screw up.

"I'm twenty-four, yet he calls me a boy………. A BOY?" The irritation in his voice was easily detected, as there was no attempt to disguise or hide it. I tugged on his sleeve to get him to calm down but he ignored me again.

"Is there something you'd like to say to me boy?" the king

asked. "That reaction of yours says something to me, you seem a bit aggravated."

"WELL I…." Jason bit his tongue and paused for a moment. He glanced at me but looked away immediately after. "I do have something to say but I will refrain from speaking my mind," he continued. I slapped my hand against my forehead and sighed. Our goal was to stay irrelevant, unnoticed and certainly not a problem, but we seemed to be the exact opposite. People began to murmur and I hated every second of it.

"Really, you won't tell me?" The king diverted his attention towards me with narrowed eyes, evaluating me from head to toe like a hawk would assess his prey. "You vented loud enough to your friend for me to hear and now you're telling me that you have nothing to say. A coward, that's what you are."

"Why do I need to repeat myself when you already heard me?" Jason retaliated. He subconsciously raised his voice and took a few steps forward till he stood chest to chest with the king. "I am no coward. Don't you ever forget that!"

I grabbed his arm and pulled him back straight away, he was heavy, but in the heat of all that confusion I managed to do it.

"What are you doing!?" I squeezed his upper arm but his muscles were too tough to dig into. "Relax!" I scolded. The murmuring in the room increased significantly. The king kept his eyes on us and didn't blink once. I avoided eye contact at all cost, but Jason stared back.

"Young man, do you have any idea of who I am? I can make your life a living hell."

"There's a golden crown on your head, everyone knows who you are just by looking at you." Jason answered. "I know what you're capable of, and you can surely try." My nerves took over and my senses left my body, before I knew it, I slapped him with my right hand against his left cheek. I didn't realize what I did until he responded to my reckless outburst against him. His upper eyelids rose with long heavy breaths resting on my face. I didn't know who to fear more between Jason and the king but I knew the king would do a lot more damage than he would.

I fell to my knees, I wasn't sure if I bowed properly but I did it similar to Hezron when he cowered in fear.

"I'm sorry, please forgive my brother…."

"Don't apologize for me." Jason insisted. This time he lowered his voice, but he was loud enough for everyone in the room to hear him. He fell to his knees afterwards and bowed "I apologize if I…"

"I don't want to hear your apology. You two get up." The king's voice wasn't as stern as before but a sense of irritation was still there. "Did you mean everything you said?" he asked.

"Yes I did," Jason answered. There was no sense of fear or regret in his words, just a blunt and honest response.

"Good. I think I like you. You remind me of my son." The king's words confused me but as long as he wasn't mad, I had nothing to fear. "No one ever stood up to me without their knees buckling….I mean, some did but they all died." He looked at us and grinned, his eyes weren't intimidating to look at any more. "I haven't killed someone with my bare hands in a while, I miss that feeling…" His voice became calm, like a normal person having a casual conversation but his words didn't give off that same vibe.

"Same," Jason responded. The king subconsciously arched his brow and said nothing for a few seconds. I was lost for words but too scared to put my hands on him again. He scanned Jason from head to toe keenly till a smirk appeared.

"You really are strong, I don't know why you're here but I look forward to seeing what you'll bring to the table. Not as an enemy but as an ally, soldier or whatever it is you can be. You may be of good use to me one day." With those words he diverted his attention to Hezron and his companion. "You two, what are your reasons for interrupting this major event that I'm hosting?"

The two guards stood there trembling nervously and mumbling words that no one understood.

"Speak Up!" His patience decreased drastically and despite my own moment of humbling I enjoyed every moment of their humiliation.

"W-w-we, they were..." Linden mumbled, he was lost for words but still attempted to say something.

"Speak properly! That same young man that's called a peasant spoke to me without hesitation and owned up to everything he said. I sensed not one ounce of fear in him and yet, here you are, a soldier who can't even look me in the eye properly and speak. Don't make a bad repute for the soldiers in my kingdom." After dealing with Linden, he shifted his attention to Hezron. "And you...you're a noble. Not an important or high-class noble but you're still a noble so act like one."

"I wonder if Joel is considered an important noble." I whispered.

"He should be. He's the prince's right hand man, basically his chief assistant in everything he does." Jason explained. We looked at Linden and grinned mockingly, we knew he heard us and couldn't do anything about it.

"Now I'll ask again. Why did you two find the need to interrupt this critical gathering?" the king continued.

Hezron stared with his cold eyes piercing deep into our souls.

"My king, those two were constantly talking since they entered so we..."

"O really?" the king interrupted. "Even though they were talking, they didn't manage to interrupt anything. No one heard them, no one noticed anything until you two caused a scene."

"I heard them!" Linden intruded. I looked at that scrawny old man and cringed, he just wouldn't shut up when I wanted him to.

"Linden you hear every damn thing. Now that I'm thinking about it, you interrupted us, not Hezron. Hezron didn't talk at all actually, he just stood there and watched you make an outburst," the king stated. Linden's eyes widened in fear, slowly becoming watery, but he blinked continuously to avoid the leakage of a tear drop or two. He cleared his throat and gathered the courage to come up with an explanation. He was desperate for a way out so of course he'd play dirty.

"Don't you want me to tell you what they were talking about? They seemed a bit sinister to me, that's also why I interrupted them. I'm sorry, I didn't expect to make as large of a scene as I did," he explained

I glanced awkwardly at Jason but his eyes squinted with furrowed brows in pretence to seem confused. It was all part of his tactics. I fixed my face and relaxed my muscles to seem innocently calm and deny everything he had to say.

"Whatever they were talking about is their business," the king disclosed. "Hezron, next time make sure that your companion keeps his mouth shut. There better not even be a next time."

Hezron bowed slightly and nodded in agreement, "Yes your highness."

"Addressing this situation is beneath me," the king continued. "Usually I'd let one of my nobles deal with this, but this is an important day for my children so I'll do what's necessary at this time."

"I-I apologize my king," Linden stuttered.

"Let this be a warning to everyone. If anyone spoils or attempts to ruin this evening, there'll be no more warnings, just immediate consequences." The king cautioned. I preferred warnings. Actions definitely wasn't my thing but Jason was the opposite.

Even though being in the presence of the king was quite nerve wrecking, based on my first impressions and his handling of the situation, I actually liked him, or at least I appreciated him. Everyone stared as he disappeared into the crowd then reappeared next to his lovely wife on higher ground. She was gorgeous, with luscious long golden blonde hair and green eyes. Her eyes sparkled and complemented the genuine smile she showed, I wished I knew what made her smile because it looked so real. Her ageing showed slightly but her beauty made it easy to ignore. The crown she wore was almost identical to the king's but smaller in size. My only concern now was that the preceding circumstances now made it impossible to keep a low profile.

Chapter 10: No such Thing

We stood there for almost ten minutes listening to a speech about things we didn't care for. A history lesson on the royal family's generation, the rival kingdoms that raged war against us but failed and most importantly, how great this kingdom was and how blessed we were to be here. I drowned in boredom just waiting for some sought of escape to appear but then Logan finally said something that caught my attention.

"Many of you have no clue what this gathering is about," he stated. A lot of murmuring began but I didn't quite understand. It just didn't make sense. Jason and I knew why we were here, at least that's what I thought. At this point I hoped that I was right about the perceived objective and we were not victims of some kind of strategic deceptive marketing ploy. Logan did say earlier that our names were on the list, so we were expected to be there. I just felt extremely out of place since even the servants looked better than us.

"Raise your hand if you have hopes to marry into the royal

family one day." Logan instructed. I gasped by the instant show of hands raised proudly in the air. Only the hands of middle-aged people and senior citizens remained low at their side. Logan's eyes travelled the crowd till he paused and stared in our direction. His pupils shifted downwards, drawn to our hands that remained at our side. He grinned and continued with the most mischievous smile on his face.

"This may come as sad news for you all but it's happy news for me. Most of you will never have that opportunity. Only twenty-four young women and twenty-four young men are eligible in all of Mandora to marry into the royal family. They already know who they are and are hidden in the crowd among us."

Murmuring quickly turned into a bold uproar as they lowered their hands slowly, searching helplessly through the crowd to figure out who the individuals were. I bit my bottom lip to prevent myself from laughing or showing too much teeth. It was even more amusing to see my brother do likewise. Logan raised his voice to silence the crowd and continued.

"This may come as bad news for many of you but If you were not selected, it's because you're not good enough and never will be. I don't mean to sound harsh but I need to be quick and straight to the point. Catrina was very specific in her process of selecting these individuals after her final prophecy. Each one of them was born either under a blue or red moon."

"We haven't seen a coloured moon in decades!" someone shouted.

"Which is exactly why this needs to happen. The selected are between the ages of twenty to twenty-eight. The last coloured moon appeared twenty-one years ago, rare gems are basically extinct. The very few we've found over the past few years are powerless and even if they weren't, there's too little of them remaining to create another miracle."

Scornful eyes shifted in my direction, I never understood what a rare gem was, I just knew it had something to do with people that looked like me.

"A war is coming, we don't know when but actions must be taken to prepare. To secure the future of a strong bloodline, there's no other choice. The enemy is strong, stronger than anything we've ever faced and we ask that you all do as much training as possible to prepare."

"Then why don't we just gather every strong person and train them to fight when that day comes? Why does it have to go as far as marriage?" Someone else interrupted. I was happy to see that my questions were voiced by others who shared the same concerns that I had. Voices of others agreeing with him quickly turned into another uproar, but mostly from young women and parents that had their dreams crushed before them.

"That's something we plan to do soon but the marriage must happen. Let's not forget we haven't seen a coloured moon in decades, it's only wise that they marry one of the gifted. The prince and princess must choose their spouse wisely or else all efforts would be in vain. Unfortunately Catrina couldn't go into much details in her final moments but she did state clearly that this must happen."

"Are you saying that they must make a lucky guess between all forty-eight individuals to save our kingdom in the future?"

"There's a chance of winning with each one of them. Some will just bring forth better or worse results than others." Logan answered confidently with answers only politicians could pull off.

"What if the chosen refuses to get married?" My ears tickled by what could've been the most important question of the day. My heart raced anxiously as I desperately waited for Logan's response.

"We'd let the royal family make a decision on that matter if a situation like that ever occurs. Judging from the show of hands earlier, I don't think that'll ever be a problem. Catrina's prophecy cannot be ignored. We must do our part to prevent devastating casualties in the future."

He mentioned this woman called 'Catrina' and the word 'prophecy', talking about her as if she was valuable and her opinions were greatly respected. I had absolutely no idea who she was, but to be fair I didn't even know any of the nobles or high ranking people of my land. I was only aware that we had a king, not even a queen, prince, or princess.

"They expect me to marry someone I've never seen before? That's just uncalled for." Jason complained softly. I elbowed him in his rib, completely caught off guard by his hypocrisy.

"That's how I felt, but you wouldn't listen to me." Even though I spoke up to remind him of his words, he kept venting as though I said nothing. I didn't understand, he told me that he didn't mind having to fight for the princess's heart, not necessarily fight, but participate. We were just in it for the wealth that we were promised. But now he finally realized that we had no choice but to marry if we were chosen, at least it seemed that way.

"This is ridiculous and the most selfish shit I've ever heard. If I say I don't, at the alter, what are they going to do kill me? I will burn this whole place down..."

"Your power isn't fire Jason...." I interrupted. I knew what he meant but I couldn't pass on the opportunity to get under his skin.

"You know what I mean. I will tear this place up before they get me to marry someone I'm not attracted to." I always knew he was more concerned about the princess's looks over anything else.

"For them to want us, we have to make them want us, the same way we can make them not want us. We went through all of this already Jason, just relax," I tried to calm him, knowing that if he kept fussing he'd cause another unwanted scene.

"Yes we did, but the possibility is still there. We can make it as low as we possibly could, but we can't rule out the fact that we may still be chosen."

I couldn't help but laugh when I heard Jason speak. His opinion on the situation shifted when he saw that it affected him as well. I made sure to be very subtle with my laugh so it was just a soft grin. I couldn't bear to draw any additional attention to ourselves because of that nosey guard Linden.

The king hovered over Logan's shoulder and leaned forward slightly. Logan crossed his eyes lightly to the right as he acknowledged that the king needed his attention but in a discrete manner. They both whispered secrets into each other's ear that no one could hear. After their brief interactions the king stepped forward and spoke in Logan's place.

"As you all know, Mandora has never…EVER been defeated. That can change if the wrong person is chosen. Another concern that Logan left out, but only because I told him to, is the probability that some of the selected would turn on us and help the enemy. I'm sure you've all heard the term, keep your friends close and your enemies closer."

"So basically what you're saying, is that some of these chosen individuals are potential criminals, or maybe they already are. Why don't we just kill them all to prevent this issue from happening?" someone asked.

That was the most brutal and ignorant crap I've ever heard. I didn't know if to feel scared or angry, but ever since I got here the mindset of these people was just too insane for me to understand. They were all so selfish, rude, filled with pride and most of all, ignorant. Even though Jason and I didn't expect to be here for a long period of time, one year seemed like it would be too much to tolerate. I was actually hurt that someone would say something like that. I understood that war always had collateral damage, and to many who knew that they were not numbered among the chosen, it might make sense to kill forty-eight people and save the kingdom. His logic wasn't that bad, but I wasn't ready to die.

"I will kill everyone in this place before I allow them to lay a hand on you," Jason vowed. His energy became cold and as he talked I noticed the frost leaving his mouth. "I won't be surprised if they brought us here to kill all forty-eight of us." he continued.

"Relax!" I whispered harshly. Jason always had this violent mind-set that bothered me. Whenever he felt threatened or thought that someone wants to act in a violent manner towards him or the people he loved, he never hesitated to return the favour. I always looked for alternatives to avoid that worst case scenario. Violence was never the answer for me.

"Let's hear him out before you make any rash decisions. Joel is a noble and he did say that he and his sister is a part of this selection. Do you really think they'll kill them too?" I asked.

His eyes pitied me in distress and annoyance. "Amaris you are so slow and sometimes so stupid that it bothers me," he muttered. My breath was taken away for a quick second. I couldn't understand why he'd say something so hurtful, but the king responded to the question at just the right moment, preventing me from responding to my brother's hurtful remarks.

"There are suitable matches for my children among the forty-eight individuals chosen. I will not rob them of that opportunity to find love among the most gifted in Mandora. Secondly, what good would it do our nation to kill them all when only a few are guilty. That doesn't seem very fair to me. After we kill all youths born under a coloured moon, what defence will we have when the enemy has extraordinary power of their own? We may as well surrender if that's our plan." The king's words granted me the perfect opportunity to reason with Jason.

"You see, there's no issue," I whispered. His face was still stern but his muscles weren't as tense as they were before however frost still escaped his lips when he spoke.

"I still won't let my guard down, but I'm calm. I'm always calm," he lied. He wasn't always calm, he just learned to master the art of hiding how he really felt. I actually felt inspired in a way, but I was not sure if I could pull it off.

"I'll agree that you're calm when frost stops escaping your lips when u speak," I stated. His head shifted towards me with expanded eyes.

"Am I really...?"

"Yes you are, so control yourself. Please, let's not cause another scene," I softly scolded. He let out one long sigh in my face and the last of his frosty breath was set free. I shivered slightly and groaned. "You didn't need to do that."

"BEFORE I CONTINUE...." The king caught our attention with the aggression in his tone. I saw his eyes as he looked down on us sharply from the higher platform on which he spoke. I wouldn't be surprised if he saw Jason and I talking the entire time.

"I need my children beside me, this event and our future revolves around them. I promise you all that everything will work out for the good of Mandora." When my mother was alive, she always told me not to make promises I couldn't keep. I hoped he understood the actual significance of the word promise.

I flinched at the immediate ear-splitting sound from golden, strangely shaped metals that the soldiers blew into. It was the first time I had seen such instruments or heard the sound reverberating from them. As fancy as they looked, I wasn't impressed.

"LADIES AND GENTLEMEN, WE PRESENT TO YOU… . PRINCE JOEL AND PRINCESS ROSELYN BLADE!" the herald announced.

"What did he say? Prince Joel?" I stammered. My heart was racing and my ears were on the verge of bleeding from the words spoken.

Jason hovered over my shoulder and whispered his nasty secret. "I probably should've told you, but there's no such thing as a prince's right hand man."

CHAPTER 11: Well Played

My heart pounded intensely until my chest pained. Eventually the music faded into silence allowing me to process my thoughts for a while. Jason's words kept replaying in my head non-stop like a tormenting headache.

"Did he really lie?" I questioned softly. I couldn't believe it, I had to see it for myself. He had no reason to lie. There was no way he could possibly benefit from it. In my twenty-one years of living, Jason was the only person confident enough to lie to my face but of course his reasons were somewhat practical. He either lied to protect me or lied to prank me.

"Why do you always assume the worst in people Jason? No one will lie for something like…" I couldn't complete my statement. My jaw dropped as the golden curtains opened revealing the prince and princess as they made their entrance. I didn't expect the princess to be so pretty. Just because someone is royalty, doesn't mean that they'll be gorgeous or anything, that's just fairy tale stereotypes. My expectations for everything were low and I seemed to be wrong about almost everything.

If the princess wore makeup, it was not noticeable and she still looked better than almost all the ladies in the room. Her ash brown hair was quite thick and full. It cascaded almost to her waist, ending in curly waves. Her eyes were Hazel brown just like her father's and they seemed to beam brightly whenever the slightest bit of light came in contact with them. The small crown on her head was the perfect accessory. Her dress was the only thing that wasn't simple, each layer of it was very detailed. The top half was fitted but not tight and the bottom piece from her waist down was a beautiful flare with a shimmer of gold. Her entire dress was gold but the shimmer stood out the most along with her sheer sleeves that fitted her arms perfectly. The most exceptional thing about her however, was her smile that seemed absolutely genuine. It made me want to be her friend.

"I don't mind marrying her," Jason stuttered. I yearned to respond to Jason's cunning remark, but I couldn't. I was speechless when I laid eyes on the prince. He took my breath away but not in a prince charming way. His malicious green eyes and sharp jawline were easily noticeable. As I scanned him even further his hair was wavy and blonde with slight hues of brown and still styled in that messy bun. But above all, what stood out the most was that sickening smirk that he just wouldn't get rid of. I was flabbergasted, I didn't know what to think or believe. His gaze kept traveling the room restlessly as if he was looking for someone. I flinched as Jason pinched my arm.

"Bow...everyone is bowing," he hissed. I was brought back to reality instantly and noticed that everyone's back was already arched. I arched mine quickly, not out of respect but only to blend in. I was still so trapped in my thoughts that I didn't notice when everyone rose. Jason grabbed me and shook me vigorously, forcing me to accept my rude awakening.

"Get yourself together!" he scolded softly. My eyes widened and I blinked twice just to make sure that everything was real, that everything was really happening the way it was.

"Okay...let me go now, you're making a scene," I quietly complained.

"You were about to make one yourself when you were still bowing even though everyone was up. Get your shit together and relax. He lied to you, so what? You should've seen the signs from the beginning. He tricked you. I do the same all the time. What do you do whenever I trick or make a fool out of you?"

"I get you back..." I answered.

"Good, now get a hold of your emotions and get back at him. Don't allow him to see you like this. You're too bothered and obviously affected. It only makes his victory even sweeter." He loosened his grip and finally let go. He was right, and maybe I did over react a little. Joel had no idea what he signed up for. Playing games with people was my specialty and he seemed to have made his first move. I raised my head and acknowledged his presence, his eyes were already on me, his restless endeavor for the person he searched for in the crowd ended. His sinister smile expanded until it unraveled into a shy grin.

"Well played Joel, well played," I sneered. It was as if he was laughing at a joke that only he and I knew about. I stared at him sharply, but it wasn't an angry stare, it was more like a... I acknowledge you and you've got my attention kind of stare. He returned the look with a mutual glare, I felt as though we talked without saying anything. If I was right and we both understood each other, it's safe to say that war began. His sister noticed him grinning and followed his gaze which led her straight to me.

Her eyes widened at the sight of me and a slight smile appeared on her lips.

"The princess is looking here," Jason stammered. "No… she's not just looking here, she's specifically looking at you."

I caught her attention unintentionally, but she was so pretty. Her beauty made me nervous. I didn't know what to do so I avoided eye contact. "Maybe it's because my skin is dark brown Jason, it's nothing new," I tried to play it off.

"Yeah but she's still looking. The king and queen noticed you but they didn't stare for long. Oh…don't bother, she isn't looking at you any more." His last few words eased the cumbersome feeling in my veins and all heftiness was gone. The king talked unnecessarily about his children, boasting about how great they were but nothing he said stood out. It amazed me that he was in my presence for over an hour and I didn't even know his name but in two minutes his children's name were already announced. After a few minutes of unnecessary yapping, the king eventually clarified the information that Jason and I looked forward to.

"We know that this new adjustment may be slightly difficult for you all to get used to. I'm sure you all had your scheduled way of living before you were chosen for this, which is why we have plans in place to make up for the inconvenience as best we can. Every month you will be awarded or in other words gifted with allowances and merchandise. It should be noted that not everyone's allowance will be the same, it varies depending on how well you impress my children."

I was grateful for his transparency, based on our allowances I knew it'd be easier to estimate our place in their ranks with enough time granted. Our motive was money, that was our agreement, but I couldn't help but wonder if Jason had a change of plans after seeing the princess for the first time.

"What are your chances of falling in love with the princess?" I asked. I had to weigh the pros and the cons. If Jason fell in love with the princess, he'd want me to get along with the royal family.

"She's gorgeous...so very high," he teased. "Don't worry I'm not going to try to win her heart or fall in love. I'm just going with the flow and taking the money as we go."

"Going with the flow?" I snapped. I was slightly triggered. How could he just 'go with the flow'?

"Relax Amaris," his voice was rough and I sensed a bit of irritation. "If we just relax and be ourselves we'll be fine. Everyone else will try their hardest to make an impression, they all want the crown. We'll never stand out, we'll fade away and be easily forgotten if we're just ourselves. The only thing that makes us stand out is that we're poor and low classed. Your skin looks like chocolate and I look like..." he paused for a moment. "And I look like vanilla or so, I don't know. Your hair is naturally like cotton or something like that and mine is straight, that's the only thing that'll make you stand out."

"Yes but I flat ironed it so we'll stand out less..." I interrupted.

"Do you plan to keep it straight for our entire stay here? Once water touches it, it gets puffy and big again," Jason stated. He was right. Whenever my straightened hair interacted with water it always reverted to its natural state. If one day I got caught in the rain, I'd be screwed.

"Yes." I was being unrealistic but it was a risk that I was willing to take.

"Anyway," Jason continued. "In a few weeks they'd get accustom to our drastic difference and your appearance as well so it wouldn't matter. You are a rare gem but looks alone won't make someone want you, but it does play a big part. Once we stay chill and be ourselves with no intentions of impressing anyone, the others will over shadow us eventually and we'll be irrelevant."

He was right and that stirred a bit of excitement in my bones. I'd be living lavishly in the castle for a while and all I had to do was have fun being myself while the others try their best to stand out and be chosen. In the end, I'd be sent home rich enough to start a new life.

"Are you ready to be rich just by having fun?" I giggled softly.

"I was always ready. I'm only concerned about how long our stay here will be. One year will be enough, I think it's more than enough actually," Jason implied.

"If we make it to two years I think that'll be a problem," I explained. "At that point we're clearly one of the favourites and at risk of being chosen. Do you think we'll develop certain feelings towards them too?" I asked.

"Definitely. Then that will be another issue for us...somewhat. Because if we aren't chosen and you're in love, I'd have to deal with your heart broken ass crying every day for weeks." He chuckled. Me, heartbroken over someone a lot of girls will be fighting over? Never!

"Don't think so lowly of me Jason. Last time I checked, you were the one with a leakage of tears running down your eyes over someone you loved," I said my words with the biggest sarcastic smile on my face. He cleared his throat and said nothing more. His silence satisfied me, looked like I won this one. I rarely ever won our petty playful arguments and even on this rare occasion I couldn't enjoy the feeling of victory as long as I wanted to. It was instantly taken away by the King's request.

"It'd be an honor to have the chosen at our side at this moment. Please, make your way up here so that everyone knows who you are."

My heart skipped a beat followed by my shortness of breath. I stood there in disbelief hoping that I heard wrong but everything was made clear the moment two people with similar features, black hair as dark as the night sky, similar to their eyes approached first. My hair is black but it seemed dull compared to theirs. They were quite fascinating to look at, I never saw hair that dark and even their nose and lips were the same, but they're twins so it's to be expected. At least Jason and I weren't the only siblings taking part in this…whatever this was.

I spotted other young adults moving through the crowd and up the stairs to the podium. I watched as they all climbed the stairs and bowed within five feet of the royal family then walked away respectfully and stood behind them. The guard marked each one of them sharply to prevent any mishaps or casualties from happening, but I'm pretty sure the royal family was capable of protecting themselves. I stood there frozen, intimidated by everyone, I knew that the moment we stepped foot on those stairs we'd instantly be judged by everyone. I felt a tugging on my arm that changed into a heavy pull as Jason took hold of me and gave me a slight push on my back, forcing me to take a few steps forward.

"Come on let's go," he insisted.

Chapter 12: Are you dumb or are you Stupid?

"They're watching us really hard," Jason whispered.

"I know, that's why I'm keeping my head down. I'm pretty sure they're judging us by our rags and dull attire. I don't even have makeup on."

"You don't even know how to put on makeup, if you keep your head down you'll look like a coward. So far everyone can see that you're intimidated, do you really want to seem that way?" He was so manipulative with his words but he was right. He placed his hand around my neck and raised my chin, forcing me to look up. "Raise your head and keep it that way. Now isn't the time to act timid."

"What are you doing?" I stuttered. "You're causing a scene."

"We are already the scene and more specifically you. You're always the centre of attention upon meeting new faces so pull yourself together. Those aren't just new people, they are high ranking civilians and nobles."

"But that's why I'm nervous...."

"So what? Are you going to use that excuse to look like a sissy? You're such a weakling," he teased. He knew exactly what he was doing. Using his words to get the reaction he wanted. No matter where I was, people would always stare, but I already knew that.

"It's complicated...." I complained. He tried to dissect and figure me out but I wasn't in the mood to be examined, especially as we made our way up the stairs.

"I know what the issue is. You grew accustom to everyone staring anytime they laid eyes on you, but ever since you got here, you're so self-conscious. It has nothing to do with the difference in your racial appearance...."

"I never said that..."

"I'm not done," Jason interrupted. "You feel embarrassed because we're poor and surrounded by all these wealthy people. Judging by the other contestants, they look well off and marriage material in the eyes of many. I'm also aware that we'd be instantly judged the moment we step foot on that podium. We're being judged right now, but we can't do anything about it and we shouldn't care." His words were abrasive, but accurate, I didn't like hearing the truth and neither did I enjoy having a conversation about it.

"We're almost there so stop talking. We have about six more steps to climb...."

"Then let's not climb them," Jason insisted. He paused and just stood there looking at me. His timing couldn't be any more off than it was. He took a firm grip of my arm, preventing me from going any further.

"Jason people are watching," I hissed. "You're causing a

spectacle."

"As I said, we were always the scene. How long we exaggerate the scene is up to you. Fix your face and stop over thinking. We're poor... so what? No matter where we go and who we meet we'll always be judged for any and everything. The moment you lay eyes on someone you subconsciously judge them, off their looks, place of birth, the way they talk and how they carry themselves. Financial status is just another category that we have to deal with. It's simply human nature and that will never change."

"Okay..." I sighed. I covered my face with the palm of my hands and groaned. His piercing words dug deep, slowly seeping into my heart. I wiped away the worry from my face and substituted it with an unfazed appearance.

"That's better...Now let's go." Jason took his few steps forward and I followed. I wondered if we looked disrespectful when we paused for a few seconds and whispered, but everyone was clapping as we ascended the stairs so I was pretty confident that no one heard anything. But I still knew that although they didn't hear us, just seeing us stop for a moment to whisper would've raised concern. There was the probability that someone could read our lips but the only person that maybe knew exactly what we said was that old guard, Linden.

As we made our final step to the podium, the royal family welcomed us with beaming smiles. I wasn't sure if they were all genuine but the pleasant expressions reduced my nervousness allowing me to relax a little. I avoided eye contact with Joel as best I could but I knew that sooner or later I'd have no choice but to look him in the eyes. We paused within a distance of five feet and bowed for the sake of respect. My eyes met the king's first and he nodded with a smile, I smiled back and then looked at the queen. She did the same with her beaming green eyes, I felt comfortable in her presence. My gaze shifted to princess Roselyn, the smile on her face seemed so forced, almost as if she faked it to be polite but couldn't perfect her pretence.

Her eyes travelled from my head to my toes and they seemed to be growing colder each second. She clearly wasn't impressed nor was she happy but she eventually looked me in the eyes again but without pretence. From the narrow, frigid look in her eyes, I was clearly dismissed. I gave her a piercing stare and watched as her eyes twitched as she blinked twice in disbelief. I dismissed myself with a smirk on my face, it was a shame that such a pretty girl could be so disrespectful, but royalty or not I could be disrespectful right back.

I glanced over my shoulder and watched as Jason interacted with her. I wondered if she'd treat him the same or be more welcoming towards him. My brother acted like the flirtatious fool he is and winked at her with a blush on his face. She rolled her eyes and looked away, I couldn't help but laugh but I made sure to keep it as a subtle grin.

I glanced at Joel and noticed his green eyes beaming brightly at me fuelled by mischief. I didn't bother to stare long. I refused to give him that satisfaction. I walked passed him immediately without looking back and joined the line of contestants. I would admit that they were all dressed in the finest of clothing, covered in jewellery and drenched in expensive scents, but I didn't want what they wanted. They wanted the crown, all I wanted was money and a fresh start to a new life. Some would call me selfish but I'd call it surviving. The moment Jason stood beside me, I couldn't help but take the opportunity to address that ridiculous stunt he pulled.

"Are you dumb or are you stupid?" I boldly stared into his eyes, just to tease him some more. I remembered that embarrassed expression on his face when the princess rolled her eyes at him and tried my best not to laugh out loud.

"What do you mean?" he stuttered. He was clueless, had no idea what I was talking about so I came to the conclusion that he had to be stupid.

"A wink? Really? So you just had to be the flirtatious play boy that you are huh? What did you think was going to happen?"

"First of all... I didn't wink at her," he lied. I prepared myself for the bullshit excuse that he was going to come up with. "I blinked because something was in my eye."

"So you blinked at her because something was in your eye and you even smiled too. That thing in your eye must've felt really good to make you smile," I countered.

"I smiled to address her politely, that's what the smile was for. I was in no way flirting with that gorgeous young lady," he blushed. We stared silently at each other till one of us couldn't hold it in any more. It was me, I grinned first because that look of embarrassment replayed in my mind constantly until I cracked.

"That's why she rolled her eyes at you, because you're stupid," I teased. He laughed back and looked away.

"I guess it's safe to say we may not be their favourite after all," he grinned. "That should calm your worries for a while."

I remained optimistic and entertained. For many years I looked forward to seeing Jason play his flirtatious game and be turned down by a beautiful woman and it finally happened. It was bold of him to even try that with the princess. The rich wanted nothing to do with the poor. They always dismissed us like we were nothing, and for some of them, being in their presence seemed to be a form of disrespect. Based on the silent interaction from the princess and the way she looked down on us, I felt certain that she had no desire to see us within miles of the castle. Jason was aware of all of this but arrogance and pride made him stupid. Your looks could only take you so far and this time it wasn't enough, but I also knew him to be a clown, so I had no idea what his true intentions were.

Cringe worthy words were issued from the king's mouth in such a proud manner. "Ladies and gentlemen, I present to you THE LEGENDARY CONTESTANTS FOR THE CROWN!"

We were greeted with a loud and powerful applause. I was tempted to cover my ears but I knew better. I squeezed my fists to relieve a bit of the irritation I experienced but it didn't help. The king raised his hand to silence the crowd and draw everyone's attention, the noise faded immediately.

"Finally," I muttered. I let out a long sigh of relief and relaxed the palm of my hands.

"Now we celebrate," the king continued. "After the celebration, the pursuit for the crown and the heart of my children will finally begin. In the meantime, let's have some fun." He turned and faced us, the so called legendary contestants. "You are free to go back now." He didn't need to tell me twice, Jason and I were the first to leave without hesitation. We hated it up there. We preferred to remain in the shadows and blend in with the crowd although that was almost impossible for us in this environment. As we headed down the stairs, the others followed.

"And one more thing," the queen interrupted. It was the first time I heard her speak so she had my full attention. "The king said that the pursuit for a spot in the royal family starts after the celebration, but that's not necessarily true."

I watched as the king's eyes widened in confusion. Joel and

his sister had a similar expression, but she continued. "The first planned activity starts after the celebration but there's no need for you to wait that long. Feel free to make your move, maybe you can give them a reason to look forward to the activity that we have planned later you know. Make them want to see you, but do so in a respectful manner. May the best man and woman win!"

"I agree. There's no need to wait. If you want it badly, you'll find a way to make things happen. Your journey for love and a spot in our family has already begun, do what you must to win, but whatever you do, be genuine. Now... let the party begin," the king announced.

"I already made my move, I'm not making another," Jason insisted. "There's no need to go after the princess. She's pretty but I don't feel anything towards her so why waste my time trying to win her over."

"I agree," I admitted. "Let's sit back and be entertained as the others fight for a spot in the royal family."

CHAPTER 13: Unreal

All preparations for the ball or celebration, whatever they called it, were completed in approximately ten minutes. I was impressed but not surprised, it was the Kingdom of Mandora after all. Anything was possible in this country. Not many changes were made; the place looked the same with just a few additional adjustments. Food was everywhere, there were at least twelve stations set for food, or maybe I lost count because it seemed like a lot more, but the tables were set for appetizers, main meals, drinks and even deserts. Jason and I were in man-made heaven, free food was paradise to us.

We swayed to the music as the talented musicians played their instruments. I guessed that classical music was their theme for the night. We had no experience in dancing so there was nothing more we could do. Servants walked around with trays of appetizers and desert for those who were too lazy to serve themselves. A slim redhead with pale skin approached us with a tray of bread and smiled. The scent of garlic tickled my nose, arousing my taste buds even before I saw the source of the aroma. It was garlic bread, one of my favourite type of bread. I smiled back and gladly accepted without thinking twice. I was starving since I had only eaten an apple for the day.

"Thank you," I responded, graciously accepting the treat. The bread felt so warm and freshly baked yet soft and tender with a little bit of crust at the corners. It was definitely made with top quality ingredients. The flavour was intense, or maybe we just weren't accustomed to that kind of food. The last time Jason and I had something so tasty was on my thirteenth birthday, when our parents were still alive. We struggled to have decent meals for years but due to our circumstances we settled for basic, tasteless food that lacked appetizing ingredients, but we still survived, that's all that mattered. As she turned her back towards us I pleaded for her to stay a few seconds more.

"Wait! Please don't leave yet," I requested. "I'd like to have some more. Is that okay?" Her eyes expanded in shock at my sudden request but then she smiled.

"Of course you can, it's an all you can eat buffet. Take as many as you want, its fine." Her words were like music to my ears. I took two more slices. I didn't want to seem too greedy or desperate, although I probably still did. Jason stretched his arm over my head and took four more. His mouth was already stuffed with two slices.

"Jason, don't be greedy," I scolded. Even though we were given the opportunity to eat as much as we wanted, I thought that we should at least be discrete about it. There were no plates or napkins in our hands, but that didn't prevent him from awkwardly filling his hands with the mouth-watering treat. It amazed me that he didn't drop any.

"I'm just appreciating how well the food tastes and there's no better way to do that than to partake of it. At least allow me to eat in peace, everyone else is so why can't I?" he muttered between swallows. He stuffed his face with another slice as crumbs fell to the floor.

"Umm excuse me... I don't mean to interrupt but you should taste our chocolate cake, or maybe even the ice cream..." The server suggested. She was so shy but cute at the same time. Jason's eyes lit up when she mentioned the ice cream. She talked so softly in a nervous manner that I was forced to strain my ears to hear what she was saying. "Would you like me to get some for you? You won't have to go anywhere if you're comfortable where you are. You're a selected pair, I'd love to serve you for the night," she pleaded.

"Thank you so much. We'd love to and we appreciate your services to us as well, you're so kind," Jason commended. She blushed uncontrollably and walked away.

"Ugh, here we go again," I complained. I never understood how he did it. He always left an impact on females and then gloated in my face.

"You see? I'm a natural at this," He looked at me with a broad smile that was quite sickening. I wished there was a way to wipe it off.

"The princess doesn't even look at you," I clapped back. "You being in her presence is upsetting to her. I hope you feel proud about that too," I grinned.

"I didn't come here to win her over or anything so I don't care," he retaliated, stuffing another slice of bread in his mouth.

"But yet you still winked at her before the words hello my name is, came out your mouth," I stated. He avoided eye contact with me and folded his arms as he took a while to swallow the last slice of bread in his mouth.

"I'm a flirtatious person by nature but that's just how I make friends," he explained. He always had an excuse to justify his actions but I couldn't help but laugh. Friends? Definitely not. He always left a trail of girls disappointed or hurt and didn't even notice.

He tapped my shoulder and pointed to an area across the room. "Look, it has already begun. How do you think it'll play off?"

I strained my eyes in the direction in which his finger guided and searched through the crowd till something stood out. I didn't know what I was looking for but something did stand out, or rather someone. Joel stood in the centre of the room with a smile so bright that I felt certain that even his wisdom tooth was showing. He was talking to someone, a very pretty girl. Having taken in the scene, I forced my brother's arm down. He was too obvious.

"Stop pointing…. That's low key rude," I stated. He put his hand down and placed it in his pocket.

"It's not really that I care, but I'm pretty sure you saw what I'm talking about," he said.

"Yes, I'm seeing it as we speak." I observed them even more. She was the prettiest girl in the room after the princess. Her dainty nose was cute but her eyes were so pretty. Something about her eyes just stood out the most. Her eyelashes were long and thick and her pupils were golden brown. I never saw anything like it, hazel brown was a nice eye colour but golden brown was my new favourite. It was even better than the green and blues. Even her hair matched the colour of her eyes, I just couldn't stop staring. Her red dress exposed her shapely figure and hugged her body perfectly with its soft and stretchy material. She wore red gloves and red high heel shoes to match her dress.

There was no doubt in my mind that she had a top quality fashion designer to help her out. Even if she did choose her dress personally, nothing would change the obvious fact that she had money, lots of money. Her face was heavy on the makeup just like all the other women in the room but her face was flawlessly done.

"Why are you staring at her like that? Are you intimidated….or are you jealous that she has his attention," Jason teased. He played along with his words like a joke to spark some sought of reaction out of me. "Or are you developing a crush? You've been staring at her for the longest while. Is there something you're not telling me? Are you by chance swinging that way or curious about what you like?" he grinned. I pinched a muscle in his arm to make him stop and watched as he flinched at the unexpected pain he felt.

"Stop. I'm not intimidated by anything or anyone and you know I'm not into girls…at all," I responded.

"Yes, I know you don't swing that way but you were staring for so long. It's okay if you're jealous of him talking to someone else, I won't judge you. I'll just harass you." His words burned my ears from the nonsense he spewed.

"I'm not jealous, I'm staring at her because she's pretty. You should be happy she isn't available to flirt with, that will save you from humiliation…. again." I looked at him as his eyes twitched to my words.

"Look Jason," I pointed. My attention had already shifted from the prince. I tried my best to hold in my sinister smile before I dropped the bomb on him. "A different guy is flirting with the princess and he's been doing so for over two minutes now. Two minutes may not seem like a lot but she wouldn't even look at you for two seconds. She'd just role her eyes and look away."

I felt his deep breaths escape his nostrils as it rested on my face. He forcefully pushed my finger down and grunted. "Put your damn finger down. Didn't you say pointing at people is rude? Earlier you were afraid of me causing a scene, now look at you, pointing at people and being disrespectful."

"Stop nagging and just watch," I retorted harshly as I observed the interaction between the princess and the contestant. His warm undertone of beige skin complemented the colour of his eyes and hair perfectly. He was tall, lean and strong almost about Jason's height. I tried my best not to blush but he was a fine looking man. His suit was the same shade of red as his sister's dress. Everything about those two was well coordinated. I was surprised to see another pair of siblings since coloured moons were so rare. When he spoke to Roselyn he wore a charming smile on his face that seemed quite genuine but Roselyn's smile looked obligatory.

"She's not talking much, she just has this faint smile on her face and then she nods every time he says something. I'm pretty sure he's forcing a conversation right now, he can't even take a hint that she doesn't want to speak to him. Or maybe he's just desperately looking for a way in," Jason indicated. My brows rose unconsciously as conversation became loud in the room.

"I can't believe those two are candidates to join the royal family. Uncultured swine, not even third class people, clearly the lowest of the low."

Jason chuckled a bit at their stupid remarks but nothing was funny to me. I turned to my left and faced them with the broadest smile I could offer. It was a middle aged woman with her husband holding hands beside her. They grasped each other's hand so tightly that their bond was noticeably fake. It must've been an unstable marriage since they tried so hard to seem perfect. I raised my middle finger and stuck out my tongue as Jason joined me. All they could do was flinch at our reaction. It wasn't long before others in the room noticed and gave their remarks.

"Those two don't belong here, I would never bow to her if she became queen."

"I hope the royal family sees, it'll make the elimination process much easier."

"While the others choose to make their moves and talk to the prince and princess they choose to stand there and disrespect the guests. Not surprised though, poor people never know their place."

Each statement meant the same thing. To them, we weren't fit for the royal family but I didn't care, we came for the money. My opinion of the rich in Mandora was abysmal. They acted all high and mighty as if they're worth much but most of them got their title and wealth from their ancestors, not because of their own personal achievements. I was not impressed.

"Umm, here's the chocolate cake and ice-cream," a girl squealed. She caught me off guard but her familiar face and tray of ice-cream brightened the mood.

"Thank you soooo much," my voice trembled in excitement.

"Mmm, this is good, really good." Jason muttered. His words were muffled and unclear. I looked at him to get a better understanding of what he said. His mouth was stuffed with chocolate icing smeared at the side of his lips.

"I didn't even see your hand go into the tray. When did you take?" I asked. The server covered her mouth and grinned.

"I took a slice right after she said cake and ice-cream. You should try it, it's really good." He kept talking with his mouth stuffed; fortunately no food flew out of his mouth this time.

"Jason you didn't just take a slice, there's two more slices of chocolate cake in your hand. Stop talking with your mouth full and wipe your mouth, you have cake crumbs and icing in the corner of your lips." I grabbed a slice of cake from his hand and watched as he wiped the crumbs off his face.

"Give me back my slice," he demanded. I looked at the cocoa brown fluffy cake in my hand fascinated while the chocolate icing stained my finger-tips.

"No." I bit into the cake and smiled as I did my happy dance in his face. The cake melted on my tongue and the sugary sweet taste danced around on my taste buds.

"It doesn't matter, I don't need that specific slice of cake. I can take another slice from the tray, a bigger one," he acknowledged. The pretty red-head servant just stood there grinning at us. She searched through the tray and selected the biggest slice she could find.

"Here you go," she offered. Jason took it immediately then arched his brow and smiled at me indicating that he got the last laugh.

"Thank you… May I ask, what is your name?"

"My name is Susan," she said softly. She was so timid, our personalities must've been too much for her.

"Well Susan… my name is…"

"Jason, your name is Jason," she intervened. "And your sister's name is Amaris," she said her words with great confidence and then stumbled again. "I'm sorry, I didn't mean to interrupt you I just…."

"That makes me feel special, I promise to remember yours," I grabbed a glass of ice-cream and winked at her. Perhaps I tried too hard to be nice.

"I'm shocked too, I wasn't expecting anyone to learn our names so soon." Jason admitted. I stared at the white milky substance melting in the glass cylinder that it was kept in. Reality felt unreal.

"Is something wrong?" Susan asked. I kept looking at the ice-cream without taking a bite, she must've been nervous. "The flavour is coconut ice-cream. I'm sorry, I should've asked you what flavour you preferred."

"If you don't want it I'll take it," Jason suggested. He held an empty silver container in his hand with little to no remains of ice-cream.

"You ate all already?" I stammered.

"Yeah what's taking you so long?" Jason reached out and took another. "It's okay if I grab a next one right? If I'm taking too much just let me know."

"No it's fine, there's no rule about how much you can eat," Susan repeated. I gripped my silver spoon and took a taste.

"It's been years." I muttered subconsciously.

"I know, let's embrace it until it's over." Jason's words were always so practical. I stood there without moving a muscle, trying not to expose myself in a vulnerable manner.

"Amaris are you okay?" I sensed the concern in his voice but I couldn't respond, I didn't know how to. "Susan, thank you for everything that you've done thus far but can you leave us for a moment?" Jason asked.

"Sure, I'll give you two your space."

A leakage of tears escaped my eyes and ran down my cheeks as I stood there in a state of shock. Jason placed his arms around me and pulled me close. I planted my face in his chest and cried while he rubbed my back.

"I know exactly how you feel," he whispered. I knew he did. "We won't have to starve any more." I whimpered.

"No, no more going days without eating, no more worrying about a place to sleep or even a place to shelter from the rain and the snow. We're safe here and I promise you that when we leave this place, we will never go back to the way things were. We'll live comfortably for the rest of our life," Jason squeezed me tighter and wouldn't let go. He too was fighting with his emotions and needed that hug just as much as I did.

"I'm causing a scene aren't I?" I sniffled. I removed my face from his chest and raised my head. His eyes weren't watery but his cheeks were red.

"No, you're not making a scene...."

"There's no need to lie. I can hear them talking, they're not exactly whispering. How bad is it?" I asked. Jason stayed quiet for a few seconds and then let out a long stressful sigh.

"Everyone in the room is watching, including the royal family. And also...."

I flinched at the random tap to my shoulder. "Are you okay? Joel asked.

CHAPTER 14: Intentions

His eyes showed that kind of gentle concern my mother's always had. When he came in my presence, he brought the attention of everyone else with him. I didn't want that, I didn't want to be seen as the crying girl that the prince talked to out of pity. I didn't want to speak to him, I didn't want his help or his concern. I bowed in respect but hesitated to speak.

"She's fine, we're sorry for causing a scene but we're fine now." Jason said softly. Everyone in the room was already quiet, trying to gather information as best they could so we tried to be as discrete as possible.

Joel spoke through his clenched teeth with great irritation. "If she's fine then why hasn't she answered me yet? I'll change my question this time, what's wrong?"

Jason pinched my arm, forcing me to say something. I raised my head slowly to process my thoughts but his eyes were already sharply fixed on me.

"I am fine your highness, I'm sorry for worrying you," I

sniffled. More tears ran down my face but I wiped them away immediately and made sure that they were the last of it.

"It doesn't seem like nothing, would you like to talk about it?" he asked. Irritation boiled through my veins, I didn't want to talk about it and I definitely didn't want to talk about it to him. My pride was already broken the moment everyone in the room saw me crying.

"No." I spoke more assertive this time. As strong headed as I was, I flinched as his eyebrows arched sternly.

"Once again, we're sorry if this caused you any inconvenience," Jason said.

"Excuse me your highness…." I mumbled. I wasn't sure how he'd take what I was about to say but I had to let him know how I felt. "I mean no disrespect, but I'd like to be alone right now."

"Well… that explains a lot," Joel's voice raised slightly. I pleaded with him with my eyes to tone it down a little.

"What does this explain?" I asked. I was confused but deeply concerned about where his head was at but he brushed it off like it was nothing.

"It's nothing, I'm probably just over reacting," he stated. I didn't know what to say, everything just felt so uncomfortably awkward.

"Uh…okay," I mumbled. "I'm fine, I really am. I'm just a little too embarrassed to talk about it but I… I think I'm happy, overwhelmingly happy."

"So those were tears of joy?" he asked. Confusion was written all over his face, I wanted to clear everything up but I didn't want to make myself vulnerable in the process.

"I'm just relieved, for the first time in a long while I am… relieved. I am also overwhelmed so…"

"So that's why you two are the only contestants that haven't approached my sister and I since the celebration began." His tone seemed less stressed all of a sudden. I didn't think about it too much, I was just relieved that the tension was gone.

"Bro, we had the longest conversation with you than anyone else. We laughed, had conversations, argued and almost got into a fight," Jason grinned. We all laughed, it brightened the mood for a little while. "O shit... I'm sorry," Jason stuttered.

"What? What's wrong?" Joel asked. His face was as puzzled as I was, Jason didn't say anything offensive.

"Your highness, I meant to say your highness. Sorry it'll take us a while to adapt to this new setting, especially having to call you things like your highness and bowing to you and whatnot."

"It's fine. I'll give you as much time as you need. I understand that my true identity may be shocking for you two," he tilted his head towards me and wore his favourite sinister smile across his lips.

"It wasn't a shock to me." Jason explained. "You need to come up with better lies, there's no such thing as a prince's right hand."

"There is," Joel confirmed. "We've had it for two generations, I'll be selecting one soon."

"What's the criteria for that position?" Jason asked. I knew he'd be interested but I wasn't sure if that's what I wanted for him.

"You have to be strategic and smart but you must know how to hold your own if trouble comes. That person must have great leadership skills, not someone that would flee and leave their soldiers for dead. Maybe I'm asking for too much but I don't want my people to be led by a coward in my absence." Joel explained. I agreed with him. I wouldn't want any of my loved ones to be lead in battle by a coward who was willing to sacrifice everyone.

"You're not asking for too much," Jason right hand maned. "It's actually reasonable."

"Are you interested?" Joel continued. I hated where the conversation was heading. It would've been a great opportunity for my brother but he'd be exposed to danger too frequently. I remained there as a third wheel just waiting for their conversation to be over, there were no openings for me to join. With the prince in our presence, eyes remained locked in our direction. I must've looked so awkward just standing there, not talking to him. The general expectation was that a contestant to marry the prince would make a move.

"Interested, yes. But do I want the position? I'm not sure." I wasn't happy with Jason's response but I wasn't upset about it either.

"I'm not sure my father will be pleased about this conversation, but I'll take my leave now. I have other people to attend to, see you two some other time."

"Are we supposed to bow before you walk off on us?" I asked. I had to be safe because everyone was watching, one wrong move and we'd be judged instantly. They already had a negative impression of us, but now the prince was in our presence talking and laughing right after I made a scene by sobbing like a baby. He grinned at me with his white teeth exposed and then gave a response.

"You really do have a lot to learn but yes, usually you give a slight bow before a noble departs from your presence."

"Thanks for the clarification," I said with my back already arched downwards. He gave us a slight nod then slowly disappeared into the crowd. The harsh stares remained for a while. I waited until he was out of sight before addressing my concerns with Jason. "Are you out of your mind?"

"What's the problem this time Amaris? I'd like to go at least two hours without having confrontation with you," Jason complained. He protested as if I always had an issue, but he always gave me a reason to.

"So now you're talking to the prince about positions in the castle? We haven't been here for twenty four hours but you're already taking big steps."

"I'm searching to see what options I have available. Wouldn't it be nice to have a secured job before we leave? That will lessen our worries." His reasoning made sense but something about that position was a bit of a stretch for me.

"Yes but…"

"I know what you're thinking," He butted. "That position is a little too much, maybe I should search for something else. Yes, the thought of working as the prince's right hand man is nice. It actually seems like the perfect job for me but it doesn't necessarily mean that's what I'll settle for. I'm keeping my options open till it's time to choose one."

"Okay…fine. That can work," I admitted. He was thinking ahead, that was smart but maybe he was moving a little too fast. "Do you think we should talk to the princess? Maybe it'll look bad if we talked to the prince but had no interaction with the princess," I stated. Jason responded quickly without even thinking about it for two seconds.

"No."

"No? What do you mean no?" I stammered.

"She's rude, you saw it yourself. We interacted already, I gave her a wink and she rolled her eyes then looked away. Would you want to talk to someone that obviously doesn't want to talk to you? Maybe if I was interested I'd try a thing, but a pretty face and a title is all she has to offer. She knows that everyone approaching her wants to win her over or at least be on her good side. I'm not going to let her think that about me."

His petty behaviour was quite laughable but I appreciated his pride. We weren't there to impress, we were there to invest. "I agree, let's not boost their egos when we don't even want them."

"But you gave the prince an opening to speak to you though." His words startled me, it's not like I broke down in tears on purpose.

"He only approached me to look good. Comforting a crying contestant is what any prince in his situation would do." I made a forceful attempt to switch the conversation and I knew my selected topic would be effective "We've been here a good while now and all we've eaten so far was garlic bread, chocolate cake and coconut ice-cream. They have a lot more to offer so let's have the feast we deserve. Look! There is a lot of meat over there," I pointed to a table across the room where a variety of meat was being served.

A fat roasted pig layed in the center of the table with its stomach already cut into large serving slices. Surrounding the roasted pig were huge platters of fowl stuffed with savory fruits and nuts. I thought it was a weird combination but food was food at this point. On the far ends of the table roasted beef was drenched in barbecue sauce, Jason's favourite. Goat was also on the menu, stew goat which we've never tried but intended to. We made a conscious decision that we must sample everything they had to offer.

CHAPTER 15: Something's not Right

"Jason, are you seeing what I'm seeing?" I asked. The room was much brighter, the music, much louder and everyone around us multiplied. "Why are they moving like that?" I sipped the remainder of my juice slowly. It burned as it touched my tongue and made its way down my throat.

"Yeah, but many of them are leaving."

My chest and stomach felt cold, but not just cold, I was wet. A sweet, strong but surprisingly not pleasing scent leaked off of me. "Why do I smell like that?"

"You spilled the juice when you tasted it. You thought the drink was expired so you panicked and spilled some. But a few hours later you kept spilling more on yourself for some reason," Jason explained. I looked down and scanned my dress and noticed the red stains all over, from the top of my chest area to the bottom of my belly.

"Ahhh shit. I don't think I'll ever be able to get this stain off!" I vented. Jason kept swaying side to side and bumping into me each minute. He leaned forward to respond and tripped on his left leg but he didn't fall.

"Well if you weren't clumsy none of this would've happened. We didn't pack enough clothes to last us A WEEK!" he suddenly raised his voice as if he was upset or something. I cringed at the loud ringing in my ears but worst of all, I cringed at his stink breath. It smelt just like the stain on my outfit.

"Jason your breath is nasty, get out of my face" I demanded. He didn't say anything for a few seconds, he just kept staring till he eventually snapped.

"MY BREATH DOESN'T STINK! YOURS DOES!"

The stench of his breath lingered longer on my face. The people that passed by kept staring as they walked away, some even stopped and spectated longer.

"Stop shouting!" I yelled back. Maybe I shouldn't have but I tried to match his volume. Some may have seen it as unladylike but it was a quick and not thought out reaction. He kept drifting slightly but looked at me and said nothing. He wrinkled his nose and one of his brows arched higher than the other as if he was confused. Something definitely wasn't right.

"I'm not shouting, you are."

My head felt heavy, it was quite odd. Everyone seemed to be shaking subconsciously and that raised a lot of concern in my brain. Either something was wrong with them or something was wrong with me, with us. My ears were ringing for whatever reason and my eyes felt weighed down somehow. I forced myself to keep them open. Overall I felt drowsy, very drowsy but that was the least of my problems. Nothing made sense and I felt so light headed to the point where I looked at people and saw two of the same person drifting in and out of each other. I existed in a world where everything slowly faded. It worried me but fascinated me at the same time.

"I'm not feeling well," I admitted. "Something is wrong with me. I think I'm seeing things and my head is pounding."

"Seeing things?" Jason asked, still tripping on nothing. "Seeing things like what?"

"I see two of you and you keep swaying in and out. It's weird, I think I'm hallucinating." I didn't want to explain it any further, everyone looked fine and I seemed to be the only one with problems. I didn't want him to think I was crazy.

"You are a bit shaky but everyone is fine, it's just you. I wasn't talking loud either so I don't know what that was about. Your hearing can't get extremely sensitive all of a sudden. The celebration is over so I'm sure we'll get to bed soon. Right now we're just waiting on further instructions," Jason whispered. He tried to comfort me but I still wasn't focused on anything he said. "Don't think about it too much, you're probably just sleepy. You've never been out this long," he said. "If you can't stand straight, just lean on my shoulder till they assign us to our rooms to sleep."

I tried to rest my head on his shoulder but he was too tall so I leaned my head on the side of his arm. It stopped me from swaying but I knew I couldn't remain standing for long; my body just wasn't strong enough for that. My gaze travelled across the room and stopped when I laid eyes on Joel. He leaned on a pillar with his arms crossed. He was already staring at me, I wondered how long. He was grinning again, something about his genuine laugh just made me smile. I was embarrassed about my situation but he made me realize the funny side of things. I noticed his sister Roselyn on the other side of the room standing beside her mother. I didn't see the king but I knew he was somewhere around.

"So I've been acting a fool around these people this whole time?" I asked. I didn't bother to speak softly because my voice was already weak and difficult to hear.

"Don't worry about it, all you did was shout and lost your balance every minute, then you kept bumping into me. You stumble a bit whenever you take a few steps forward but I won't say that you acted the fool," Jason explained. Although he was polite and reassuring I still couldn't make sense of what he said, so I just said okay. I felt as if he looked down on me sharply. "What did I just say?" he asked.

"I don't know," I admitted. He didn't tell me anything for a while. His silence bothered me and I felt uneasy. I felt the pillar on which I rested my head shifted. My body tipped over slowly and before I hit the floor Jason grabbed my shoulders and shook me vigorously. The reeling sensation that I felt increased. He finally let his hands off me and I tipped over once more. I didn't know what was happening and I couldn't fix it. The control I had over my body left. Jason brought me closer so that I could lean on his shoulder once again.

"Something's not right. Why are you the only person acting this way?" he muttered. I didn't bother to reply, it was too difficult to get the words out my mouth. It's not like I knew what was happening anyway. I blinked a lot more and constantly lost focus. Joel's sister rolled her eyes at me again, upset as if I had something to do with the way she felt. I couldn't do anything so I shifted my gaze to the queen. Her eyes expanded with raised brows, I didn't notice any anger but she did look a bit concerned.

The other guests had already left the room. A few people that looked wealthy enough to be nobles, and the royal family remained. I guessed they all lived there. Some were still eating and drinking as they continued to carry on their conversations. It was minutes past twelve on the clock. Back at home I would have been sleeping on the mattress or the ground by now. I heard constant murmuring at all corners of the room. I heard some of their words clearly but I still didn't understand what they were saying. As time passed I saw nothing, the sudden silence in the atmosphere grasped the little attention I had remaining.

I opened my eyes slowly, they were so heavy. I noticed Joel approaching from the corner of my eyes but I couldn't keep them opened for long.

"What's wrong with her?" The panic in Joel's voice almost made me blush a little. I kept a still face and surrendered to my body's demands to keep my eyes closed.

"I don't know. Maybe you can tell me," Jason responded. "I don't understand why she's the only person acting this way."

"I think I know," Joel grinned a bit, treating my situation as a joke. "I think it's her first time. Is it your first time too? You look slightly affected but not as bad as her."

I was in my own world separated from everyone else. My eyes shut closed again and the glass I held in my hand slipped away and shattered. Jason's arm couldn't hold me anymore, my head slipped downwards and my body followed. "I'm sorry." My apology was soft, I wasn't sure if anyone heard me. I thought that this time I'd hit the ground, but Jason caught me.

"Amaris, can you hear me?" Jason squeezed me tightly. I heard the panic in his voice. He rarely ever showed that side of himself.

"I don't think she'll be able to stand anymore," Joel said plainly, calm as if nothing was wrong.

"Why is she the only person acting this way!? I think someone poisoned her but I tasted everything before she consumed it."

"Relax, she'll be okay. She's just drunk." Joel explained. They kept talking, but eventually their voices faded away and I sensed nothing.

CHAPTER 16: Congratulations?

The moment I opened my eyes I wished I never did. I felt disoriented as my eyes burned when it made contact with the bright lights above my head. The golden chandelier in the center of the ceiling and the white light on the wall to my right just left me confused and instantly annoyed. Why should two coloured lights be on at the same time? Why should two lights be on in the first place, isn't one light enough? I endlessly found reasons to complain despite how grateful I was to be there.

I heard a loud banging sound to my left as a door I didn't notice between the walls swung open and slammed against the wall. Sudden shock left me frozen until the person behind the door made his appearance.

"Amaris are you here?" Jason asked. I wanted to beat the crap out of him for scaring me unnecessarily. Surely we were raised to open a door better than that.

"Yes. I'm fine so you can relax now. Do you remember how we got here?" I asked. He sighed loudly to release whatever stress he had stored within.

"I was just about to ask you that same thing. I don't remember much from last night, do you?" he asked. I took a trip through memory lane, trying to recoup whatever recollections I had of the previous night but unfortunately my mind was somewhat blank.

"I only remember eating cake," I stated. "Do you think someone placed something in our food? Maybe its…"

"Now that you've mentioned it," Jason interrupted. "It wasn't the food. I remember Joel saying something about you being drunk."

"D-DRUNK!?" I stammered. "No one told me they were serving alcohol. I just drank what I saw others drinking. Didn't you drink too?"

"Yes I did, I even drank more than you but I wasn't drunk so why can't I remember anything?" Jason paced around the room trapped in his thoughts. I could tell that our lack of memory bothered him. It bothered me too but at least there wasn't anything noticeably wrong with us.

"Do you think someone wiped away our memories?" I asked. When my words met his ear he stopped suddenly and just stood there with his fingers rubbing his chin. I couldn't see his face but his energy became heavy. I had other concerns but I refused to mention anything more till I knew what he was thinking. He removed his hand from his chin and faced me with an assertive but troubled look on his face.

"I don't know what happened that night or what caused us to forget but if there's something shady going on that can cause us any harm I will kill……"

His statement was cut short by the sudden breeze that gushed through the room, my door was swung open with a great intruding force. An aggressive voice pierced through our ears with a question that sounded more like a threat.

"Kill who?"

My eyes quickly followed the voice of the man that intruded our privacy. It was Logan, bold enough to open the door and take a few steps in without an invite. I should've known it was him the moment the sound of his voice passed through my ears.

"You're quite bold to enter our room without permission," Jason stated. "You didn't even knock, how inappropriate for a noble like you."

Logan's face turned red instantly as he held his breath, trying to hold back laughter but his attempt to keep a straight face failed after five seconds. "A noble *like* me? Hahahaaa, funny you say that. Do you even know who I am for you to say a noble *like* me?" he grilled. "Yes I'm a noble, but you don't even know my rank or position in the kingdom. You have no clue about what I do. That was a bold statement you made there….."

"I don't need to know what you do," Jason interrupted. "I observe how people react around you. Another noble was trembling in your presence, I'd assume that a noble *like you*, is high in the ranks. And I thought that a noble *like you*, would have enough manners to at least knock and announce himself before entering someone's room."

Jason stressed on the words, 'like you' as if he was giving a lecture. I laid in bed nervously as I watched my brother express his disappointments to a noble without hesitation. It was such a great way to start our morning.

Logan cleared his throat harshly with sharpened eyes fixed on Jason. I still felt uneasy with a reaction of goose-bumps on my skin just by looking at him. We were in a different environment now, we couldn't just react however we pleased. My brother arched his back to bow in Logan's presence, I was still too tired to just get up instantly and bow but I had no choice. My body felt heavy as I struggled to crawl out of bed within three seconds and properly acknowledge the noble before us. I had a feeling that getting used to this type of life would be quite bothersome.

"That's more like it," he responded. Our silence was loud, neither of us felt comfortable. "From today you can consider yourselves nobles. Congratulations, in less than twenty four hours you two went from peasants to nobles," his face lit up with a huge smile. The enthusiasm on his face left me confusingly happy. He was the first noble, the first person in the castle that showed any sought of acceptance to our presence with hints of joy.

"We're nobles?"

"Yes from today, till you two leave this place you're both considered nobles," he stated.

"Since we're both *nobles*…. What's our position? What's expected of us?" Jason queries were spot on, you couldn't call us a noble and not explain the extent of our power.

"It's not about positions, you haven't been given any specific responsibilities to uphold, it's about your level of importance. You're actually more important than more than half the nobles in Mandora."

"I understand. They don't call us the legendary chosen or whatever for nothing I guess." Jason admitted.

"Exactly,"

"I think I understand too," I blurted. Something about Logan just made me nervous but at least I built the courage to speak.

"This may sound confusing but even though you're more important than other nobles, you're not particularly at a higher status than them. But they aren't higher than you either so they can't boss you around. There's no need for you to bow to them

119

and they don't need to bow to you. You're somewhat mutual to all nobles at this point."

"Then why did we have to bow to you a few seconds ago," I asked.

"I was just about to ask that same thing," Jason responded.

"I am the King's right hand man, there's no need to show courtesies to anyone other than royalty and myself," Logan explained. He looked so glad, he just couldn't get rid of his proud smile.

"So you're the highest ranking noble in the kingdom aside from royalty?" Jason asked.

"Yup that's right, and I even requested to be your advisor." His smile expanded playfully with mischievous eyes.

"You're the highest member of the council and you want to advise us?" Jason crossed his arms and pranced around him slowly with the sharpest glare. "I don't trust him."

I didn't trust him either, but I wasn't bold enough to say it out loud to his face. I kept quiet and allowed whatever to unfold.

"Don't think about it too much, you two are already late for breakfast. We spent too much time talking and not enough time preparing. I'll leave these two servants with you and meet you guys later, there's a lot to be discussed."

CHAPTER 17: Friends?

It was only our second day here and once again we were late for something important. Our attention was so fixed on Logan that we didn't notice the two servants behind him. After turning his back on us, we had no choice but to acknowledge the two individuals before us were dressed in similar blue uniforms. I should have noticed the familiar pale skin and red hair the moment Logan first opened the door.

"Susan!" I squealed, then I gasped. I had no idea why I was so excited but she was the most welcoming female to be around. Not once did she make me feel uncomfortable or judged. Her face lit up when I called her name as though our feelings were mutual. She curtsied immediately and the person beside her followed her gesture.

"My lady, it's nice to meet you?" she smiled

"My-my lady?" I muttered. The person next to her was a lean tanned man with rough, short, straight hair. He lacked some muscle structure but he still looked eye-catching. His navy blue suit matched the colour of Susan's blue dress. Her dress seemed puffy at the bottom but still stiff, with a white apron around her waist. Their fabric seemed a bit rough but still better than anything Jason and I could've afforded.

Everything about our new encounter caught me off guard. "My lady? I've never been called that before. Aha, it makes me feel like I'm old or something." I laughed a bit to disguise my confusion.

"That's how we've been trained to address you mam," the young man stated.

"I guess our lives as nobles begins now," Jason commented.

"You two are potential royalty, that's why we need to address you both with respect," Susan added.

"Well there's no need to address me so formal in private. We can be informal in private," I suggested. I saw her as an equal and preferred to see it that way. I refused to let an overnight change of status ruin my potential bond for a genuine friendship.

"Please talk to me normal in private as well," Jason requested. It was a big change for him too, we weren't ready to adapt to this lifestyle so quickly, especially since we didn't have intentions of staying here too long.

"A-are you sure?" The young man continued to stutter with wobbling legs. The more I observed him, I could tell his nervousness grew as our conversation prolonged. Requesting him to do the opposite of what he was trained to do must've been too much to ask for our first encounter.

"What's your name? We know Susan's but not yours," Jason mentioned.

"M-my name is Peter, s-sorry for not introducing myself earlier….."

"Well Peter, my name is Jason. No need to apologize, it's not like we gave you a chance to introduce yourself anyway."

"Well, we're here to serve!" Susan interrupted. She must've been much more excited to start our relationship on friendly terms than Peter was.

"What exactly are your duties?" I asked. Her vague questionable statement left me longing for some sought of clarity. For many years my brother and I had learned to get by on our own so I was certain that we wouldn't need much help.

"I've been instructed to assist Amaris and Peter was instructed to attend to Jason. If Jason feels uncomfortable with a manservant attending to him then he can request a female instead." Susan explained. Peter kept his eyes fixed to the floor with pretence that his shoes were more interesting to look at than to acknowledge what Susan had said.

"Why would I not want a manservant?" Jason questioned. "I'm not a pervert. Gender won't matter once the job is well done."

Peter raised his head slightly and struggled to hold back his shy smile, he looked a bit relieved to me but he still avoided eye contact with everyone.

"As your servants we bathe and dress you, we also..."

"YOU WHAT!?" Jason and I stammered.

"That's why I said if you have issues with a manservant, you can switch," Susan explained. I caught Peter in time to see him place his hands in his pockets to hide the increased trembling.

"Peter how old are you?" Jason's interrogation started on Peter, who raised his head and finally along with his voice.

"I- I'm twenty-three."

"So you're a year younger than me. Why are you so timid? I won't bite," Jason grinned trying to make light of the situation. "As a twenty-three year old you should speak confidently, especially as a man, there's more pressure and expectations of us in that aspect," Jason advised.

"I-I'm just a bit nervous sir, I really need this job so I'm trying not to mess up. I've been rejected eight times already because most male nobles don't want man-servants….. Well unless they're gay," Peter mentioned. Susan jabbed his rib with her elbow and hissed at him to keep his secrets to himself.

"You're saying too much," Susan scolded softly, but she was still loud enough to be heard once we strained our ears.

"Let me be honest, you're already messing up, well at least for me," Jason stated. My jaw dropped, embarrassed by Jason's harsh feedback.

"Jason! Why would you say something like that?" I scolded. His cold remarks were random and out of character, the last thing I wanted was his overnight change of status to affect his brain. Peter's eyes slowly turned wet like a barrel of tears ready to overflow. His breaths deepened followed by heavy panting. He must've really needed that job.

"You're messing up by being too timid," Jason explained. "I want you to speak to me normally without hesitation. Secondly don't call me sir in private. I said my name is Jason. Opening up may have been a problem with other nobles but I appreciate the honesty and that's what I want from you. To the public you may work for me, but a friendship is what I truly want. I can't be friends with someone who's too nervous to speak to me."

Tears escaped Peter's eyes trickling down his cheeks. "Are you suggesting that I be myself around you sir?"

"I said DON'T call me sir, at least not in private," Jason insisted. "And friends don't bathe each other by the way, I can do that myself. Believe it or not, I also know how to dress myself." I couldn't help but laugh at his attempt to get away from a man giving him a bath.

"B-but that's our job," Peter stated.

"If for some reason we dress ourselves wrong......" Jason's face turned red as he struggled not to laugh. "Y-you guys can adjust our clothes after."

"Okay deal!" Peter was relieved, his energy shifted to excitement and certainty. Susan jabbed his ribs with her elbow and protested while he groaned in pain.

"But that's our jobs, we'll get in trouble if our superiors find out," she argued.

Peter developed some base in his throat and spoke confidently standing his ground. "Susan, why are you fighting this so much? They're offering us to work less and with the same pay. Let's take this opportunity to fetch their clothes for breakfast while they bathe, they're already running late. Besides, if I see another dick I'll probably go crazy."

We laughed till our lungs ached then quickly separated to prepare ourselves for breakfast.

Chapter 18: Wrong Choice?

I wasn't ungrateful or anything, but I found it odd that Jason and I were placed in the same apartment. I wasn't going to speak on it till Jason muttered something smart under his breath.

"Freedom ain't freedom if I'm still stuck in a room with you," He had just finished taking a shower and slammed the door on his way out heading to his room with a towel around his waist. His body was drenched and stained the floor with his wet footprints.

"I couldn't agree more. My chances of peace just flew out the window once again," I muttered. I chose not to speak loudly because the last thing I wanted was an argument so early in the morning, we didn't even eat breakfast yet. Susan gave me three dresses to choose from and I chose the dress with the simplest design. She expressed that those were the only dresses remaining and apologized. If she brought one dress I would've been fine, besides, two of the three dresses were too flashy anyway. I preferred something simple for breakfast; this was not a fancy dinner with a fashion show.

I chose a yellow dress that fell slightly below my knees with a white belt securing a bit of shape around my waist. The sleeves were short and rested on my collar bone but I fell in love with the fabric. The silk was soft and smooth, the most comfortable clothing I ever wore and I had no desire to take it off. Susan advised me not to pick that dress because it was too simple but I'd rather be under dressed than overdressed for something as simple as breakfast.

She brought me two pairs of heels, both black with a nice sheen to them and a sandals. I choose the brown sandals, only because it was comfortable to walk in. I never had the opportunity to wear heels and I wasn't going to start now. I styled my hair in a low bun since there wasn't enough time to do anything fancy.

"Are you sure you want to go like that?" Susan asked. She looked so unimpressed with a screwed face and folded arms.

"It's breakfast Susan, not a ball. I'm sure everything will be alright so stop overreacting," I explained.

"Ha! Me Overreacting?" She laughed but I could tell my statement wasn't funny to her at all.

"Well my friend, it's not like I'm here to impress anyone."

Her brows arched and her left eye twitched at my words. "Well are you at least going to apply any makeup?" Susan asked. The only thing I knew how to apply was powder, blush and lip-gloss.

"I don't wear makeup," I stated plainly. She took a deep breath with swollen red cheeks taking a few seconds to process her thoughts before she responded.

"How you look reflects how I do my job, please don't embarrass me," she pleaded. I didn't see the big deal. The royal family's main concern should be the candidates of the bride to be, not their maids or stylist.

"If someone has a problem and wishes to punish you just tell them that I insisted to wear this even though you were strongly against it." I thought it was a fair solution to her problem honestly.

"No, that's not –"

"Alright let's go." Jason interrupted. I didn't expect him to get dressed so quickly, but judging by his appearance he didn't make much of an effort either. His hair was still wet and leaked unto his clothes, leaving a stain on his collar and chest area. He wore a plain navy blue suit with a black tie and a glossy black shoe. His hair was laughable but it's the best I've ever seen him dressed. Susan sunk to the floor and groaned in frustration.

"You have got to be kidding me!" she protested. "Couldn't you at least dry your hair and style it in some sought of way?'

"I'm going to eat, not take part in a fashion show," he stated. He glanced at me for two seconds and then looked away. "You look....cute."

I couldn't tell if he meant it or not but I said thanks anyway and complemented him on his attire. "You look good in a suit. It'll be nice to see you in those more often."

He ignored my words and left the room. "Let's go, I'm ready to eat." I followed behind him and a few moments after I could hear Susan's heavy footsteps and frustrated muttering behind me.

"They're going to make me lose my job."

Chapter 19: HOW DARE YOU!?

We paced through the halls in a rush to arrive at our destination at a reasonable time although we were already late. The sandals I wore and the shoes on Jason's feet allowed us to comfortably move at a fast pace, but Susan was falling behind in her heels. Her steps echoed loudly behind us but eventually got fainter by the second.

"Take off your shoes if it's slowing you down." I suggested.

"I can't its part of my uniform," she panted. "We have a strict dress-code that I must adhere to."

"Would you rather us reach late or be on time. You can just put on your shoes when we're there." Jason suggested.

"But my....."

Jason cleared his throat and spoke assertively with a slight aggression to his tone. "Peter knows the way, so just meet us there. I won't allow you to slow us down any more."

"If you arrive without me I'll definitely lose my job!" I no longer heard her footsteps so I looked over my shoulder to see if we lost her. I was willing to wait. The last thing I wanted was for her to lose her job. Her determination shocked me, my eyes expanded as she took off her heels and held them in her hand. She quickly increased her pace and sprinted towards us. "This job pays too well for me to go back to the streets!"

It was difficult to keep up with Jason and Peter in my dress, since it wasn't really made for running. I was certain that Jason didn't care about the time, he just wanted to eat. The heavy meal we ate last night would've lasted us three days, but I didn't blame him for taking advantage of the opportunity to eat another meal.

Guards at each corner laughed and scorned at us as we passed them by. They already had an idea of the situation, and were brave enough to voice their unwanted opinions.

"They'll definitely be gone in the first elimination. The royal family will never choose them."

"At least they have some time, those servants will be gone by tomorrow, we'll never see them again."

I knew Susan was already stressed about keeping her job so I couldn't remain quiet. "Just ignore them, they want to get under our skin for their amusement."

"It's not like what they're saying is a lie," Susan muttered. She couldn't even look at me, she didn't want to, she kept warning us of what would happen and we didn't listen. I refused to let her lose her job because of our selfish ways.

"We're almost there," Peter pointed out. My heart sunk to my feet after his words processed through my brain. I wasn't ready for what was to come, my stomach tightened and I took deeper breaths struggling to breathe. I looked at Jason and he couldn't help but smile.

"It's almost time to dine."

Their abrupt stop without warning caused me to bump into

Jason's back. My nose burned from the collision and my eyes watered, my vision was temporarily blurred until Peter announced our arrival.

"We're here."

We stood before a closed silver door with the kingdom's crest engraved into it. It was clear that their favourite colours were bronze, silver and gold.

"Good morning, we're here for breakfast," Jason explained. He stood directly in front of me making it difficult for me to see who he was speaking to. Judging by the rough deep tone of the individual, I knew it was a man but Jason was taller so all I saw was the armour at his side.

"I'm sorry but who are you? You don't look like you're dressed for breakfast with the royal family, please leave before I escort you out myself." I shifted to the side to see what was happening, locking eyes with the guard. He beamed with excitement mixed with fear. "Wait a minute... you're the peasants selected that everyone was talking about."

"Ugh, here we go again." Jason groaned. I understood his frustration but at least the man finally knew who we were.

"Can you please let us in, we're already late," Susan insisted. The man couldn't help but laugh at our situation.

"I'll admit, even though you're late I support you two because I was once a peasant too." He turned his back on us with a smile and turned the doorknob. My pores raised while the door opened smoothly without a creek. The brilliant light streaming through the room as the door opened was all I could see since I was too shaken up to concentrate on the actual scenery in front of me. I trembled as I took two steps back ready to back out and call it quits.

"I can't do this..." I whispered. Jason grabbed my arm and

forcefully pushed me in front of him. I stumbled as I made two steps into the room struggling to stay balanced.

"Yes you can, I'm hungry." He insisted. Before I could face him and respond to his unethical manners, the guard rushed before me and bowed.

"The last two are finally here your majesties," he announced. If I wasn't focused then, I was definitely focused now. I bowed immediately with Jason beside me, Peter and Susan stood behind and bowed as well. The harsh voice of an angry king pierced through my ears with shivers down my spine.

"You two have some nerve showing up like this!"

"My apologies my king, it won't happen again." Jason expressed. I had nothing to say, whatever was happening, I just wanted it to be over.

"I don't remember giving you permission to speak. Raise your heads and look at me when I'm talking."

The food I ate last night was ready to leave my stomach, I raised my head slowly and turned to the direction of his voice. His hands were clenched tight and his muscles printed tensely through his golden suit. His eyes were sharply focused on Jason, I was worried for him but I couldn't look at my brother to decipher what he was thinking. From the corner of my eyes I noticed that the other contestants were either grinning or smiling. They must've enjoyed our humiliation and viewed us as contestants they'd never be intimidated by. The king then drifted his attention to me and slapped his forehead with the palm of his hand.

"What are you wearing?"

"I- I chose this dress because it was the most comfortable option." I explained. My heart was racing, breathing was proving to be a task that increased in difficulty as the tension grew.

"It should not have been an option in the first place. Do you think my son would have any interest in you wearing that?" I found his question to be quite insulting, I wasn't interested in his son but I dared not say that.

"I'm sorry my king, because of the rush I decided to wear something simple to get dressed faster since we were already late.:

"Don't apologise to me, apologise to my son, I feel disrespected just by looking at you right now, I can't imagine how he feels. Your only purpose is to help him make a decision in choosing a wife, but all you can do is make him not want you."

"I'm sorry for upsetting you my king, but doesn't that help him make an easier decision in picking his future wife?" I felt instant regret as the words left my tongue, I didn't mean to say it like that but my words had already travelled through everyone's ears in the room. Numerous gasps and murmurs echoed through the room, the jaws of many were dropped with swollen eyes. The immediate silence of the king bothered me as his lips separated to speak an unspeakable awe enveloped the room.

"Excuse me?"

"I-I'm just saying that if he doesn't like me...." Jason covered my mouth and pulled me closer.

"That's enough," he whispered. "I'm sorry my king, she didn't mean it like that."

"Let the girl speak!" he demanded. No one was grinning or smiling any more, nothing was funny.

"The prince can only choose one wife, seeing things he doesn't like will make the elimination process much easier for him anyway." I explained.

133

"Did you just say anyway? As if you don't care?" the princess snapped. She caught me by surprise. Throughout the tension I didn't even notice her presence.

"I'm not saying that I don't care, I'm just being realistic. Do you want your brother to like us all and accidentally choose the wrong woman to marry?" I asked. I felt proud as I thought that I had explained myself to the best of my abilities without being offensive. The king slammed the table and leaned forward almost spilling his drink.

"How dare you?!"

I hated people shouting at me because it triggered my anxiety. My eyes watered but I refused to let the tears escape to show any signs of weakness.

"Father please relax, you too Roselyn, I understand what she's saying there's no need to be upset." Joel interrupted. Even though he didn't speak to me directly his words calmed me with a bit of hope that the tension would ease. Our eyes met each other but he looked away immediately. It was the first time he didn't have that sinister smile on his face.

"A- are you defending her!?" Roselyn stammered. I didn't know what it was but she despised us the moment that she laid eyes on us.

"I agree with Joel," the queen intervened. Those simple four words granted me a brief moment of happiness. "We invited two peasants into our castle to live with us for a while, this is all new to them. You saw how they came here yesterday, this is probably the best they've ever looked so I don't blame them for being comfortable in what they're wearing right now." The queen looked at me and smiled, "When you wore that dress and looked at yourself in the mirror how did it make you feel?" she asked.

"I- I felt pretty."

"She looks beautiful in my eyes," Jason commented without permission. I looked at him immediately but he kept his gaze on the royal family without fear. He rarely ever complemented me but he did so twice for the morning.

"That shade of yellow complements her skin tone beautifully. Joel are you upset with her choice of clothing?" The queen asked.

"I see no issue with her dress. I'm not going to choose a wife based on what she wears."

"Joel, are you going to choose someone that doesn't make any effort at all to please you?" Roselyn interrogated. She always had the urge to stir up something. Her presence just irritated me.

"I don't remember her saying she didn't make an effort, she felt beautiful in that dress and chose to wear it," Joel answered. It surprised me that he even bothered to defend me. His response to every comment targeted to belittle me were perfect. I never thought he'd defend me in a room full of people that didn't matter. I assumed he was only nice at the celebration to make himself look good among hundreds of people. This time only the contestants willing to fight for the throne and his family were present.

"He's right," the king stated. His words confused me since he hated me a few seconds ago. "If we are to blame anyone we should blame their servants."

I looked at Susan immediately, her hands were trembling, but I was relieved to see her shoes on her feet, she must've put them on in the midst of confusion.

"I agree, we should fire them to prevent this from happening again." Roselyn suggested.

"No, I like them and I want them to stay," I insisted. I spoke more assertively this time with a slight demand in my tone.

"Same." Jason voiced. The king stared harshly at Jason and clenched his jaw in disgust.

"You have no right to say anything. Your hair is wet leaving stains on your suit, I can't help but think there was little to no effort on your part."

"I actually feel insulted just by looking at him," Roselyn commented. "The mere fact that he's a contestant for marriage makes me feel devalued."

From the corner of my ear I heard him grinning which eventually swelled into a boisterous laugh. His reaction scared me because I knew he was upset, I just hoped he wouldn't say anything out of line.

"You think I made no effort? I forced everyone out the room and insisted we run through the halls since we were already late. We had to deal with a lot of guards shouting their insults at us through it all, but I guess because my hair is wet I made no effort. My apologies, I thought you'd be more upset about us being late than my hair being wet, next time I'll make sure to fix my hair."

The awkward silence in the room left an uneasy feeling in my stomach. Jason even had the audacity to sharpen his glare at the king and the princess, they stared back at him but neither of them blinked.

"I'm sorry my king, this is all my fault." I followed the eyes of the familiar voice that made that statement and saw Logan leaning on the wall with his arms folded.

"Logan, please explain yourself," the queen entreated. The king kept his fixed gaze on Jason, both of them still refusing to blink but the princess gave up.

"I drank too much last night so I woke up too late to organise everything for them in time. I assigned Peter and Susan to serve them an hour before breakfast so it was impossible for them to be on time. That's also why Susan couldn't find the best dresses for Amaris to wear. She wasn't left with much options to choose from."

The king broke his stare from Jason and diverted his attention to Logan. "You're my right hand man and already causing issues for this selection, simply because you can't handle your liquor. Are you sure you want to be their advisor?"

"Yes, I see something *special* in them, especially the boy. No one else wants to be their advisor anyway. Please allow me to continue to look over them." Logan requested. I blushed like a fool not knowing how to control my facial expressions after being called *special.* I didn't care that his complement was more directed to Jason. He was the King's right hand man and saw something special in us.

The king cleared his throat and looked at us with his right brow arched almost to his hairline. "You two may have a seat, there's no reason for us to refrain from eating our meals any longer. Logan, you and I will have a talk after this."

"Yes your majesty," he bowed one last time.

Jason brushed pass me easily, without thinking twice before taking a seat. There were only two seats remaining, they only catered for the expected attendance for breakfast. Luckily for us, the remaining seats were the furthest away from the family, the opposite end of the table. The women sat to the left and the men sat at the right side of the table. The only available seat was next to the pretty girl I saw at the beginning of the ceremony when she climbed the stairs. Her features were easy to recognize since her hair resembled the midnight sky. I sat quickly and avoided eye-contact with everyone.

The table before us was stacked with food, not as much as the feast last night but it was still a lot. I had so many options to choose from, pancakes, bread, cheese, bacon, baked chicken, fruits and even cake. Everyone else already had food on their plate. I noticed that the women ate in moderate amounts while the men stacked their plates with food. I didn't have much of an appetite so I took an apple and a few grapes. Jason sampled almost everything on the menu except for the fruits, he made sure to get as much meat as possible too. There was more meat than anything else on his plate, but it amazed me how he still managed to fit everything on his plate without anything falling off.

"It's okay son, the food won't run away," the king mentioned, looking at Jason in disgust. I couldn't stop myself from laughing so I let out a subtle grin.

"Does that mean I'll be able to get seconds after this?" Jason asked. Roselyn's jaw dropped as she heard his words.

"You have got to be kidding me," she complained. "I'm glad he's all the way over there and it'll stay like that till his stay is over."

"You're quite a judgmental person aren't you?" Jason responded. I kicked his knee under the table and hissed at him to shut up. I couldn't believe the audacity I witnessed before me, the nerve he had to say those words to the princess. His careless statement triggered an unnecessary uproar, many young men stood to defend the princess. It was all for show anyway, she didn't seem worth defending.

"How dare you!" some of them shouted. If shouting was their only way to appear chivalrous and gain the princess' favor, they had a lot more work to do.

"You should apologise to her immediately!"

"That's why you're seated at the end of the table and will forever stay there until they kick you out!"

"That tongue of his should be ripped out his mouth."

"A peasant like you should be happy that you even get to be in the same room with the princess, but yet you sit there and disrespected her. I'd love to make you eat your words in a duel, then force you to crawl to the princess on your knees and apologize." This was the lengthiest protest to Jason's voiced observation and it came from a candidate that sat closer to the royal family, whose sister also felt the need to say something. After getting a proper look of her, I realized that she was that pretty girl with golden brown eyes that kept a long conversation with Joel at the ball.

"You and your sister have done nothing but cause problems since yall got here, of course the princess will feel disgusted just by looking at either of you. The presence of you two alone just upsets me," his sister added. After she included me in this mess I just had to say something.

"Do you think talking down on us gives you more points for the prince to like you? If so that's cute."

Her brows twitched when she looked at me and her face slowly turned red. "Look at where you're seated and look at me. If anyone has to try hard to be liked, it's you."

"What's that supposed to...." My mouth was frozen, I could no longer speak. I looked at Jason and his mouth was frozen too, covered in frosts from ice. It wasn't just us, but everyone except the members of the royal family had frozen lips with frost gradually spreading around our mouth.

"That's enough," Logan announced. "I will not allow this nonsense to continue any longer. Jason what you said was out of line and very bold of you, I'm actually disappointed. You two will never move up if you keep acting this way."

"There's no point in scolding them now, nothing will change," Roselyn grinned. "Do they look like they can even adapt to this new lifestyle? I suggest we get rid of them now." Logan ignored her nasty comment and continued where he left off.

"You two were late so you have no idea why you're at the end of the table. Where you sit, is a reflection of how the prince and princess feels about you compared to the others. If you're seated right next to them then you're their favourite…"

"I'm guessing that we're the least favourite since we're at the end of the table," Jason interrupted.

"H-how are you able to speak?" Logan stuttered.

"That ice you put around my mouth restricted me from eating so I got rid of it," Jason answered as he took a large bite a chicken leg in his hand, already exposing the bone. His mouth was immediately frozen again and the leg fell on his plate.. This time the barrier was larger, the ice covered his mouth like a chain restricting a prisoner.

"Yes, the further away you sit from the prince or princess, shows that everyone before you is who they favor over you. And right now you two are last on the ranking, congratulations on being the first last pick."

"Are we being ranked individually or together?" Jason asked. I slapped my forehead with the palm of my hand, he should've just stayed quiet.

"H-he broke the ice barrier again…" the king stuttered while his eyes expanded in confusion, his mouth was left slightly opened as his eyes remained fixated on Jason. Joel grinned and covered his mouth as though he enjoyed watching Jason cause trouble.

"I'm sorry, I'll keep quiet," Jason stammered. His mouth was slowly frosting till it turned frozen, this time he froze himself. Roselyn's jaw dropped to the floor but she quickly covered it with her hands and fixed her posture.

"To answer your question, yes you'd be judged individually. Not everyone has a sibling that's been chosen to take part in this selection with them. It's rare to even have multiple children born under a coloured moon unless they're twins. By some miracle, they might marry a brother and sister but the possibility of that is extremely rare. The prince ranks the women and the princess ranks the men, but this is just a first impression so it'll change every month. This will remain your seat till the end of this month."

I finally felt the ice slowly melting off my lips, granting me the chance to speak if that's what I desired. I looked at Jason and he continued devouring his plate of food as if nothing happen. I kicked his knee again and whispered.

"Don't you have something to say?" I asked.

"O yes," he muttered as he swallowed his food. "I apologize for upsetting you…my princess," he spoke as if he wasn't sure that was the right thing to say. "I promise that I will try to not cause any trouble in the future."

"Your apology will be accepted when your actions start matching your words," she said. Her words irritated me but I no longer wanted to draw attention to myself negatively so I stayed quiet.

"Don't worry they'll behave now, especially after that eye-opener, I don't think they'll continue to play the fool after being ranked last," the king mentioned. Jason forced eye contact with me with his cheeks swollen and face slowly turning red. I wish he didn't do that because now I struggled not to laugh, the grinning caused me to choke on my apple and then Jason couldn't hold it in any longer. Soon we were both laughing with tears streaming down our faces. If they thought our reason for being there was to fight for love, they'd be disappointed through our entire stay there.

Chapter 20: Your Darkest Fear

Jason sat in his chair in a slouched posture and continued to eat his meal until he was full. It seemed that everyone in our immediate vicinity was prepared to kiss ass and say anything to be in favour with the royal family. "It's an honor to be here, your majesty, I'll do my best to please you all," the girl sitting next to me stated as she leaned forward. Her statements were too ingratiating for me to respect, so I awkwardly turned to the side to cover my amused yet horrified face.

The king responded, "Thank you for your considerate and agreeable sentiments. We look forward to seeing what you can contribute in the future. The other women seized the opportunity right away, saying anything they could to gain attention.

A girl in the centre begged, "Can I say something, please?" She sounded quite soft, I barely heard her. She had her red hair styled in waves and wore heavy makeup, but despite my dislike for it, I had to admit that she still looked appealing to the eyes. Joel leaned forward and smiled, as if he actually cared. "You may speak, there's no need to ask permission, we're all having a conversation." His charming demeanor annoyed me, if only they knew how much of an asshole he could be.

"I'm very happy and honored to be here, but I'm curious to know what guided your decision in our first rankings. I'm only asking so that I can improve and do better in the future." Although it seemed like a desperate question to ask, I didn't blame her, we've been there for less than twenty four hours, so they shouldn't have been able to make a proper decision that early. I couldn't remember much of what I did last night, but I guessed it was enough to be ranked last. I didn't want to be chosen but I also hated the idea of being the least desirable.

"Whatever, they hated us since we came here, especially the princess, they probably think we're not worthy of their time since we're poor," I vented softly. I flinched immediately after Jason kicked my leg under the table.

"Why do you look so tense?" he whispered.

"Mind your business," I snapped, but quietly enough to not cause a scene. Joel leaned forward some more and cleared his throat, I guessed he took his time to calculate the right response that would be comforting to everyone.

"Honestly, it's been less than a day since I've known you all. I'm being honest, I still don't know any of you so I made my decisions based on the very short conversations we had. Most of you said the same thing which was….Good evening your highness, I'm honored to be here, I'll do my best to please you in the future."

I grinned ridiculously after hearing him mock the voice and actions of women without shame. "You all said the same thing but with different words, well except for Jason and Amaris of course." My chest tightened at the sound of our names escaping his tongue.

"I'm surprised that you even remember their names," Roselyn pointed out. Her face was sickening to look at while she stared at us, without making any attempt to disguise the repulsion that she obviously felt.

"It's not hard to forget when they left a strong impact to rank them last is it? So don't pretend you don't know their names either," he responded.

"Fair point." She sat back and chewed on a luscious black grape. I only hoped that the single grape would keep her quiet for the rest of the conversation, maybe even choke her a little.

"Back to what I was saying before my sister interrupted me for no reason." The long pause was comical while they stared at each other with nothing but frustration displayed on their faces. "Because there wasn't much info to make a decision, I judged you all based on attraction, your overall looks at the celebration last night. But with that being said, today's a new day and if I were to judge based on attraction again the ranking would be a bit different. It's amazing how women can change their appearances so drastically with makeup, but many of you are wearing less this morning, which is nice."

"Joel, that's enough I believe they understood," Roselyn interjected. I loved his honesty despite the fact that his explanation broke many people's dignity at the table and revealed just how cold he could be. After his comments, the air became a little dense. I made an effort to suppress a grin, but the circumstances were just too amusing.

Luckily for everyone the tension was quickly interrupted by a random soldier that burst through the door unexpectedly in a panicked pace, causing my heart to skip a few beats. He made it to the king's side in a few seconds, quivering at his feet.

"Please excuse me for interrupting you my king but...."

"Now is not the time Cordell, please leave," the king commanded. Upon having a closer look at him I noticed the blood stains on his neck and armour, even the palm of his hands were covered in stains of smeared blood. Whatever he had to say I wished he'd say among us so that I too would know what was happening.

"I-I don't think this matter can wait my king. *He* left us with a message." The man squirmed.

"Is this message the reason why you've entered my dining room like this? Covered in blood at my feet?" the king asked. He must've been evaluating how important the matter was before he allowed it to go any further.

"Y-yes my king," the soldier stammered.

I needed them to address the matter immediately if I was to feel somewhat at ease. I noticed the king gripping unto the table cloth tightly and Roselyn kept fumbling with her hands. Her worry was more visible than the king's subtle signs of agitation.

"Damn it, this can't wait. We need to address the situation now," the king announced. The queen leaned forward with confusion written all over her face, but she managed to ask questions to gain clarity.

"Are you going to talk about this here right now? Or are you going to....."

"Let's just talk about this now, they deserve to know. Many of them will be here for months so they should know the danger we're facing." Joel suggested. I guess he wanted to get this over with as much as I did. Anxiety was killing me.

I looked at Jason. His elbow was pressed against the table with his palm under his chin. All lessons on etiquette and manners seemed to be forgotten or laid aside for the moment, although there were no signs of concern about this current situation.

After sitting in unbearable silence, mixed with confusion, for what seemed like an eternity, the words that I'd been longing for were finally spoken by the king.

"Alright on your feet. Report to me what happened and then read the letter he left us."

As the guard stumbled to his feet, I noticed the blood stains he left behind on the floor from his boots. "At the front gate, one man slaughtered seven of our guards. His face was hidden under a silver mask and a black robe, so we couldn't see him. It could've been him or one of his men, but he left as soon as our reinforcements arrived."

The king unwittingly twirled a few beard hairs while rubbing his chin. "He easily dispatched seven guards, but then fled you said?"

"Yes my king, we only got there in time to witness him jump over the gate and flee, leaving a note behind with one of the bodies."

"Did you send any of the men after him or did he just escape with ease?"

"T-the two men that went after him got their heads detached from their bodies, we cannot confirm if he managed to do this alone or had help on his way out," the soldier stammered. His body was still trembling with fear, I couldn't believe that one man alone did this.

"Father you're asking the wrong questions," Joel interrupted. "How long ago did this happen?"

"T-This all happened ten minutes ago my prince." My chest ached as I processed his words through my brain. I faced Jason immediately to see his reaction but he leaned back and smiled. There was nothing to be smiling about, I didn't feel safe.

My pores raised instantly after the king slammed the table and got to his feet. "TEN MINUTES AGO? That's not enough time for him to escape our lands. Send twenty of my silver armoured men, he won't stand a chance."

Those reassuring words were all I needed to feel safe for a while. Jason kept smiling the entire time, violence always excited him.

"Leave the message with us, I'll read it," Joel suggested. The soldier pulled the blood stained letter from his pockets and left it with Joel before he rushed out of the room to gather more soldiers.

As Joel took his time to unravel the letter, I noticed him cringing at the blood stains on his fingers. "I'll have to wash my hands immediately after this," he complained. "Should I read it aloud or should I just explain what it says after?"

"Please read it aloud, I have no interest in hearing your sugar coated words to make us feel better about the situation," Jason requested. My mind went blank by the demands of my brother. I thought of ways to save him but it didn't seem quite possible.

"If you keep this up I'll have your tongue ripped out of your mouth. Your presence already upsets me so it'd be best if you keep quiet," Roselyn snapped. The giggles my brother made with a sinister smile was the prefect signal to pray on his behalf. The moment his lips separated I crossed my fingers and hoped he'd at least say something sensible given the current situation.

"How will you be able to kiss me then?"

I felt like I died, got resurrected, and died again. I kicked his knee cap as hard as I could under the table, but he only flinched and smiled even more. Joel was grinning in the corner with his mouth covered by his bloody hands.

"It seems to me that you're using this opportunity to be rude and cocky. Keep it up and you won't last more than a month here," the king scolded. He spoke more calmly to him than I expected. He must've been too concerned about the threats to focus his negative emotions towards Jason.

"I wish it were possible to have them gone in a week," Roselyn complained.

"I wasn't being disrespectful, I just asked a reasonable question. There is a chance, no matter how small that I'd marry her one day. I cannot kiss comfortably without my tongue. I need it for my special tricks." Jason explained. At this point I had died and been resurrected too many times. Joel's grinning slowly turned to laughter until his mother sharpened her eyes at him, silently indicating that he should shut up. Everyone else at the table was speechless, including the king. Roselyn sat there with her jaw dropped and finally had nothing else to say. Although I was embarrassed it felt good to see her in that state. Joel cleared his throat and held the letter below his chin to break the silence.

"I've chosen to read the letter aloud to give everyone clarity of our current situation. And it states...."

Hello Your Majesty, or whatever it is they call you in your castle, I don't really care. If you're reading this letter it's because many of your soldiers are dead and their blood are on your hands. This all could've been avoided if you just gave me what I wanted. You allow everyone to enter your kingdom but not me? That's rather bold of you, but I'm flattered since it's obvious that you fear me. I'm searching for something but I haven't found it yet, even after searching through 4 countries. What I'm looking for belongs to me, so please permit me to continue my search in peace in your kingdom. I'm sure you're already aware of what happened to those four countries. It wasn't my intention to take over, I simply asked them to comply with my demands but they didn't listen. Honestly, I'm only asking to be nice, I've already had access to your kingdom without your permission and I'll be here again soon. There's word going around that this is the strongest Empire in our region, but your soldiers seem rather weak to me. Fix that before things get uglier for you. But as I stated earlier, I'm only here to collect what's mine, no harm will be done to you or your people if you comply. Your general is dead, I had one of my men pretend to be him for a while. No worries you won't be seeing him again so I suggest you choose a new general. I'll be here again soon, hopefully there won't be any more blood on your hands, just be a good pet and comply.

….your darkest fear, Jhovaise."

"His handwriting is cute, reminds me of royalty," Joel commented. He didn't seem worried but Jason and I locked eyes immediately when the name *Jhovaise* passed through our ears. The smile on his face was no longer there, his face slowly turned red and his muscles were tense. I looked at the other contestants and their faces were plastered in fear.

"I'm seeing a lot of weak faces around me, how many of you can fight and are confident in your skills?" the king asked. All the men at the table raised their hands except Jason, he stared at the table with frost escaping his fingertips. I counted fourteen women with their hands raised but their nervous faces couldn't convince me that they were confident. It was still a large number to consider, I was always under the impression that women were taught to look pretty and impress men, especially the women of their kind.

"With all that mouth you got, it surprises me that you won't raise your hand. You displayed your abilities to everyone a few moments ago, are you afraid?" Logan directed his question to Jason, reminding us of his presence. The temperature dropped significantly and frost leaked from Jason's mouth with every breath he exhaled. People began to shiver in confusion but I knew what was happening.

"Logan what are you doing!?" The king shivered slightly, he forced himself to appear strong while everyone else struggled to keep warm and shivered tremendously.

"It's not me, it's Jason."

"S-so instead of simply raising your hand, you intended to show off," Roselyn stuttered, I wished she was more like her mother and kept quiet. The dining table and all its food slowly became frozen, I had to find a way to release Jason from his mental cage. I had no choice but to lean over the table and slap him.

"Jason relax!" I scolded with crossed fingers hoping that he wouldn't retaliate since he was always unpredictable in that state. He blinked twice then took a deep breath and the temperature went back to normal.

"I-I'm sorry, what were they saying?" he slapped his cheeks to pull himself together. "I'm sorry for ruining the food."

Joel stretched out his arm and led a ball of fire over the table until the food was warm again. "Don't worry it's fine. My father was just asking how many of you can fight and are confident in your skills. All you need to do is raise your hand."

Jason raised his hand in silence and lowered it slowly. His eyes squinted when he looked at me with his brows arched. I knew what he was thinking but I wasn't willing to do it. I shook my head sideways to indicate that I wasn't comfortable to raise my hand. I am familiar with a sword, but wasn't confident in my abilities to actually kill someone so he rolled his eyes and looked away. I understood his reason for disappointment since he thought me how to defend myself but I was pretty sure my abilities were only good enough to defend myself against an inexperienced person.

"What about your power?" Jason whispered. There was no reason for him to mention my ability since it never could've helped the situation. I ignored him to avoid conversation but he brought it up again.

"If you don't want to talk about it now we'll talk about it later," he insisted. I preferred the idea of peace, but after the king's question I don't think peace was on his mind.

"Before I say anything further, what do you think should be done about this situation?" he inquired. Hands were immediately raised all around the table but Jason and I had nothing to say. For someone who's excited about combat, I thought he'd be the first to speak up. The first person to speak was the girl that sat next to Joel, his favourite pick.

"He disrespected you and killed many of your men. I don't think we should comply with his demands. Giving him what he wants will just make us look weak." I cringed at the words that came out of her mouth. She wasn't wrong and her points were valid but I preferred peace with no casualties. After her statement, there was a unanimous vote with everyone voicing their agreement but Jason and I said nothing. Jason leaned forward to whisper his own conversation and I was very much intrigued.

"Did he say that the guy's name is Jhovaise?" he asked. I knew what he was thinking but now wasn't the time to lie. I calculated my response in a way that might keep him at ease.

"Yes, he did, but there's probably more than one person with that name so we can't be sure that it's him."

"Jhovaise isn't a common name Amaris, of course it's him. You know what he's capable of."

"Is there something you'd like to share with us?" the king interrupted. I faced him immediately hoping that his question wasn't directed to us. "You two seem to be having your own conversation while there's an important issue to address and you're the only ones that haven't given any input on this matter."

I didn't know what to say so I gasped and covered my mouth hoping that he'd be satisfied with my silence but Jason took this opportunity to finally speak up.

"Just to be clear, did you say that his name is Jhovaise? Is that the person we're dealing with?"

Before responding, the royal family exchanged quiet glances and mutters with one other. Even though I was certain that we heard Joel accurately the first time, we only needed a yes or no response to confirm.

"Why does the name matter? Do you know someone by that name?" The king asked. I looked at Jason hoping that he'd acknowledge that I wanted him to lie but he kept his eyes fixed on the king and gave his honest response.

"Yes."

"No," I interjected, I didn't want to talk about him. Joel looked at me and his eyes twitched in confusion. The king let out a long frustrating sigh and asked again.

"Do you, or do you not know him?" This time Jason observed my body language and noticed my hands trembling while I tried to come up with a suitable response. We stared at each other for a few seconds and concluded that I should answer him instead.

"We know of a guy named Jhovaise, but we're not sure if it's the same person you speak of," I said. A lot of murmuring began and stares from everywhere were directed at us, which was exactly what I tried to shun.

"What does he look like?" the queen asked. I wasn't really good at describing people and it's been a long time since I last laid eyes on him so my description wasn't as detailed as it should've been in these circumstances.

"He's 6'3, muscular and tanned with brown hair," I explained.

"That could be anyone," the king dismissed. I could tell he was annoyed, but that was the best description I could put together at that moment. I blurted out the first thought that came to mind as a result of my increased anxiety from his murderous glare.

"He also has a birth mark on his lower back." Laughter was heard all around the room, I noticed Joel covering his face with the palm of his hand, completely forgetting about the blood stains. I sank into my chair with shame consuming my thoughts. On the bright side I figured they wouldn't take us seriously any more and drop the topic.

"Hopefully you could sense by the vibe in the room how stupid that comment was. You two don't need to worry, I never anticipated anyone in this room, much less two country villagers, to know him. He and his family has taken over five nations and no one knows where they truly reside, anyone that came close to figuring it out were all slaughtered," the king explained. I quickly turned to Jason with a sorrowful gaze to apologize for the embarrassment I brought upon us but he wore a disturbing smirk on his face with sharpened eyes directed to the king. He didn't say anything, he continued to listen to the king's words with an unnerving look of mischief on his face.

"We've already come to a unanimous vote by this table, so no further input from you two is needed. It won't make a difference to anyone here so let's not continue to waste everyone's time."

Jason's sneer became more obvious as the table's laughter increased while they mocked us. "I have one more thing to say, but it's more of a question," Jason implied.

"Don't waste your breath, we've heard enough from you two," Roselyn interrupted. I hated her guts as much as she hated ours. The laughter continued but this time Jason laughed with them....or rather at them. The only people without a look of amusement on their faces were Joel and the queen.

"You're laughing as if this is a joke, please do not continue to waste our time," the queen insisted. Jason ignored her request and proceeded to speak.

"I would admit that my sister failed to give a proper description, but it's my fault for failing to ask a more accurate question, so I'll ask again....... Is the person you're referring to *Jhovaise Pierson?*"

The sound of the king's fork clinking as it fell to the floor defeated the room's silence. Joel tilted his head to get a better look at his father who was now speechless and Roselyn's repulsive grin finally left her face. The queen leaned forward and muttered words into the king's ear causing him to blink twice before he said anything.

"W-what did you say?"

Chapter 21: Us Against The World

"I'm not sure that I'm reading the room correctly but it looks like we have the same person in mind. Just to be certain there's a few more questions I'd like to ask." Jason smirked.

"H-how do you..." the king was lost for words and I supposed they stopped viewing us as a joke. My brother enjoyed every minute of their reaction and so did I, but I had a gut feeling I'd come to regret it in the future.

"I may be wrong but is his Father's name Dexter Pierson? I believe his mother's name is Eve and he has a younger brother named Lucious, I think he's around my age or just a few months older." Jason explained calmly, but judging by his tweaking lips, I knew he was trying not to smile.

"Amaris do you remember the names of his cousins? I can only remember Heather and Andrew." I didn't expect him to put me on the spot, but I willingly answered.

"Don't forget about Damien and Darion," I added.

"O yes! Damien is the shapeshifter! He wasn't around as often as the others so that's why I forgot about him.

Murmuring began, Jason had gotten a little too comfortable with his words. Anyone would believe that we're friends with the enemy. From the corner of my eyes I noticed a few guards approaching with their hands on the hilt of their swords waiting for an indication from the king to make a move. I looked at him nervously fearing what his response might be to Jason's words. His eyes twitched in our direction but his silence didn't last long. He spoke a lot harsher this time and his simple question seemed more like a threat.

"What did you say?"

Before either of us could respond, Joel intervened in a calm manner but it was clear that he shared the same level of concern as his father. "You're asking the wrong questions, you heard him loud and clear. It's obvious that they know our enemy better than we do, maybe even on a personal level. A better question to ask would be how do you know them?" Joel sharpened his glare at Jason and avoided eye-contact with me. In the back of my mind I just wished Jason wouldn't say too much this time. There was a lot of valuable information that he could've said that would work against us, especially me. I kicked his knee under the table to get his attention, but he only looked at me for a split second, I shared a harsh glare to let him know what I was thinking and he nodded in acceptance.

"We've known them for six years. We were much younger at the time. When Amaris was about ten years old, she ran away after a heated argument between us and met Jhovaise when she got lost. I don't know much about how their first meeting went but he dropped her back home.

After some time he sneaked away from home to spend a few hours with us but we had no idea who he was at the time, but our parent's and other villagers warned us to stay away from him. We never saw him as a threat so we kept spending time with him. When his family found out about us, they hated the fact that he spent hours of the day with peasants like us so they cut off our communication for a few months. As time passed we got an invitation for his birthday celebration. He was turning fourteen and apparently he told his parents that he would not celebrate his birthday if we weren't allowed to be there so they gave in. After our mother died and our father disappeared, we were invited to sleep over every weekend and we did, but we ran away after a few years when they killed everyone in our village during a night that we slept over. We haven't seen them since," Jason explained.

It surprised me that they allowed him to speak without any interruptions. His explanation may have been long to everyone but it was short and sweet to me since he left out the important parts that could've made us vulnerable. I sighed in relief and whispered a thank you, hoping that they'd be satisfied with his explanation. The silence in the room was loud as everyone waited for the king's response. He rubbed his beard and stared sharply, he must've been trying to read us to see if we were lying or hiding something from them. The queen intervened, needing to satisfy her curiosity. She didn't speak much when the matter was addressed so I was eager to know what she had to ask.

"Are you talking about the same massacre that happened five years ago deep south in Mandora? If so then why did he kill them?"

"Yes, the Pierson's are responsible for their deaths. After Amaris was bullied and beaten by some of the villagers, they ordered men to slaughter them all." It made me happy to see Jason take control of the conversation, as an over thinker I wouldn't respond fast enough to please them.

"You two must've been really important to them," the queen deduced. Those thoughts were what I tried so hard to avoid but I understood why she felt that way.

"At that point in time yes, but not anymore," Jason responded. He was quick with his words. We couldn't afford to have them think misleading thoughts about us. The king finally spoke after his long period of silence.

"Based on your story, it seems like you have no reason to hate them, his family even killed on your behalf so why should we trust you? Do you even feel comfortable fighting against them? It seems to me that there's a greater chance of you turning on us in the end."

"Why would we tell you all this personal information when we could've kept it to ourselves and play pretend in this place to our benefit?" Jason countered.

"It's an easy tactic to use to gain our trust. You only told us what you wanted to. I won't be surprised if you're hiding more information. I noticed the interaction you two had before you spoke. I know you haven't told us everything." Joel stated. "I don't care that you left out some information in your story, but I have questions and I expect you to answer me honestly," his tone was harsh and stern, I wasn't prepared for his questions but Jason answered the previous questions well so I left it in his hands.

"Your village was slaughtered by the Piersons because of Amaris and you slept over in their territory on weekends. Are you saying that for years they've been living in Mandora?" Gasps were heard all around the room as the contemplation of our enemies living among us for years loomed over their minds. My eyes watered by the way he structured his question, he basically blamed me for the deaths of those people. I had nothing to say and neither did I want to say anything.

"Yes, they lived in Mandora, deep into the woods beyond the villages. When we looked for them a few months after the massacre they were nowhere to be found," Jason answered, he smirked a bit before leaving them with a shady remark. "It's shocking that people find it almost impossible to discover their location but I guess no one bothered to look among the poor villages since those areas are often overlooked. Maybe they gave into the stereotype that strong wealthy people don't live among the poor, but that's understandable. Their home was a mini castle made of stone, but not tall enough to be seen through the woods. It was hidden well among the oak trees."

Joel scoffed a grin and looked away. "I have one more question, this time I want Amaris to answer, you seem to be doing all the talking when you two shared the same experience with these people."

My heart sunk to my feet. I didn't expect him to put me on the spot among all these people to continue his interrogation. The longer he took to ask his question the higher my heart rate became. I never performed well under pressure, and the weight of these questions was heavy. Given the situation we were in, I knew my answer had to be calculated and precise. He locked his eyes on mines and they seemed as cold as ever before opening his mouth to speak.

"Jason said that you two looked for them a few months after you ran away, why was that?"

My lips trembled before providing him a response, the truth could never be told. Along with the pressure of everyone staring at me, I felt it most at the corner of my eyes from Jason's worried glare. I didn't have time to calculate my answer because they wouldn't believe me if I took more than three seconds to respond so I came up with the best lie I possibly could.

"I wanted to collect the blanket my mother made me. I left it there when we ran away. We weren't left with much things to remember her by when she died," My eyes watered at the thought of her, even though I lied I still had pain mustered inside me about her death. I wiped away my tears and looked away, I despised being vulnerable among people, especially among strangers but my mother was my greatest weakness.

"I see, well I have no more questions to ask," Joel stated, his harsh tone died, probably just out of sympathy, but his father had more to say.

"As embarrassing as this may be to admit, you two may know them a lot more than anyone in Mandora. I've already made my decision but what are your thoughts on this matter, do you think we should fight or give them what they want, whatever that is?" The king's question was directed at Jason. He paid no attention to me but I was relieved that he didn't. Jason obviously showed that his abilities could be very useful if a battle were to take place so his input must've been more desirable than mine.

"I want Jhovaise dead, whether or not you choose to take part in it is no concern of mine. The next time we meet, blood would be shed, more of his than mine," Jason revealed sternly. I wished he hadn't said that because although he's strong he's also too arrogant, I feared that one day he'd eventually meet his match. The king arched his brow and broadened his shoulders.

"Based on your story, you two haven't expressed enough reason to want him dead but you seem to have a strong urge for revenge."

"As Joel stated, we only told you what we wanted you to know, but trust me when I say….I want him dead. Mandora is arguably the strongest country in our region, but the Piersons took over Phraga in less than a week, they boasted about it during our stay so they're not an easy foe to deal with."

I flinched as the king slammed the table and got to his feet. He gripped unto the table cloth and tightened his fists as his words changed from mutters to a loud outcry.

"WHAT DID YOU SAY!?"

Jason looked at me in confusion but I was just as confused as he was. Joel passed his hands through his hair aggressively, I noticed his chest expanding through his increased deepened breaths. At first I thought they were upset but it seemed like they experienced a trivial moment of panic.

"D-did you say they took over Phraga?" the king stuttered. "How long ago did this happen?"

"Roughly eight years ago, that's the first country they defeated. Didn't you say they took over five countries? I thought you knew," Jason responded. The king took a seat and muttered obscenities.

"Phraga is our ally, we've been doing business and trading with them for over six years. Some of their people even reside here for months to help us with our projects. Their king is even invited here for dinner at least three times a year as our sign of our appreciation," Joel explained. His voice became weary, almost as if he was on the verge of giving up. A shy smile appeared on Jason's face but not a happy one, he seemed to have figured out the riddle that everyone sought answers for.

"Well I guess now you know who the spies in your kingdom are," he hinted. This entire conversation felt like a meeting between the royal family and my brother and I. The other contestants were irrelevant spectators in our midst who stayed quiet or muttered their worries to each other.

"Logan, after this meeting I trust you know what to do," the king stated plainly. Logan leaned off the wall with a beaming smile and arms still folded. He reminded me of my brother, excited by chaos.

"Of course, I'll have this issue handled in a delicate manner within three days. We seem to be playing a game of chess and losing. We gave them a long enough head-start, head-starts are for the weak."

"What are your thoughts about the general?" the king asked. "I didn't see that one coming either."

"I always had my suspicions about him. He asked too many questions that he should've known the answer to, so I didn't feed him with any new information. But still, I never expected him to die. His wife had been lying beside a stranger all this time but she did complain about him rarely being home and blamed us for keeping him away from his family."

"What's even more shocking is that they've taken over more countries than we expected. Phraga, Etdon, Cedeinuz, Locilita, Farude and Vedane all fall under their reign," Joel admitted. "How can we be sure that our other allies aren't stained by the Piersons' control?"

At this point my existence was irrelevant and I preferred it to remain that way. Listening to their conversation without them wanting my input was much more comfortable to endure even though it did not remove or decrease my apprehension about the developing situation.

"Our allies are secure. If there was any chance of them falling into the hands of the Piersons they would've written us a letter requesting our support. The king of Phraga is just a puppet on a throne. We've been deceived but now we can use them to our advantage."

"That may be true father, but we need to prepare for the worst case scenario."

"And what may that be?"

Joel filled his glass with wine and drank in large gulps till it was empty within a few seconds, slamming the empty wineglass unto the table. "Us against the world."

Chapter 22: You're A Coward

An hour had passed since the breakfast meeting and we were given the freedom to do whatever we wanted until 8pm that night. Apparently there was a celebration happening later that we were required to attend. We were informed that whatever we did apart from our assigned tasks would also be judged, although no details were given. Every decision made would also be examined and judged for determining the ranking. Not that I really cared, but comments about encouraging the prince as he takes a significant step later that evening, left me somewhat intrigued.

Given the freedom that we had, I never expected Jason to spend the first few hours on dorm with me. But of course that was his intention. He waited for the right moment to speak about everything. To be honest, I wasn't sure if I was ready but I knew it wasn't a conversation I could run away from. After a while of roaming around and invading my space every few minutes, Jason finally decided that it was time to confront the issue and get the words out his mouth.

"Why didn't you raise your hand?"

"Do you really think I'm able to go against one of the *Pierson*'s men?" I asked. I knew for sure that I couldn't.

"The lack of confidence in yourself is the reason why you're not ready." Jason critiqued me like a tutor as to why I'm not a good enough student. I couldn't help but laugh, surely I wasn't good enough to fight against the enemy.

"So what if I get stabbed and bleed to death? You'd feel so bad if I died."

"You know damn well that you of all people won't die from being stabbed. It's not easy to kill you...."

"But it's easy to hurt me. Do you think I like to feel pain?" I interrupted. He knew I wasn't ready for violent environments, but because it's not easy for me to die he didn't care about how I felt.

"There's no way for you to get better if you don't try, you're lucky it isn't easy to kill you. People only get better with practice and experience, unfortunately some die in the process but you can survive because of your ability. You can become the perfect weapon, but you're too much of a coward to improve yourself."

I rolled my eyes and looked away. His words weren't as motivating as he hoped they would be.

"I wanted peace with the Piersons, so why would I volunteer to fight? All we have to do is allow Jhovaise to search for what he's looking for and then watch him leave, but for some reason everyone prefers bloodshed. We both know what they're capable of so why put the citizens of Mandora through that potential massacre?"

"Blood has already been shed by the Piersons. Peace was never an option, especially for Mandora. Why would the strongest country in the region back down after being disrespected? How do you think the families of the deceased would feel about us doing nothing about it and helping the enemy...."

"He was never the enemy until y'all declared war! He killed those men in self-defence. They knew what they signed up for when they chose to be soldiers and so did their families."

My words kept him quiet for a few seconds. The silence was awkward but also peaceful. He had quite an increasingly stern change of tone but I avoided eye-contact with him to prevent him from intimidating me further. "You're defending him a lot, how am I to trust that you won't defend him on the battlefield?"

His words were nothing but comedy, I faced him again to see if he was serious and I couldn't help but laugh at his sharp glare towards me. He, all of a sudden, didn't trust me because my words made sense.

"You won't be seeing me on the battlefield, I'm a runner not a fighter, the only person I'm defending is myself if I'm forced to," I explained. "Why would I help the Piersons? There's nothing to gain from it and we both don't like them."

"I'm just making sure you don't get in the way of me killing who I please. You know I wanted him dead a long time ago."

"You're upset because of what he did to me, but I've already moved on and you should too." I didn't want to bring up the dark areas of our past, but he just wouldn't get over it and I feared that one day it'd get him killed.

"You only moved on because you're a coward, a weak one too. You let people take advantage of you and allow them to get away with it. You should've stabbed him in that moment, you had your pocket knife but yet you did nothing."

"S-stab him!?" His bold words caught me off guard and I stuttered as a result of his foolishness. He kept reminding me of his toxic traits that he'd probably never be able to change.

"Why would I stab him, when the house was full of Piersons? We both would've died that day. That's why I'm worried about you. You don't think before you act and if you keep this up it's going to get you killed. You're not the strongest man in the world."

"You should be the last person to worry about me. You can't even protect yourself so worry about that. I may not be the strongest person in the world but I will be eventually."

The conversation wasn't going anywhere, he was too arrogant to understand, or maybe he just didn't want to.

"Well you do you, and I'll do me," I suggested. The conversation was dead to me and I believe he felt the same.

"Good. Just stay out of my way." His cold response crawled my blood but I was relieved that the conversation was over. Just when I felt like I could finally relax, there was a disturbing aggressive knocking at our door. I sighed.

"You're already standing so you should see who's at the door," I groaned. I didn't look at him but I heard his footsteps becoming heavier as he approached the door. I glanced over my shoulder as I heard a creak to see who could possibly be disturbing my peace at that moment. It was a gentleman in his basic copper armoured uniform with a flyer in his hand to relay a message.

"Good Morning Sir, My Lady," he bowed. "The king suggested that I leave this flyer with the contestants. You're not obligated to attend but it will be an entertaining battle."

Jason's voice screeched in excitement, "A battle!?" he asked? "Let me see the flyer."

So far I heard nothing that interested me, I never cared to see people fight nor did I understand why people were entertained by it. My ears flickered as Jason gasped and expressed his interest to attend.

"The winner will become the prince's right hand and awarded one hundred pounds of silver!? "

I couldn't take my mind off the prize money, it was more than enough to make a down payment for a home. I leaned forward and sat on my bed to listen to their dialogue more carefully. I was still adamantly opposed to attending, but it seemed like Jason had a plan in mind.

"Can I take part?" he asked. My heart raced rapidly, I looked forward to the possibility of him winning but I was worried that he'd be dreadfully hurt in the process.

"Of course you can! This is an open event for anyone that's willing to take part. There's over two hundred people registered, but it's going to be brutal."

"Has any of our competitors registered?" I asked. If Jason was interested the other guys would've been interested too, some might've seen this as an opportunity to prove themselves and please the royal family to gain points for the ranking.

"Of course they did, Jason is the only male among your contestants that hasn't registered yet. There was a young lady among you that also signed up, this isn't an invitation that's only for men, if you're interested you can be registered too. The location in the castle to sign up is written on the flyer."

"If he's looking for the best of the best why is there an age requirement on the flyer? It says open to anyone thirty and younger, I guess it may not be as brutal as you say," Jason mentioned. I rolled my eyes at his continued arrogance, it seemed like he'd never stop.

"The prince voiced that he doesn't want to work with anyone extremely older than him. Many nobles will be participating, people are already betting on who the winner will be. Even though I believe that the chances of you winning are slim, I suggest that you take part and receive some bonus points from the royal family by showing them how serious you are."

"I don't really care about that, I just want the money and a stable job," Jason admitted. I grinned at the soldier's arched brow and squinted left eye.

"O-okay, well good luck," he stammered.

"If you're up for some money, I suggest you place your bets on me," Jason suggested. A smirk peeled off the soldier's lips followed by gentle laughter.

"No thank you. That's too risky, I think a safer bet will be Luke Blake, he made it on the list of our top ten warriors at the age of twenty-four. He became the general of a thousand soldiers just last year, there isn't anyone in your age group than can defeat him. Take my advice and avoid him on the battlefield if you want to last as long as possible before getting knocked out of the competition."

I couldn't help but laugh as I had a feeling that Jason may do the opposite just to prove a point. Although I chuckled, worry was hidden in my laughter because I didn't know the potential of Luke's strength. I knew that Jason feared no one.

"Tell that to the weaker contestants, your advice doesn't apply to me. You can even tell Luke to avoid me on the battlefield to save himself the embarrassment of being knocked out too early. I only fight people that are worthy, he needs to prove himself to me first."

The gentleman's face was swollen and red as he tried to hold back his laughter. He turned his back towards us and prepared to leave. "I admire your confidence, I wish you the best." After he closed the door on his way out he was comfortable enough to let out his boisterous laugh.

"I'm going to enjoy having the last laugh," Jason vowed. He

took a closer look at the flier and his smiled broadened. "This event is three hours away, looks like I'm gonna get that money soon."

"This isn't just a money making opportunity for you. I'm gonna make money from this too," I hinted. He looked at me bewildered, but I maintained my composure to convey the seriousness of my position. He appeared to have the wrong idea, but I couldn't help but entertain it a little after his uncertainty. He groaned and tapped his forehead, exposing his displeasure written all over his face.

"You have got to be kidding me, don't tell me you're going to register for this too. If you want the money we can split it, but please stay out of this, I can't be bothered by having to protect you, I want to fight in peace and enjoy myself," he pleaded.

"Didn't you say that I'm hard to kill? Why not? Maybe it's a good idea." I teased. His face burned red and his squinted brows arched upwards to his hairline. My eyes watered as I tried not to laugh but it only pissed him off even more.

"It's hard to kill you but it's very easy to knock you out to the floor," he mentioned. He didn't realize how hypocritical his words were but I had no issues explaining that to him.

"What's that? Are you eating your words? A few minutes ago you were trying to convince me to fight and get strong, now you don't want me to take part in this money making event?"

"That's not what I meant when I said I wanted you to train to prepare for the war, not jump into a battle and hurt yourself for money you'd never win. Don't test me, I'll knock you out myself and have them drag your unconscious body out of the ring."

"Is that a threat?" I giggled. As funny as his reaction was, I did feel intimidated.

"It's a promise so stop taking me for a joke. If you keep playing with me I might just knock you out before the competition and leave you here." His words cut deep. Knowing my brother, he'd definitely do something like that.

"Relax, I'm just teasing you. I have no plans to take part but I'm going to place a bet on you and win some money in the process," I explained. The muscles on his face were still tensed while he squinted his eyes at me in confusion.

"With what money? We don't have anything remaining, unless you hid some from me."

"I don't have any money, but I do have something valuable....the *ring*."

"After all this time when we've been struggling and starving, you kept it for so long? You do know that it's worth over fifty pounds of silver right?"

I wasn't sure if he tried to guilt trip me but I had my reasons for keeping the ring. "Mummy used a piece of leather and turned it into a necklace since it became too small to fit my finger. Why would I get rid of something she made for me? We weren't left with much memories of her, all you have is the scarf she made you and your chain."

He lowered his head and sat next to me as he let out a freezing cold sigh, I must've triggered the emotions he concealed within. He looked at me with nothing but sorrow in his eyes.

"Are you sure you want to bet on me with that ring?" he asked.

I returned his question with a gentle smile as my eyes watered. "Are you sure you're going to win?"

"Losing was never an option. Let's make that money." he got up and placed the flyer in his pocket. "I'm going downstairs to sign up."

"I can't believe you'll be employed tomorrow and one of the

richest men in Mandora." I commented. Before I knew it I was on my feet and ready to go, this opportunity was my wakeup call, I couldn't afford to spend my time here and not find ways to better myself.

With the few hours we had remaining I decided it was best to go job hunting and see what job opportunities were available. I was confident that Jason would work in the castle alongside Joel, but I had no idea what my future would be like when I'd be sent home within a year. I didn't want to depend on my brother's money to survive. Eventually he'd have a wife and children and I couldn't be a leach, depending on my brother's wealth.

"Can I come with you," I requested, knowing that he was always that mean brother who wanted space and freedom from me any chance he got. He looked at me, still holding the ring in my hand and his response was barely audible, although plainly stated, "Yes please, I'd appreciate your company."

I had expected some form of protest but instead I was pleasantly surprised by his concurrence. I quickly put on my sandals as I noticed him approaching the door to leave.

"Let's go, there's no time to waste." He left the room and I quickly followed with my ring in hand.

Chapter 23: Jealous?

Fortunately for us, finding the venue to sign up for the event wasn't difficult. I had second thoughts about everything as soon as we reached the corner after rushing down the last flight of stairs. The line to register was unbearably long, extending almost to the entrance gates of the castle on the right. The line for placing bets was on the left and was just as long, but I comforted myself with the notion that at least they were both in the same location.

I understood the frustration in Jason's voice as he instantly voiced his irritation at the scene before us. "You've got to be kidding me."

I tried to leave him with a few words of encouragement to lighten the mood but I wasn't sure if it did much. "Waiting in line for an hour will be a small price to pay for a hundred pounds of silver coins." I even had second thoughts about standing in line to gamble and place my bet, but if Jason was willing to wait in line to register there was no logical reason for me not to. This was a once in a lifetime opportunity and we'd be fools to walk away from it without making an effort.

"Both lines are too long for you to waste your time standing beside me. We should split up," he suggested. I couldn't agree more since there was no point to me being in the line to register then joining the line to place my bet. I also hoped to have some time to myself before the event since I had a few plans of my own that I hid from him.

Between both lines was a clear passage way for anyone to pass. My jaw dropped slightly as I scanned the contestants in the line that Jason had to compete against. I saw men of all shapes and sizes with deadly weapons at their sides. Almost all of them had battle scars on various parts of their bodies. Jason's words echoed in my mind when he mentioned needing experience to survive. They all seemed to have a high level of experience, possibly more than he did, but I wondered if they ever struggled as much as he had.

Jason's eyes were beaming as he chuckled, while walking through the line. Fear seemed to be an abstract idea that had no effect on him despite the calibre of contestants, many of whom appeared to be skilful and highly motivated. Although he was smaller in size compared to most his competitors, that was not my greatest concern. In the past he had defeated many men that were practically twice his size. However, as I surveyed the contestants, I realized that each of them had not only their weapon of choice, but also armour for further protection. Jason had neither of these. I wished he had a sword but he had sold it a few months prior to put food on our plates.

"I wish you at least had some armour like everyone else but we can't even afford it right now," I sulked.

"Armour is for the weak in need of extra protection, I don't need it. It'll slow me down anyway." I admired his confidence

175

but I knew that deep down if we had the money he would've invested in some kind of defence.

My line was shorter than his but it provided the opportunity that we both wanted, which was obvious to me as Jason expressed what his intentions were after completing the registration process. "Looks like we'll be apart for now, I'll see you later, I don't think I'll be going back to our dorm immediately after so there's no need to wait for me," he declared. His back already faced me as he quickened his footsteps to join the lengthy line. I was curious to know what his plans were but I avoided asking. I already had plans of my own which I knew he'd disagree with.

"Okay no problem," I kept my response simple and headed to the back of my line.

Initially, I thought standing in line for an eternity would be a hassle, but I didn't take into consideration how hot the sun would be. It was only 10:00 a.m. and it seemed to get worse by the minute. I crouched beneath the shadow of the person in front of me, it didn't do much, but it was a lot better than nothing. Everyone else in line had wooden umbrellas and palm fronds to protect them from the sun. Although there weren't many wealthy people in line, some servants placed bets on their employers' behalf. Most of us were there for the same purpose, we just wanted some fast cash and an opportunity to have a better financial situation by end of day. Both lines moved much faster than expected. It didn't take long to just sign your name and make a payment.

The sun stung when the man before me lowered his head causing his shadow to drift away slightly, I couldn't see what was in front of him so I adjusted my head and leaned forward to receive more shade. Another shadow loomed beside me but

I kept my head down until a familiar voice called out to me.

"I'm surprise to see you of all people here," he stated. I raised my head gently to address the man, but upon laying eyes on him I was instantly annoyed. "Who are you placing a bet on?" Joel asked. One of the female contestants stood beside him and welcomed me with a smile, it didn't seem genuine but I smiled along. She was the same pretty girl with dark hair that sat next to me, it seemed like Ms. Second to Last secured some alone time with the prince.

"My brother of course," I answered confidently. I thought I noticed a smile escape his lips, but if had, he concealed it immediately but he couldn't hide the impressed look on his face.

"Interesting, do you even have enough money for that?" His question irked me, why would I be in line if I couldn't afford it? I dug into my pocket and showed him the necklace my mother made with the ring.

"I don't have money but hopefully they accept this." Joel squinted his eyes as the reflection from the gems blinded him slightly.

"Where did you find something so valuable?"

"I didn't *find* it, it was a gift. My mother made it into a necklace when the ring could no longer fit my finger," I explained. I flinched as his eyebrow arched with his judgemental glare.

"So you're willing to give up something so valuable even though you may not win..."

"He's going to win." I couldn't allow him to finish his statement after sugar coating his doubts about my brother. I stood in line because I believed in him. There was no room for doubts to plague my mind.

"I admire your confidence but it's a stupid idea," he dug into his pocket and pulled out his golden sack of coins. "Here, take this. They'll charge you five coins to place a wager, with the remaining funds, treat yourself to something lovely." His sack of coins was awkwardly extended to me, but I refused to take them all. I inserted my hand and removed exactly five pennies, although it was heavier than I anticipated. I smirked and shoved the stack of coins to his chest, "Five coins is all I need. I appreciate it, and I'll pay you back when this is over."

He frowned at my attempt to return the rest of his money, "There's no need to pay me back, it's my gift to you."

"I said I'll pay you back so I will," I insisted.

"And I said no." His eyes sharpened as we warily stared at each other for a few seconds. "Come on Pia let's go." He turned his back towards me and walked away with her at his side. I glanced over my shoulder to monitor his movements only to notice him making another stop to talk to Jason. I didn't stare at them for long, I didn't want to seem too nosy but someone appeared behind me and gently tapped my shoulder.

"Excuse me young lady, the line is moving," he said. Upon getting a better look at him I felt a blush escape my lips, it was quite embarrassing but I couldn't help it. He didn't look like the rest of us in line, he was definitely wealthy, his entire outfit was made of silk and the royal blue colours complemented his blue eyes perfectly. His brown hair was well polished and the veins in his muscles made sure to say hello. His smile broadened as his eyes met mines but I refused to stare for too long and make things awkward.

"Oh m-my apologies," my brain malfunctioned as I tried to get the words out of my mouth. He didn't look a day older than twenty five yet he chose to call me young lady as if he was a middle aged man. "I thought you were at least in your forties when you called me young lady," I grinned. His face turned swollen as he tried to contain his laughter but he failed and let out a boisterous laugh. I was so relieved that he had a good sense of humour. Apart from Susan and Peter he was one of the few strangers that seemed nice to me.

"Hahaha, I guess that's what I get for trying to be polite and showcasing my well brought up manners."

My head tilted as I noticed the harsh stares from Joel and my brother. I did nothing wrong, we were just having a friendly conversation. "You seem to be very interested in the Prince," he commented. "No wonder you didn't notice me. I'm not surprised though, a lot of women are obsessed with him."

"I'm not looking at him, I'm staring at my brother, he's next to the prince," I protested. It may have been half of the truth but I didn't want him to categorize me with everyone else. He turned around to get a better look and sighed.

"Why are they so bothered?"

"Maybe because I'm talking to you." My chest squeezed when his brow arched to his hairline with confusion written all over his face.

"By any chance were you born under a coloured moon?" he asked. I felt like this was probably one of the unluckiest moments of my life. It pained me to answer but I couldn't lie.

"Y-yes." I had a feeling he'd be disappointed. His eyes widened as he shook his head.

"I see. Okay."

Just when I thought our heart-warming conversation was over, he grabbed my wrist and walked quickly to the front of the line. His sudden movements confused me but my footsteps followed, I figured it'd be better to walk alongside him than be dragged if I refused to move my feet.

"W-what are you doing?"

"I'm under the impression that you're not from here since you clearly don't know who I am. I didn't come here to wait in line, I have things to do." He quickened the pace until we arrived at the front. I expected people to complain about us skipping but they didn't. The teller at the table stood to his feet and bowed slightly.

"Are you here to place a bet my Lord?"

Their interaction caught me off guard but I should've known better. Despite his friendly manner to me, his physical appearance revealed that he was of a person of means and title. "W-who are you?"

"Don't worry about it, people call me Mr. Yinward but just call me Brandon," he smirked. I wasn't satisfied with his answer. I yearned to know every detail about him in order to put an end to my intense curiosity. My imagination was running wild and I just needed to know.

"Tell me who you are," I insisted.

"Maybe another time, today is a busy day." he directed his attention to the teller. It must've been rude to keep everyone waiting longer than they had after we had already skipped the line. "I'm here to place a bet on three individuals but I'd appreciate it if you let the young lady go before me."

"That's fine," he looked at me with a forced smile and provided his assistance. "What's your full name and who are you betting on?"

"My name is Amaris Yearwood and I'd like to place a bet on Jason Yearwood." He grabbed his pen and wrote swiftly, I was relieved by how fast and easy the process was.

"Your information is registered, the payment required is five silver coins," he scanned me from head to toe with a slight scornful look in his eyes, I assumed that I still looked poor. I dug into my pocket but Brandon interrupted.

"I'll be covering the cost," he stated. I couldn't help but blush. The independent woman in me was non-existent at the moment.

"Thank you!" I beamed with the brightest smile. I stood beside him until he was done placing his bets.

"It was nice talking to you. I guess we'll see each other again if we're meant to cross paths in the future. I hope we do."

I waved at him as he walked away and grinned. "I hope so too, better sooner than later." My smile was still evident as I watched him walk away. He seemed to be headed where I was going since he left the castle's gates, but I didn't want to follow him and give him the wrong impression so I waited at the side for a bit. Jason and Joel still stared at me harshly but I paid them no mind even though they were quite intimidating to look at. Pia rubbed Joel's shoulder to grasp his attention but his eyes were fixed on me.

"There's no way he could be jealous," I thought.

Chapter 24: They Killed him. My father is Dead

After stalling for what felt like five minutes, I was finally ready to make a move. Jason was still in line but I no longer saw him from the angle I stood due to the exceedingly tall man that was in front of him. Joel was nowhere to be seen either. I guessed he finally left to have a brief happily ever after moment with Pia. I didn't want Jason to bother me by asking too many questions so I waited for the perfect moment to leave. A couple of maids in their blue uniforms brushed pass me and I quickly followed behind them like a shadow with my head facing downwards to avoid making eye-contact with Jason, wherever he was.

If I could possibly count the steps I made, I couldn't have made it passed twenty before I felt a rough tug on my arm as Jason forced me to his side.

"What are you doing!?"

I fumbled a little as I tried to regain my balance and come up with the perfect lie. "I-I'm going to the garden."

"Then why are you behaving in such a sneaky manner? It's a bad look, too much is going on right now, especially with this Jhovaise thing, for you to look so suspicious." he scolded.

"I'm only sneaky because I wanted to prevent this from happening. I knew you'd bother me by asking too many questions." My words were only half-truth but I managed to speak convincingly, at least to my own ears.

"So you're sneaking around because you want to go to the garden and not be bothered by me?" His eyes thoroughly searched mines for hints of lies. Intimidated by his harsh unconvinced stare, I heard my voice increase in pitch as I tried to sound believable.

"Yes."

"You're lying. Are you going to meet that man you were talking to earlier?" As funny as his question was, I'd rather him believe I was going to meet Brandon than go searching for jobs.

"His name is Brandon but I'm...."

"I know what his name is," he interrupted me. "Joel already told me, he's also the general's son." My eyes popped in disbelief, but a bit of pity stained my heart. I wondered if he knew that the Piersons had his father killed and a shapeshifter impersonate him for weeks. The scenario in my mind wasn't realistic, it was impossible. The news had only reached us this morning when Joel read the letter.

"What? All of a sudden you're speechless," Jason nagged.

"I didn't know who he was, he only told me his name."

"Oh well, now you know. Do you plan on running after him now and continue flirting?" Jason's words irked me, I had no intentions to remain in the sun and tolerate his baseless accusations much longer.

"I said I'm going to the garden, after that I'll go wherever I please, but don't you dare accuse me of running off to flirt with any man!" I shocked myself by how harsh my tone was, but I didn't bother to wait for a response. I turned my back towards him and kept walking, refusing to look back. He muttered a few words but he wasn't bold enough to say them aloud so I paid him no mind. I quickened the paste of my footsteps till the sweet scent of pollen slipped through my nostrils.

After two minutes of walking I finally made it to the garden. Just when I thought the coast was clear and there'd be no more obstacles to prevent me from escaping the castle's grounds, I saw Joel with Pia beside him.

I knew without a doubt he'd never allow me to leave but luckily for me his back faced me as he indulged himself with what seemed to be a very enjoyable conversation with Pia. It almost looked like Pia was blushing but as her eyes met mines her smile faded. For a brief moment she seemed to be sulking at me, but she had nothing to worry about since I had no intentions of interrupting their joyous conversation. Joel noticed the sudden change in her facial expressions and turned his head slightly.

As he started turning in the direction that she was looking, she yanked his arm suddenly and wore a forced smile to keep his attention as long as possible. She seemed quite fazed by my presence and although her actions were quite amusing, I was also extremely grateful that she didn't allow him to see me.

If I wanted to leave the castle's grounds, I'd have no choice but to find a way to move past them unnoticed. The chances of Joel seeing me were extremely high considering I'd eventually be in front his view. Even though Jason proclaimed that being sneaky would give me a bad look, I found myself tiptoeing towards the rose trees and crouched behind them to properly hide from Joel's glare.

To prevent myself from looking too suspicious I sniffed a few roses to seem as if I was only there for the plants. Pia noticed my every move and wore the most confused look on her face as her eyes squinted in my direction. That was enough to grab Joel's unwanted attention since he suddenly tilted his head my way. I quickly crawled away to the other bushes but my quick movements caused the plants to ruffle a bit. Pia must've thought that I was spying on her, she even had the perfect opportunity to rat me out and make me look bad. A few humming birds seeped through the branches and flew around the flowers to collect pollen. Their timing couldn't have been more perfect.

"What's bothering you? Your attention seems to be elsewhere," Joel pointed out. My chest tightened the moment I realized that the success or failure of my plan laid in Pia's hand. She now had the perfect opportunity to rat me out and embarrass me. I kept crawling to escape their presence, I figured that the further away I was before she snitched would provide me with a better chance to get up and run away without being caught.

"I heard some rustling in the bushes but it was just the birds," she lied. I wasn't sure she lied for my sake or hers, but her lie saved me. I continued to crawl until I almost made it to the exit, I knew that others could see me but I didn't care, as long as it wasn't Joel. I peeped through the spacious areas between the leaves and branches to time the perfect moment to get up and sprint away. Their backs turned towards me with her arms locked in his while they headed back inside. A heavy weight of frustration left my body and I got up instantly, ready to implement the final steps of my escape plan.

I quickly got rid of the dust that clung to my dress and hopped over the plants to find myself back on the path to leave. Pia looked over her shoulder as the slight thud from my hop reached her ears. Joel followed her posture and turned his head slightly, his eyes hadn't met mines yet and I refused to give him the opportunity so I ran as fast as I could without looking back. I knew he saw me leave but I tried too hard to prevent him from stopping me. The guards weren't fazed by my sudden movements nor did they bother to stop me. Today was a day where many people were expected to enter and leave the castle to make bets or register for the tournament so they must've thought that whatever reasons I had for leaving could've been something related to the events.

It didn't take me long before I reached my destination, I stopped about three times to catch my breath from all that running but after noticing that no one chased after me, I took my time and walked in peace. The copper trail indicated to me that I was close to the city, when I finally got there it was a lot more crowded than the last time. I never expected the city to be as busy as the castle today. The clothing stores were full of ladies trying on expensive dresses and jewellery, probably for the event later in the evening but the men were in almost every store that sold weapons and armour.

The food places weren't doing as great as the other businesses but they still had customers. My eyes met the old lady fruit vendor as she screwed her face at me. I lifted my chin and rolled my eyes as I walked passed her stall. I silently vowed that no matter how hard things got I'll never purchase anything from her again because of the way she spoke to me. There were no customers around her and I couldn't feel sorry for her even if I tried. The scent of pastries tickled my nose once more. I immediately remembered the bakery where I almost secured a job when Jason and Joel ruined it for me.

Without hesitation I followed the scent until it led me back to the bakery. I entered confidently and walked straight to the cash register. There weren't many people in the store either so I was first in line. Ruben stood before me with wrinkled eyebrows when his eyes met mine. Any casual observer would have guessed that he was not too happy to see me.

"Good day, how may I help you my lady?" his voice seemed somewhat aggravated but I wore the brightest, hopeful smile to greet him.

"Good day, I'm just here to discuss business. If I were to work here as someone that takes the orders of customers, what would my salary be like?"

"I'm sorry but I don't think hiring you is a possibility. You're the property of the royal family and they'd be very displeased to know that you're an employee in my organisation."

I leaned forward and whispered to avoid anyone hearing the details of our conversation. "To be honest, I don't think I'd make it past the first month in this selection. I'm just searching for whatever options I may have for work after I leave."

Ruben folded his arms and sharpened his eyes as he stared into mines. He must've been searching for unspoken answers but I had nothing to hide.

"There's always a position for you available if you choose to work here, but come back when you're no longer considered a future bride of the prince of Mandora," he insisted. "The last thing I want is for the prince to show up here again in an aggressive manner due to your actions. Why are you even here? Shouldn't you be in the castle? Don't you have any guards to accompany you and make sure you're protected?"

His questions caught me off guard. I knew he wouldn't be happy with my honest answers so I prepared to leave immediately to avoid him having any more negative thoughts about my character. "Don't worry about it, I'm going to check a few more stores to see what my options are like."

"Okay pretty, I hope at the end of it all, our bakery will interest you the most." I almost forgot about the nickname he gave me when we first met but I blushed for a split second and walked away. Most of the complements I ever received were from my mother or brother, hearing a stranger casually call me pretty as a nickname was quite unusual but also pleasing to think about. As I opened the door and stepped outside, I noticed a couple of shadows disappear into the bushes. I quickly thought about Jhovaise and the threats he made towards the royal family. Something fishy was going on and being anywhere near it wasn't an option. I walked in the opposite direction to create a greater distance between the suspicious people and myself.

If mischief were to happen caused by those individuals, I figured it'd be wise to stay as far away from them as possible for the sake of my own safety. I entered a few jewellery and clothing stores, only to be rejected because of my appearance. I glanced at myself in the window's reflection to see what the big issue was. Everyone told me I didn't look the part. I figured that I had poverty written all over my face which wasn't a good look for their store and attracting customers.

After observing myself for a few minutes, it occurred to me that my dress was quite fashionable but my sandals were basic and my hair was slowly becoming a frizzy untamed mess. My hair was no longer silky smooth like when I had just flat ironed it, it was slowly reverting to its natural state causing my hair to look like a big fur ball styled into a pony tail. The managers voiced that it's extremely important to look presentable due to many people taking notice of their stores for the sake of fashion.

I wasn't fashionable, I just looked like a girl that managed to steal a silk dress and walk around the city with a bad hair day. The stores that sold weapons and armour chose not to accept me either. They mentioned that I didn't have the proper physique to represent their brand. I didn't see how the ability to lift a sword would affect their sales. I'd make a wonderful sales person and convince customers to buy what they were selling.

They all rejected me because of my appearance. If given a proper chance I probably would've made a good sales rep for the clothing boutiques but I was just having a really bad hair day. After being rejected countless times, I sat in the shade under a large oak tree and thought about other money making possibilities. I glanced at the stingy old lady who sold her fruits, and cringed at the thought of becoming like her. I didn't overlook the possibility that I may have no other choice but to become a farmer and sell my goods to survive if I was kicked out too early.

I was confident that I'd be welcomed to work in the bakery with Ruben, but I didn't feel comfortable putting all my eggs in one basket. There was one building that caught my attention, it even excited me almost. It was a huge library with three floors. I couldn't believe that I missed it but it wasn't very appealing to my eyes. Paint was peeling off the walls and the ceiling wood was rotten with a few areas of termite territory. The sign on their glass door read 'Open' so I didn't hesitate to enter the store since business was clearly still running.

My blood crawled from the screeching sound the door made as I opened it but my smile broadened after laying eyes on the mountain of books before me. There weren't many patrons around, maybe about five people scattered at different corners of the room with a book in hand, each one with undivided attention focused on the literature in hand. If I had more time on my hands I would've joined them and buried myself in a few fantasy worlds until I was ready to head back to the castle.

I stood there frozen, amazed by the view of hundreds of books, maybe even thousands in one place until the receptionist saw me. "May I help you?" she asked. The first thing I noticed was her messy bun and frizzy hair that fought against humidity. Her pants had a few stains and the colours of her clothing looked a bit washed-out. I gave her a beaming smile, full of hope that I won't be rejected as a result of my appearance.

"I'm wondering if it'd be possible for me to get a job here in the near future."

She frowned and shook her head while she twirled a few hair strands around her fingers. "I'm sorry but we won't be able to afford it. We'd eventually have to sell this building in a few months because business isn't going well. We can't even afford to keep this building together. It looks like a dump on the outside. We need at least twenty-five pounds of silver to keep the business running. I haven't eaten a proper meal in days."

"Damn, working here would've been a dream come through for me. If you're lucky a miracle may happen...."

"Oh...my...God. This is my first time seeing a rare gem!" a young man screeched. He must've been about fifteen years old. His eyes popped in excitement as he left his book and skipped towards me.

"Maxon, please do not make this young lady uncomfortable," the receptionist requested. He ignored her words completely and focused only on me. At first he seemed happy to see me but suddenly he just left me with an odd stare.

"Why is your hair like that? I was told that rare gems have curly hair that looks like cotton. But you just have boring straight hair like the rest of us...and it looks messy."

His audacious statements made me gasp, I couldn't help but giggle in that awkward moment. The other readers in the room turned to face me while raising their heads slightly above their books. Though it was nearly impossible, I was hoping I'd be able to avoid something like this happening.

"You can save this place by working here!" Maxon jumped excitedly. "Many people would show up if they heard about a rare gem working here."

The receptionist looked at me with a hopeful glare in her eyes, she was eager to hear my response but I knew it wasn't possible. "I won't be able to work until......" My body froze as the sound of clashing swords and terrifying screams of women pierced through my ears. The cries grew louder by the second as more victims cried out for help. As I listened more attentively I heard the destruction of items and forcefully opened doors as enemies intruded.

The library's door was made of glass making it easy to observe everything that was happening, but what worried me the most was their ability to see us as clearly as we saw them. Men in black cloaks and silver masks were rampant everywhere, women and children were dragged from their homes and stores while the men fought back to protect their loved ones. They were fighting a losing battle without the help of palace soldiers. Blood was shed everywhere, I knew I had the ability to help but the chances of me surviving the attack were too slim.

Aside from the receptionist and I, everyone else in the room were young teenagers. Maxon and two other young men, each had a sword at their side, but their reaction to the chaos showed me that they weren't well equipped to protect themselves in our current situation. Two young girls sat in a corner bawling their eyes out while the receptionist begged them to stay quiet to avoid attracting the enemy in our midst.

"D-do you guys know how to fight?" one of the girls asked. Her question was directed to the three young men after noticing the swords that they carried. They lost their ability to speak and trembled as they tried to pronounce their words clearly. Maxon gripped the hilt of his sword tightly and got to his feet.

"I've been training since I was ten. B-but those men look pretty experienced, I've never fought to save my life nor the lives of others."

I was no better than Maxon, I too was inexperienced and I didn't even own a sword. The chances of survival if they ever were to attack us were slim. They probably would not have been able to kill me but I'd still face serious casualties.

"Our building looks like an unoccupied dump from the outside, whatever they're searching for or intend to accomplish, they won't find here," the receptionist explained. Her words seemed more hopeful than fact to me.

"I don't know what they're looking for but they're dragging out a bunch of women and killing anyone that gets in their way," I stated. "We're not safe with the glass door exposed, we can see them and they can see us."

"What do you think they're trying to accomplish?" the youngest girl cried. She couldn't have been older than thirteen. Her hair laid heavily on the frontal region of her forehead due to her nervous sweating.

"What's your name?" I asked.

"M-my name is Sherry, I'm not ready to die!" she cried. "Miss Hamilton, are you sure we're safe?"

"Y-yes, we'll be fine," she lied. Her body language showed the opposite of her voiced opinion as she quivered in her shoes. Her words weren't even spoken confidently. She had no other choice; she was the adult in the situation and they all looked to her for assurance. She had to stay strong for their sakes.

"They're only taking the women and children and killing the men. We haven't bothered anyone so why are they attacking us?" Maxon complained. Due to the threats the kingdom received today I was sure that this all had to be related.

"Our country is going to war soon, so the enemy is probably taking hostages for us to bend to their will," I explained, it was the only logical reason I could come up with.

"WAR!?" they all screamed. It was foolish of me to mention it since the king had not addressed the issue to the nation yet but I couldn't stand there and act like everything was going to be okay. We leaned on the walls to prevent anyone from seeing us and peeked through the windows using the curtains to cover our faces. It was a clever idea until reflex reactions controlled by emotions took place.

Sherry let out a loud cry as a waterfall of tears ran down her cheeks. "MUMMY NO!" My pores raised after realizing what was happening. Ms. Hamilton covered her mouth instantly and gripped her arm to pull her away from the window but she didn't budge. She let out another loud cry, her distress was even worse than before. "DADDY NOOOO!" Her cries were cut short as she gasped for air. "T-they killed him" she muttered. I peeked through the blinders, only to see a man with a bleeding chest coughing up blood in his wife's arms.

"The soldiers are here to protect us!" Maxon squealed. "My father is here to save us!" He leaped in excitement. All fear within him was gone. There were at least thirty soldiers in silver armour on the backs of horses leaving a trail of dust with them.

"My father is dead! Your father is useless, they should've been here sooner!" Sherry protested. Maxon responded not to her harsh words, instead he stood there trembling and stuttered words that no one understood.

"Maxon what's happening?" I asked. Ms. Hamilton pulled him away and hugged him tightly.

"It's going to be okay," she whispered in attempt to comfort him.

"T-they killed him. My father is dead."

Chapter 25: First Kill

"Is your father the man with the same brown leather wristband as you?" I asked. I stared at a man lying on the ground with blood running down his face.

"Y-yes," Maxon cried. I sighed and shook my head with a shy smile. The situation was nothing to smile about but maybe some fairly good news would help.

"He's not dead, he's just unconscious," I explained. Maxon beamed with a glimpse of hope in his eyes, but only for a short moment before fear took over his mind.

"How are you so sure?"

I hesitated at first before providing him with an answer. I didn't want to explain the potential of my abilities because I felt that if they knew what I was capable of they'd expect me to run outside and help. "I can sense energy if I focus hard enough, that way I can tell if someone is dead or alive."

He sighed in relief but it still wasn't enough to put him at ease. I understood his frustration. His father was lying on the ground unconscious and unable to protect himself from further harm.

"If he stays there they're going to kill him. We need to help!"

"No!" Miss Hamilton insisted. "If you interfere you'll die. Leave it up to the soldiers to protect your father and everyone else as well. I know this is hard but you must remain strong."

"How am I strong!? I'm just a coward with a sword hiding behind these walls, I need to do something. I rather die than do nothing at all"

"How do you think your father would feel if he survived, only to discover that you died trying to protect him? Your father's job is to protect us all with his life, to protect you." Miss Hamilton explained. I knew he was miserable but he'd only cause more havoc if he tried to do something. Just when I thought things couldn't get any worse, another young man peeked through the window and muttered words no one would ever wished to hear.

"W-we're losing...."

"W-what did you say?"

"I said we're losing, the enemy has powers too, they're too strong."

"We'd never lose, this is our territory. They don't stand a chance!" Ms. Hamilton maintained. This time her words were convincing and it seemed like she believed it and meant it. I had nothing to say, I didn't know what to say nor did I know what to think. If these were the Piersons' people, I knew better than anyone that the chances of winning this battle was almost out of reach. Seeing the loved ones of Maxon, Sherry and many others being killed or hurt worried me that Jason may get here as soon as possible if he heard about the attacks we were facing. Even though I didn't know for sure that the attacks were orchestrated by the Piersons, I had a feeling that Jason would've thought the same thing.

"The Healers and Protectors are here!" another girl squealed. She jumped for joy as the others rushed to the windows in excitement. Fear evaporated as hope and confidence in our soldiers took over.

"*Protectors?*" I asked. "How are they any different from the soldiers? Isn't it their job to protect us all?" The startled looks on their faces revealed that at my age, I should've already known the difference.

"You seriously don't know the difference?" Ms. Hamilton asked. "Come, take a look." She invited me to take a peek next to her while she further explained. I saw five individuals dressed in green uniforms with a golden emblem of the kingdom's crest on their chests; two men and three women. The green cloaks attached to the uniforms flowed with the wind which seemed to be a design flaw to me. I wondered if the cloaks wouldn't just slow them down. But I noticed that the enemies seemed to be moving around with their cloaks just fine.

"The people in green are the healers. I guess that's self-explanatory but they heal the injured."

"Ohhhh." I saw a woman leaning over Maxon's father with a green light emitting from her hands as she focused her energy on his head injury. "Why is she taking so long to heal him?" I asked.

"They're healers, not miracle workers," she grinned. "It's going to take at least seven minutes for his injury to heal. Usually when people are stabbed or suffer fatal injuries it takes at least an hour to get them back on their feet. Sometimes multiple healers would team up to speed up the recovery process if it's too serious or close to death."

My eyebrows creased in disbelief. The healers were useful

but I just wished their powers could've been more effective. "Wouldn't that make them easy targets for the enemies?" I asked.

"What do you mean?"

"The healers are forced to stay in one position to heal the injured, how can they defend themselves if they're too busy focusing their attention on the injured?"

She pointed at three soldiers dressed in cream uniforms with cloaks attached to their shoulders. Each one also had a golden emblem of the kingdom's crest on their chest. "You see those three over there? They're the protectors. Protectors form barriers around the soldiers that acts as a shield. Most of the enemies' attacks will be ineffective with the protectors around. The shields will eventually weaken after bracing many attacks but they'll be fine. It'll buy the soldiers enough time to fight back without facing any injuries. These tactics place us at a very high advantage against our enemies."

"That's why everyone calls us THE NEVER DEFEATED KINGDOM OF MANDORA!" Maxon boasted. I could see that he was very proud of our country. Everyone looked through the window excited by the chaos. They no longer feared being caught and left themselves exposed without the use of curtains as a screen to conceal their presence. Two minutes earlier they were scared with tears running down their eyes and some were even quivering. Now they all watched and to some extent appeared to be entertained, as the violence continued, all except Sherry. She sat in a corner and mourned the death of her father, she wasn't certain that her mother would survive but she couldn't bear to possibly be a witness to another one of her parent's death.

It was difficult for me to stand at the window and stare at brutality and bloodshed, like some of the others were doing. I imagined that every one of those men had a family, a mother, father, siblings and probably even children. Enemy or not they all fought for a cause. Maybe some of them were just following orders to receive compensation to provide for their families, yet people viewed a sword piercing through another man's chest as amusing. The sight of everyone jumping and screaming irked me. Furthermore at any moment the roles could be reversed and they'd be crying or quivering again. Sherry had no reason to celebrate, she suffered a great loss and it could've been anyone in her shoes, even me.

Since the enemy combatants were fully engaged in battle by our soldiers, I decided it'd be the perfect time for me to escape. I figured that if I opened the door and ran as fast as possible, no one could harm me while they were too busy fighting for their lives.

"Alright, you can do this." My words were all the motivation I needed to get up and leave. As I approached the door I felt a rough tug by the hem of my dress. Sherry's tired eyes stared directly into mine as she still wept.

"What are you doing!? Are you trying to get us killed?"

I was lost for words. I gasped at her absurd remark and took a few steps back. Before I could explain myself Ms. Hamilton stuttered as she took deep breaths to stay calm, her attention was still fixed through the window, she didn't even notice us.

"W-what's happening?"

"The protectors' shields are breaking! The healers are running out of time!" Maxon shrieked. The perfect opportunity to leave kept getting slimmer with every passing moment. I couldn't wait any longer, I had to leave now. I sharpened my eyes to see through the door before me, just to make sure I was aware of what the current environment was like before

I sprinted back to the castle. I couldn't just leave without looking for the perfect route to head back to my destination otherwise I'd get caught or even hurt. My eyes widened and my chest tightened as Maxon screamed in agony, we must've been looking at the same thing.

"NO NO NOOOOOO!"

An enemy made a strategic decision to use the protector's shield as a stool to leap over and sliced the head off the healer that had been helping his father. Her head rolled to our door as blood smeared the glass. I flinched as the blood splattered near my face but the door shielded me. My mind froze along with my body but the cries from Ms. Hamilton brought me back to my senses while Maxon ran passed me through the door, headed straight to his father.

"Maxon stop! They'll kill you!" she cried. She ran after him but came to a sudden stop by the door after her legs weakened by the sight of the healer's head at our feet. Maxon kept running with his sword in hand making crazy demands and made it to the centre of the battlefield.

"If you're going to kill my father you'd have to go through me!" Our soldiers advised him to leave, to run and never look back, but it was too late, he already stood face to face with the enemy. He held his sword with both hands quivering in fear. It pained me to watch his inexperienced stance. He was a dead boy standing. Dead if I did nothing. Jason's mocking words played through my brain.

"You're a coward. You'll never get better without experience." A battlefield wasn't the best place to gain experience for a beginner, but I couldn't just stand there and watch Maxon die. Maxon swung his sword first. His movements were slow, too easy to dodge and his stance was terrible, he lost balance with every attack he made. Our soldiers were too occupied fighting against other enemy soldiers to help.

"How old are you, boy?" his opponent asked.

"F-fifteen," Maxon struggled to speak against his strength.

"Good, you're old enough to die. I won't feel guilty when I sleep tonight." With those words he lifted his knee and sent Maxon rolling in the dust with a heavy kick as the boy's sword slipped out of his hands. As Maxon crawled to get back on his feet, the enemy raised his sword and stood above him.

I didn't know what was happening but I lost control of my body and found myself in the middle of the battlefield while Ms. Hamilton and Sherry screamed at me to head back to safety. Maxon's sword was at my feet and I grabbed it immediately. It wasn't as heavy as the other swords I held in the stores. I guessed it was beginner friendly, or maybe the adrenaline just kicked in and I found my strength. Maxon was crawling on his back with tears running down his face while he attempted to use his hand to brace himself from his opponent's sword.

The man laughed at the sight of a young man begging for his life. Maxon's father pleaded with the aggressor to spare his son but the pleas from a helpless soldier was like gasoline being poured on a fire. The vicious smile that the assailant flaunted, broadened even more. As his sword descended I leaped forward in front of the boy with his weapon in my hand, shielding him from the intended blow. Our swords clashed.

The cold eyes of the unwelcomed invader met me with an intimidating stare, but he welcomed me with a murderous smile. Regrets ran through my mind as I feared for my life. The coward in me begged for me to scream for help. The strength of my opponent was far superior and my legs wobbled as I tried to keep a stance. The more he pressed his weight against me, the more my knees buckled as if they were ready to surrender. My breaths became heavy and drops of sweat ran down my face but this was not an indication that I was exhausted. I was terrified.

My knees eventually gave in and I stumbled to the ground still bracing my face with Maxon's sword. At this point the sword was still being used as a shield, not a weapon. My elbows ached when most of the pressure penetrated through my arms to keep the sword stable.

"It's not easy to kill you." I chuckled as Jason's words ran through my brain. I've seen what these men could do, they definitely could kill me by slicing my head off but Jason trained me well to defend my weakest spot. The man scoffed in disgust after seeing me giggle.

"You must be really excited to die." He lifted his sword, allowing my arms to have a brief moment of freedom before he landed a fatal blow, but this was the moment I desperately waited for. As he raised his arm, he left his body unprotected with various openings for me to strike. My arms were weak and the sword felt heavier in my hand, but my legs regained strength. As he stood over me and planted his swords downwards I kicked his knee as hard as possible causing him to lose balance and kneel to the ground. I crawled to my feet as fast as possible and gripped a handful of sand. Just as expected, he was already on his feet charging aggressively towards me with murderous intent. I panicked and threw the sand at him too soon. He blocked it easily with his arm but a few dust particles still slipped through to his eyes.

He blinked continuously while his eyes burned, swinging his sword recklessly in his hopeless attempts to defend himself. My arms were still weak so I held my sword with both hands and ran it through his chest. I faced him with pride and his cold eyes became weary as they struggled to stay open. I sensed his arm moving beside me with his sword still intact in his last attempt to land a fatal blow. I knew he couldn't kill me that way but I still feared the pain it would bring upon me if he succeeded. I used the last bit of my strength to dig the sword deeper till it pierced through his back. When his sword fell to the ground I was sure the job was finally done.

I cautiously raised my head to make sure he was dead, but he wasn't, at least not yet. Blood splattered on my face as he coughed away his last few breaths. He was dead. His weight overpowered me and I lost my balance and fell to the ground. The smeared blood on my face burned my nostrils each time I inhaled. My dress was damp from the blood that was leaking from his body which increased with each passing second that I laid there but I couldn't move. Nothing was wrong with me physically but I felt as though I was losing my mind. At this moment I should've been happy. Happy that I made my first kill, happy that I managed to survive, happy that I saved Maxon and his father, but instead I was traumatized.

I felt my body shake vigorously as Maxon pushed the dead body off of me and pleaded for me to get up.

"We need to get out of here!" I kept my eyes closed, fearing the possibility of blood slipping through my eyes. I followed his voice and tilted my head in his direction.

"I-I can't move. T-take your father and flee to safety," I instructed.

"Did he hurt you!? You're dying, you're dying because of me. I'm so sorry," He cried. Maxon held my body and squeezed me tightly, the blood on my face transferred to his shirt allowing me to build the courage to open my eyes. My vision was blurry, everything around me seemed faded but the rumbling around me snapped me back to reality. Spears of ice arose from the ground and massacred as least half our enemies.

"Is Jason here?"

Maxon squealed as he squeezed my hand. "We're saved! You're going to be alright, the healers will save you. Our enemies are retreating it's...." Maxon choked and gasped for air while a hand gripped and almost devoured his neck, slowly lifting him off his feet. He was tossed to the side like disposable rubbish and rolled in the dirt to eat dust.

"Get away from her!" Joel demanded. My vision sharpened by the sight of Joel and Logan beside me. Joel knelt to my side and passed his hands gently over various parts of my body searching for any visible signs of injury. "Are you okay? Did he hurt you?" He diverted his attention to Logan. "Kill them, every last one of them. Kill them all."

"I already did," he answered. I looked around and every last one of our enemies were dead, even the ones that tried to run away didn't make it very far.

"I'm okay. Maxon didn't hurt me, you should apologise for hurting the one person I was trying to protect."

"I'm not talking about Maxon, I'm referring to the man you killed. I saw everything." Joel locked his arms in mine and brought me to my feet. My heart was racing. I really did kill a man.

Chapter 26: Traitors?

I struggled to keep up with Joel as he practically dragged me back to the castle. He squeezed my hand so tightly that it felt numb. The nerves in my hand were struggling to survive while I slowly lost my sense of touch. Logan remained a few feet behind to ensure there were no shady activities around that could cause us any harm. When he finally felt secured in our surroundings he increased his pace and walked beside Joel confidently and slipped his hands in his pockets. He glanced in my direction with a harsh stare then looked away.

"I volunteered to be your advisor, but you just might cause me to lose my job." I understood that my actions were foolish but I had no idea my life would've been at risk by the recent attacks displayed earlier.

"Was I wrong for leaving the castle? I just wanted to…." I paused to calculate my words and avoid potential stirred anger from the two of them. If they knew I left in order to search for potential jobs in the future there'd probably be no coming back from that. "To get some fresh air." My chest ached by the stupid excuse I came up with but it was the only lie that came to mind under pressure.

"Wasn't the fresh air in the garden enough?" I flinched as Joel squeezed my hand tighter, he must've done that on purpose. "I saw when you sneaked around and ran away. If you didn't think you were wrong, why were you acting so shady?"

"To avoid running into you." I panted. There was more I wanted to say, but I was slowly running out of breath trying to keep up with their pace. His brows furrowed as he squinted his eyes when he tried to process my words.

"Oh really? Then you must really hate me."

"Not as much as you hate me, I'm your least favourite after all," I responded, my tone was unintentionally harsh but I was a bit irritated. I tilted my head with a slightly arched brow with intentions to continue my petty beahviour.

"After your actions today you're going to be ranked last for a while. Rock bottom, the lowest of the low, congratulations."

"Thank you, I appreciate it," I wore a fake but bright smile and watched as his jaw dropped in disbelief by my words.

"ENOUGH! I've had it with you two and your lovers' quarrel," Logan snapped. "Why did you leave without your body guard? Do you have any idea how idiotic your actions were? Are you not aware of your current position? You're one of the selected, a new noble and a rare gem at that, an easy target for kidnapping. We even received a threat this morning and lost at least seven men, yet here you are, sneaking away without a body guard."

"A body guard? You say that as if there's one assigned to me. I guess I'm expected to just ask a soldier randomly when he's doing his duties to accompany me." He didn't answer me, there was awkward silence for a moment while Joel stared at him harshly. Only my heavy panting could be heard.

"So you didn't tell them?" Joel asked.

"I can't recall, I most likely forgot to. I'm an advisor in training without a trainer so don't be too hard on me."

"Amaris your bodyguard is the maid that was assigned to you. Didn't they inform you about their duties as well?" Joel asked. I didn't want Susan or Peter to lose their jobs but I wasn't educated on any of this. I spoke my words carefully to mask the truth.

"Ohhh, so that's what they meant when they said they're also there to protect us if their assistance is ever needed." I lied. I yanked my hand to get away from Joel's grip in an attempt to switch the topic, but he wouldn't budge. My elbows ached even more in my helpless attempt to set myself free from his caging hold. "Why are you even holding my hand?"

"Because I feel like it," his response was as dry as Jason's ashy knees.

"Most of the men wore masks to hide their identities, but now I understand why. They're all citizens of Mandora. They're rebels, traitors that need to be dealt with. I'm sure there's more in hiding that are plotting their next move," Logan mentioned. His words were hard to swallow, hard to process, hard to believe, hard to accept. The thought of dealing with two enemies was nerve-wrecking, first the Piersons, and now we're fighting among our own people. They made it even harder to distinguish between our allies and foes within our own kingdom.

"I know," Joel responded plainly. "I noticed it too. Father is going to lose his mind when he hears this. At least they weren't able to take any women as hostages, two attacks in a day is ridiculous."

"I regret killing them all. They were our soldiers, that's why they were so skilled. The people we fed and trained turned around and betrayed us, I want to know why. I should've kept at least one of them alive to get some answers."

"It's fine, I know of a traitor living among us in the castle, it took me a while to put the pieces of the puzzle together but I'm sure I'm right about this one." Joel commented. Logan smirked till an unrestrained burst of laughter escaped his lips.

"We must be thinking about the same person, the soldier that interrupted our breakfast. He's the only soldier that made it out alive and he wasn't on duty either. He's stationed behind the castle at night, so why was he there in the morning?"

"Exactly."

I remained silent as I listened to their conversation while they seemed oblivious of me but I took in all the juicy details to report to Jason as soon as I got back. When we made it through the entrance gates of the castle they finally slowed their pace and I no longer struggled to breathe. Sweat ran down my face and a mixture of sweat and blood dripped off my chin. While we walked through the garden I noticed that the line for registration was gone, but there was still a long line of gamblers waiting to place their bets for the battle later. We were now the centre of attention. All eyes were upon us, on me.

"Ah shit here we go. The less witnesses the better." Joel muttered.

"I guess this is where we separate for now. The event is going to start soon, in roughly thirty minutes," Logan mentioned.

"We'll talk when it's over." Joel pulled me along with him as he tightened his hold and quickened his steps, practically running. We sprinted into the hallway and up the stairs with eyes tracing our every move. He abruptly stopped, allowing me a chance to finally take a breath. Guards and other staff, positioned at every corner, looked at me with horrified expressions but they didn't stare long. The maids ran away quickly and whispered to each other while the guards tilted their heads and pretended they didn't see anything after Joel challenged them with a harsh stare.

"Take me to your room." Joel commanded.

"Huh? What for?" I couldn't think of a single logical reason for him to make such an unusual request.

"Now!" That must've been the second time he raised his voice at me and we'd only known each other for roughly twenty-four hours. I lowered my head and stared at our hands that remained locked together by his unreasonable hold.

"You're still holding my hand, why?"

"Is it preventing your feet from moving? It didn't seem to hold you back before, now walk." My pores raised at his cold response, along with a shiver that trickled down my spine. I sensed that he was still upset with me, but we were running out of time, the event was going to start soon so stalling just made everything worse. I let out an irritated sigh and began to move, I bit my tongue to avoid saying anything further, out of respect. He was the prince and I was just a poor village girl. I'd be abusing my position by voicing my dissatisfaction about the way he spoke to me. I became a recognized noble over-night, but his authority as the Crown Prince of Mandora was far superior to my current status.

"We're here." We stood before the door to my room as I waited for him to give whatever further instructions he may have up his sleeve. He stood there for a couple seconds and stared as if he was disappointed. He turned the doorknob and invited himself in as he proceeded to take a few steps forward.

"You have got to be kidding me....." he stammered. "Is this really your room?"

"Yes, why? Was there a mix up or something? Does it belong to someone else? I knew it was too good to be true, this room is bigger than our house back at home. It's so fancy in here. If you want us to leave and…."

"Amaris this is a shared apartment room for our maids. You're not supposed to be on this first floor, the contestants live upstairs, only servants reside here. The girls are separated from the guys. Do you both sleep in here?"

"I was wondering why so many maids were on this floor," Jason interrupted. I didn't see him but I heard his voice. He sneaked his way into our presence from behind and tapped my shoulder. "Are you okay? Many strangers approached me saying that I should check on you and make sure you're okay."

I completely forgot about my appearance for a brief moment. The only thing on my mind was informing him about the traitors who may possibly be living amongst us in the castle. He brushed passed us and stood before me with his eyes wide open. He wasn't upset, just concerned, but I knew it would all change once I explained what happened.

"Let me explain," I pleaded. My heart raced while I tried to form the right words in my mind to not escalate or trigger any negative emotions in his head. Joel loosened his grip and pulled his hand away and he folded his arms

"No let me explain," he interjected. "Amaris sneaked out of the castle without any guards at her side and roamed around the city alone…"

"She did what!?" Jason stammered with his brows furrowed and stared harshly at me. "So you lied to me?"

"I-It's not like that I…."

"You haven't heard the worst part yet," Joel grinned. How could he be laughing in an uncomfortable situation like this?

"While she roamed around the area, rebels attacked the city and killed at least fifteen of our men. They dragged as many women as possible to keep them as hostages, but she was in a safe place hidden until a boy ran out to save his father. She chased after him when the enemy was about to kill him and...."

"She did what!?"

"Didn't you say I need to gain more experience to get better? Don't be mad at me for following your instructions." I used his words against him in an attempt to defend myself. I was alive with no injuries, no scratches, and no pain. The blood on my body wasn't mine. I reckoned that I did great.

"She's lying. She wasn't thinking about you, she was thinking about that boy. Emotions took over her and she ran in the middle of the battlefield to save him, but maybe your words influenced her confidence." I clenched my jaw and fought with myself to abstain from spewing the disrespectful thoughts that ran through my mind.

"I was right, you really do hate me," I muttered. "What do you gain from increasing my brother's anger towards me?" He ignored my words and kept talking.

"I'm proud of her, she held her ground and killed him. It was a tough fight but she managed to survive without getting hurt, although she may have gotten a panic attack and laid there frozen on the floor covered in blood" Joel continued. I struggled to figure him out, one minute he threw me under the bus and seconds after he complemented my actions.

"I am not impressed, neither am I okay with any of this. Amaris I'll deal with you later. I'm expected to be at the stadium now with the other competitors. I expect to see you there, but who knows, you may lie and just sneak around again, so just surprise me." He brushed passed my shoulder harshly and left the room. I stumbled slightly but regained my balance quickly.

"We don't have much time. Get yourself cleaned…..and fix your hair, it looks like a frizzy disaster," Joel instructed. "Your maid should be here to help you but you being in this room complicates things. You don't even have a bell to ring when you need her assistance, so just hurry." He turned his back towards me and left, closing the door gently with a smirk on his face. I wasn't given the opportunity to respond but it didn't matter, I couldn't think of anything to say.

Chapter 27: SILENCE

I moved as quickly as I could. I even hopped into the shower when the water was cold without giving it a chance to heat up first. Cold water didn't bother me, it's what I was accustomed to, but when the warm water touched my body after a while it felt so relaxing. I could've stayed there for hours. I must've spent almost ten minutes in the shower enjoying the steam, I soaped my body three times just for the fun of it. The soap was pink and hard as a rock but it smelt like roses.

It took about two minutes for my skin to completely dry after using a fluffy red towel that Susan left for me earlier in the morning. I glanced at the clock on the wall and saw that I had roughly fifteen minutes before the event started. Usually it'd take me two hours to straighten my hair but I wasn't blessed with the luxury of time.

I quickly wrapped my towel around me and scanned through my clothing options in the closet. It seemed as though Susan made a quick update with my wardrobe immediately after our embarrassing moment at breakfast. It was stacked with luxurious dresses that I had no interest in wearing, but there was nothing else for me to choose from. I sighed in the remembrance of days when I wore comfortable baggy pants that were usually too big for me since they were hand me downs.

Most of the dresses were too glittery and long, she even added eight pairs of heels, heels that I definitely would not have been able to walk in. I made up my mind not to wear any of the shoes she selected, at least not today. They served no purpose if I struggled to walk in them so I stuck with my sandals and looked for the simplest dress of the bunch even though none had any simple attributes about them. I didn't want a dress that required to be zipped up from the back, that allowed me to narrow it down to two options.

The first option was a pink shimmery fitted dress with long sleeves and a short trail at the back of my feet. The material was a bit stretchy, but whatever fabric they used to achieve the shimmery look felt rough, I just knew it'd itch my skin and I hated the colour pink. It was a neutral pink, but still pink. The second option was another body fitting dress but of velvet material in a deep red colour resembling blood. The bottom design was like a bouquet of roses that fell at my feet, but the dress was strapless. It was a bit flashier than the pink, but at least it didn't leave a short trail for anyone to step on.

The final obstacle was my hair, I stepped before the mirror and experienced a brief moment of panic after noticing the frizzy bird nest I carried on my head throughout the day. I couldn't afford to straighten it with so little time so I immediately came up with a plan B. I dug into my belongings and grabbed my home-made flaxseed gel. I didn't have a comb on me so I gently parted my hair with my fingers and braided the front while styling the rest of my hair into a bun. The gel was able to tame the frizzy strands but it made my hair a bit wavy since it was a liquid product. I was a bit relieved to see my hair slowly reverting to curly without washing it. I crossed my fingers in hopes of escaping heat damage and permanently destroyed curls.

Since the dress had no sleeves, I thought a necklace would go perfect with the dress so I wore my leather necklace with the ring pendant my mother made me. It wasn't anything fancy but it was special to me. I had a few hand bags to choose from but I picked the smallest one. It was a leather black bag with scale designs. I quickly placed Joel's pouch of coins in the bag and ran out of the room. As I closed the door he gripped my hand quickly and locked his fingers in mine.

"You're still here?" I stammered.

"You look...." His eyes widened and he paused for a moment. "This is the best I've ever seen you look. Come on let's go," he ignored my comment and forced me along with him.

"You've only known me for a little more than a day, but thank you."

"I see you don't take complements well."

"I see you don't give them well either. When do you plan on letting go of my hand?" He ignored me again and quickened his pace. For someone that was looking for a future wife, his communication was poor, or maybe he just chose to be cold towards me. Regardless of his reasons, I still hated being ignored. I followed him quietly and brainstormed countless ways to return the favour in the future. My lips broadened as I struggled to hide my mischievous smile.

"If I knew you'd smile so much around me I would've blessed you with my presence earlier instead of spending as much time with Pia." My smile disappeared the moment his cocky statement escaped his lips and reached my ears. I was too stunned to laugh and too dumbfounded to speak, it was the perfect moment to not respond. My silence seemed to have sparked a bit of curiosity in his brain. His brows arched as he looked at me to assess my reaction but I left no noticeable expressions on my face. He studied my face for a few seconds then looked away.

"If not me, then what are you smiling about?" His voice lowered and the previous excitement in his vocals diminished. My smile brightened again as the perfect opportunity to be petty landed in the palm of my hands. I said nothing, but a slight grin escaped my lips. The palm of his hands felt warm, very warm and slowly increased its temperature by the second.

"So you refuse to answer me, that's not a good sign."

"I'll answer your question when you answer mine. Communication goes both ways, so answer me first," I instructed, I squeezed his hand to remind him of my previous question. He tilted his head downwards and finally acknowledged me while he stared at our tightly locked hands. My ears burned at his sudden burst of laughter. He paused for a moment but kept his eyes locked with mine and began laughing again. The uncomfortably warm feeling in his hand decreased and returned to normal body-temperature.

"I see, so this is how it's going to be. That's fine, let's play the silent game and see who breaks first," he insisted. Aside from being petty, I was also competitive and determined. Nothing excited me more in that moment than striking a deal with a cocky, over-confident prince.

"Deal."

I followed this man in silence with a broad smile on my face. In just a few minutes the silence was loud and unbearably awkward but I was willing to push through it. He wore that signature smile on his face the entire time. The more I saw it, the creepier he appeared to be.

I felt like I had a mini tour of the castle with no communication while he spent his time leading me to the event without speaking. The place was packed with people, all headed in the same direction but they made room with their heads bowed as we passed. I flinched as I felt a slight tapping on my shoulder.

"I didn't mean to scare you my lady, but it seems that we've crossed paths again," Brandon bowed. "Good day my prince."

"Brandon! I didn't think I'd see you so soon, will you...."

"We can't talk right now, as you can see I'm running late. I have my assigned seat to get to before my father threatens to chop my head off." Joel interrupted, there was no longer a smile on his face.

"Yes but she...." I wish I could interpret what Brandon said but Joel pulled me away and walked even faster. His unnecessary actions irked me, if he was in such a rush he could've just left me there and go to his seat. My chest burned as I kept my thoughts to myself. I refused to be the first to speak.

He led me through a weird passage way hidden within the walls. When he placed his hand on a block, the walls divided in two making room for us to enter. I stayed quiet but flinched as the walls closed shut leaving behind nothing but darkness. With the flick of his fingers the passage way lit up with candles exposing the rubies and diamonds that decorated the walls in beautiful patterns of stars and flowers. I wondered if the gems were authentic but I refused to be the one to break the silence by asking the question. As we approached a flight of stairs that led to a wooden door, the sound of a roaring crowd was getting louder by the second.

Joel dug into his pockets and held unto a silver key. "Phew, I thought I lost you and came all this way for nothing." When he opened the door bright light blinded my eyes as the sun shun directly at my face.

"My father is going to be so upset."

CHAPTER 28: Amaris will be my Property

In the heart of the castle was a battle arena large enough to hold a thousand men with a stadium like structure of seats surrounding it. I guessed this was where the soldiers trained. It was just a large area of dirt surrounded by paved walls and thousands of seats for spectators. I gasped when I noticed how packed the place was. My eyes searched the crowd for available seats, but I found none. The stadium was huge, standing in one place to search for a seat wouldn't do me any justice but I didn't mind standing to watch the event if I had to.

"We're five minutes late, let's get to *our* seats," Joel suggested. He left me confused at *'our.'* I wasn't informed about any seat being assigned to me. I didn't have a chance to ponder about what he said before he started walking and I was forced to follow along with my hand still held tightly in his.

"The prince is here!" someone announced. He was just a spectator in the crowd like the rest, I wished he kept his mouth shut, now all eyes were on us with confused stares. I already had an idea of what they were thinking. The sight of us holding hands must've been alarming. For a brief moment he finally let go but after being forced into the spotlight it felt like I forgot how to walk. As much as he annoyed me, I wanted to hold his hand again. The fear of tripping down the stairs with so many people staring tormented my brain.

"Stay calm and relax, just don't fall," I repeated those words with every step, which was the perfect indication that I wasn't calm at all. Joel gently placed his arm around my waist and held me at his side as we continued down the flight of stairs. My pores raised and my cheeks burned slightly. He led me all the way to the front, where his sister and parents were seated, with the brightest smile on his face. He seemed happy but I could tell there was a trace of nervousness hidden behind his smile. There was only one seat available next to his father and I definitely had no plans of sitting beside the king, but I was wise enough to know that the seat was reserved for Joel. High ranking nobles sat in the row above them, I counted nine, six men and three women but there was one more seat available next to a woman in an elegant green dress.

I preferred to sit among normal civilians than nobles; it'd be easier to fit in that way, or at least I'd feel more comfortable. As my eyes glanced at the seat once more I felt an unexpected tap on my shoulder.

"Looks like we won't be sitting far apart," Brandon grinned. He bowed his head at the royal family and acknowledged their presence. "I'm here to take my father's place, I haven't seen him today."

My heart sank to my stomach after hearing those words. It seemed that no one told him the news about his father yet. The king showed no emotions, he just nodded his head and silently dismissed him by waving his hand and flicking his wrist. The queen rubbed her forehead and sighed, I knew the weight of the situation affected her, probably more than it affected me. I felt sympathy for him as I would for anyone in his situation but I didn't know him.

He sat beside the lady in the green dress, in the seat I had intentions of taking which apparently was assigned to his father. My eyes travelled to the row above, the selected girls and a few guys were seated right behind the nobles. I smiled instantly with a sigh, I finally figured out where I was expected to be seated. Joel annoyed me. I thought the least he could've done was speak up and show me where to sit instead of being petty. I turned my back to him proceeding to sit with the others but he gently held my hand and pulled me to his side.

"What are you doing!?" I whispered harshly.

"I can ask you the same thing, why are you trying to leave my side?"

I blinked twice at his senseless question, there was obviously one seat next to the king which was reserved for him and the selected individuals sat two rows above where I belonged. He approached his parents with my hand still held hostage in his.

"Amaris will be seated next to me today." I must've heard him incorrectly or at least I hoped I did, but his parent's reaction confirmed that I heard right. The forced smile that his father wore to please the crowd washed away and his mother's eyes sharpened in my direction but worst of all Roselyn let out a hideous laugh. She quickly covered her mouth and apologised for her unethical outburst. The king's face slowly turned red with furrowed brows as he forced himself to smile and keep his cool.

"You've arrived in my presence late, you're the reason why we're running behind schedule to start this event and now you're telling me you want an uninvited guest to sit in our midst?" He tried to speak calmly but his tone was rough. I was clearly unwanted in their presence but I didn't want to be there either. I stood there embarrassed not knowing what to say.

"My apologies for my tardiness, there was a matter in the city that had to be handled which I'm sure you're already informed about," Joel responded. It was a pretty good excuse given the chaos that happened earlier.

"Yes so I've been told, but Logan could've handled it, there was no reason for you to be there. I was also informed that this young lady was where she shouldn't have been and came back in a bloody mess," the king diverted his harsh glare at me and in that moment I had forgotten how to breathe for a few seconds. "I don't care about your reasons for bringing her here, there's no available seat for her here, let her sit among the other girls."

I heard giggling from a row above. They laughed at me. I tried to contain my emotions but I was most upset with Joel and it felt like he did all this to embarrass me. I tried to pull away from him but he pulled me closer, forcing me to stay at his side.

"If we can't find her a seat next to me that's fine, she can sit on my lap," Joel suggested. I searched for all possible signs of sarcasm but there was none. His tone had become as stern as his father's. My jaw dropped with widened eyes as I tried to process what was really happening. Nothing made sense, I couldn't understand why he'd go this far to upset his parents, especially his father.

"I won't allow that to happen," his father protested, his voice gradually raised each time he spoke.

"No worries, we'll just sit somewhere else," Joel suggested.

"Do not mess with me *boy*."

"Joel why are you doing this?" the queen asked. I looked at him immediately waiting anxiously for the answer. His smile broadened with a gentle grin. I had a feeling that I wasn't prepared for the words that were about to come out his mouth.

"Amaris and I had a bet, so I want her beside me to see how it all plays out." I had no idea what he was talking about, but I couldn't call him out for lying and make the situation worse. The queen gently tapped her forehead and sighed.

"You have got to be kidding me," Roselyn complained. The queen glanced over her shoulder and called out to one of the guards nearby.

"Please bring this young lady a seat," she requested. I heard murmuring from the other selected women. They weren't laughing any more but they stared at me harshly so I returned their harsh glare with a mocking smile.

Joel finally let go of my hand. "Thank you mother," he said with a genuine smile.

"There's no need to thank me, I'm doing whatever I can to draw away the unwelcome attention you've caused and get the focus back on the competition. I'm pretty sure your father will deal with you later." She was right, everyone's eyes were upon us. It must've been weird to see us standing there talking for so long before taking a seat. People could've figured out that I wasn't an invited guest in the company of the royals. The king sat in silence with an angry pout on his face that he made no attempt to disguise. I felt his negative energy while standing a few feet away. As I waited in awkward silence for a seat, it felt like the longest two minutes of my life. I was so relieved when the guard showed up and placed my seat next to Joel's.

"Ladies first," he insisted. I nervously sat and endured the heavy stares of everyone around us. Joel sat beside me with a satisfied look on his face as though he was proud of himself for achieving something magnificent. After five seconds of blissful silence the interrogations continued.

"What exactly are the details of this bet?" Roselyn asked. I could handle the intense stares from the spectators but adding uncomfortable conversations meant that I was destined to have an unpleasant evening. Above all I was pretty sure I didn't want to engage in any discussions with Roselyn.

"Are you sure you want to know?" Joel teased. I figured he must've been buying time to come up with another lie.

"You have an uninvited guest among us, we at least deserve a detailed explanation from you," the king stated. I braced myself for Joel's response as I noticed him laughing gently while all this tension increased by the second. He must've been a maniac.

"Her brother is participating in this event. If he wins I'll reward her with ten pounds of silver. If he loses, she'll be my property and do whatever I say till I eventually get bored of her."

We all wore the same shocked expressions on our faces. My jaw stretched after the lies he spewed processed through my brain, but I forced myself to keep my composure before they figured out it was a lie.

"Is this true?" the king asked, diverting his harsh glare at me.

"Yes your majesty," it pained me to say so but I felt that I had no other choice.

"Joel why would you give a disgusting consequence like that? I raised you better," his mother scolded.

"Mother you and father both have slaves, I don't see the issue." Joel grinned. I wanted to throw up at that moment, I even felt dizzy.

"Oh, so now instead of your property you'll classify her as your slave!?"

"Property and slave means the same thing, I don't see the problem with this bet since she agreed. You made this event a lot more entertaining than I thought it would be. Thank you for inviting her here. I'd love to see her reaction when the winner is announced, whoever it may be. I believe Luke will come out victorious but we'll see how this goes." the king announced.

"You must really need the money to agree to a bet like that, but given your background, I don't blame you," Roselyn commented. I deserved an award for my self-control when dealing with her. Holding back on expressing my thoughts was an intense struggle but I managed to survive thus far.

"I disagree. Maybe she's just confident in her brother and took advantage of an easy opportunity to win so much money. She can start a new life with ten pounds of silver. I believe that her brother will win, she's too confident to risk it all." The queen pointed out. She was very open minded compared to the other nobles I had met so far.

"Are you willing to bet on it?" the king teased his wife with an identical troublesome smile as that of his son's.

"Ha-ha! Are you sure you want to risk losing against me? You'd have a lot to lose, I'm warning you because if I win you'd have to be my slave and do whatever I say for a week. You shouldn't have a problem agreeing to my terms since you weren't bothered by our son's bet with the girl," the queen grinned. The king lost himself in an uncontrollable outburst of laughter until tears ran down his face and Joel laughed along with him.

"Mother, are you sure you want to do this? Dad can be very

indecent at times. Please don't give him the opportunity to take advantage of you."

"I stand by what I said, I'm not afraid of your father."

"Good! Then your consequence will be the same, you'd be my slave for a week if you lose," the king clapped his hand in excitement with the brightest smile I've ever seen on his face. Given the situation, it was very disturbing.

"Mum, you have no idea what you've just done," Roselyn stammered while she rubbed her forehead in distress.

"I already feel sorry for you but I'm amused at the same time," Joel laughed.

"When my brother wins I cannot wait to see the defeated look on your faces, I'll most likely dream about it tonight in my sleep." I added. I was quiet for too long just taking in everyone's opinions. My silence was an indication of weakness and doubt, I trusted my brother. Victory was his only option.

"Hahaha, I'm already thinking about the things I'll force the king to do when this is over," the queen commented. Her cheeks were red as she shamelessly blushed when she looked at him.

"Whatever you're thinking about I can assure you it's nothing compared to my thoughts," the king teased. They seemed like a cute couple. I wouldn't mind a marriage like theirs one day, it'd be fun.

Joel leaned forward and whispered as my ears flickered by the touch of his breath. "Now that you've agreed to my silly lie, we officially have ourselves a bet."

Chapter 29: Not a Coward

"BRING FORTH OUR YOUNG WARRIORS!" the spokesman announced. His appearance was rough. I wasn't one to speak about others' appearances but he didn't seem quite prepared for the job. He stood for the announcement but struggled to keep his balance as he spoke. At least his brown suit was neatly ironed, but his red hair was a frizzy mess and covered half his face.

Joel leaned to his father's side and whispered his complaints. "Father why would you allow your drunkard friend to do this job?"

"Relax, you know he's struggling with losing his wife."

"She left him because of his drinking issues, I don't blame her. Maybe you should…."

The metal doors swung open and the crowd cheered while the contestants made their way forward. I squeezed my eyelids shot and covered my ears till the uproar ended. Maybe I over exaggerated but it felt like my ears were about to bleed.

"She's so childish," Roselyn whined. "She doesn't even know

how to act right in public."

"Roselyn relax, you don't have to vent your complaints for every minor detail that bothers you, it's annoying at this point," Her mother scolded. I smiled and fought with myself to not giggle but a gentle smirk escaped.

"Roughly six-hundred brave warriors have blessed us with their presence to compete for the spot at the Prince's side as his right-hand, but only one will be victorious!" the spokesman shouted. He tripped on nothing and quickly got to his feet as the crowd laughed.

"You see, he isn't all that bad, he's great for comedy," the king tried to make light of the situation. No one responded, even the queen folded her arms and frowned harshly. I searched the horde of men for my brother but I couldn't find him, he was lost somewhere within the crowd but I knew he'd make himself visible when the time was right. He wasn't the type to enjoy spotlight so he must've been hiding somewhere in the middle.

"Before we get started I have a few honourable mentions to make!" the drunkard announced.

"What is he doing?" the king panicked slightly.

"He's drunk, so probably something he shouldn't." Joel grumbled. "He had one job; announce the contestants forward, explain the rules and start the battle. He must really love the sound of his voice to keep talking unnecessarily."

"I need a drink," the queen said. She called for a few maids and instructed them to bring a glass of wine for each of us. The last time I drank I made a fool of myself, but in that moment I looked forward to a glass of wine, hoping that it would ease my nerves. I was anxious, worried that Jason would get hurt. The confidence I had in my brother was slowly replaced with fear. My concerns grew as I scanned the contestants while searching for him as I noticed that they all seemed strong and experienced. Many of them had battle scars, weapons and evenly matched confidence as my brother. They were there for the same reason, to win and to destroy anyone in their path while on the way to victory.

I diverted my gaze to the thousands of spectators surrounding us, just to keep myself distracted from the anxiety that slowly tormented my mind. Proud supporters held posters that showed the names and paintings of their favourite warriors. I couldn't help but notice the name 'Luke Blaton,' advertised everywhere. He must've been the crowd's favourite. There were very few posters displayed for the others, they must've been supported by their friends and family. This was one of the most important moments of my brother's life and I felt sick to my stomach due to the shame of not having something as simple as a poster to show my support. I glanced over my shoulder for a quick second and noticed that the other selected girls didn't bring anything with them either.

I thought at least one of them would've proudly supported someone but I guess it was safer to be mysterious. The guilty feeling decreased but I silently thought of ways to congratulate him in a special way when the battle was over, whether he won or lost I'd still be most proud.

"There's a lot of people here, how can so many show up for an event that was just announced a few hours ago?" I muttered to myself but Joel heard me.

"This place is large enough to comfortably hold at least twelve-thousand people, but it seems we have a little over fourteen-thousand p...."

"In our midst, we have some spectacular and important men willing to show off their strengths for the first time! I bet they're here to win the heart of our beloved Princess of Mandora since one of them is destined to be an additional member of the royal family! That's right folks, men of the selected, born under a miracle moon are also competing. Please raise your hand and let the crowd know who you are!"

The queen slapped her forehead in an aggravated manner and vented her concerns. "He shouldn't have done that, now they're all going to have a target on their backs before the battle even begins."

"That's fine, one of them is going to be my future husband. I would hate to marry the weakest of them all. Let's see how they perform under pressure," Roselyn pointed out. I ignored her words and searched for my brother. I saw twenty four hands raised but none of them was Jason's. I sat there confused and worried, not just for Jason but for me as well. I basically bet my life on this man, the least he could do was show up.

"What's this?" the drunkard continued. "I see twenty-four hands raised but one of them is a beautiful young lady, which means that one of the selected men who signed up is a coward. But this young lady is the bravest of them all, the only female brave enough to even consider taking part in this brawl. If you ask me, she's displaying that she's worthy to be our future queen!" The crowd clapped and cheered for her, she almost had a standing ovation just for being there. I took a closer look and noticed it was Pia, the same girl that sat next to me at breakfast and walked alongside Joel in the garden.

So far she seemed to be doing all the right things to grasp Joel's attention and become his favourite. I guessed being ranked second to last affected her pride dearly. If I cared about making Joel mine, she would've been my greatest competition but I was happy for her and a bit worried she'd be severely hurt by one of these men. It was rather comical to see the upset looks on the faces of the other selected girls. They tried so hard to hide it but their frustrations were painted all over their faces. As much as I wanted to laugh, I couldn't even smile because my brother was nowhere to be found.

"Okay, now he's doing too much," the king commented. He pressed his arms against the arm of his chair in preparation to stand but the queen stopped him.

"It's too late to stop him, he's too drunk to listen. No one in the crowd is surprised by his appearance, he's done this so many times so let's talk to him about it after."

"Fine," the king gave in and leaned back.

"It's a shame that Jason didn't show up, now you've automatically lost the bet and became my brother's pet." Roselyn laughed. I bit my lips to avoid snapping at her and continuously searched through the horde of warriors to find Jason. The spokesman continued to mock my brother endlessly and my blood boiled.

"It's a shame that one of the chosen men to become the Princess' husband is a coward that…."

"MY BROTHER IS NOT A COWARD!" I shouted. Before I knew it I was already on my feet and yelling across the stadium. "JUST SHUT UP AND DO WHAT YOU'RE SUPPOSED TO DO AND START THE BATTLE!" I felt a tough tug on my arm forcing me back to my seat.

"Don't you ever do that again," Joel scolded. He looked upset, embarrassed, disappointed, just a bunch of negative emotions took turns on his face. The emotionless mask he always wore on his face disappeared just like that.

"Joel please teach your pet some manners before I break it out of her," the king instructed. "Nothing about her is ladylike."

"Wait, so if Jason didn't show up, that means mum lost the

bet to dad before the battle even begun," Roselyn stuttered. She seemed a bit sorry for her mother but amused at the same time. The eerie look on the king's face while his lips quivered to hide a smile was the most upsetting thing to embrace after Roselyn's annoying comments. It was almost like he wanted us to fail but to be fair, he did place a bet with his wife involving heavy consequences.

"I'm here!" Jason announced with his hand held high. I felt a bit guilty. It may have been his intention to remain anonymous until the battle began, but the announcer calling him a coward coupled with my inappropriate response caused him to change his mind. I was right, he was hidden in the centre of over six-hundred men with two bulky men blocking his view. "I'm not a coward, I just chose not to comply with your silly request."

"O thank God," the queen sighed. I finally felt the air flowing back into my lungs, allowing me to breathe with ease. Now that Jason had made himself known, I feared that he too would have a target on his back. He must've preferred to play it safe.

"Then why would you refuse to raise your hand? It seems like you were either a coward or ashamed to say you're fighting to win the heart of the princess," The spokesman instigated. The crowd gasped and murmuring began, eyes kept travelling from the princess to Jason back and forth.

"I'm not here to fight for the heart of the princess, your comment had nothing to do with me. This is a competition where we fight to secure our spot as the prince's right hand, if the princess happens to be impressed by my performance well that's just a bonus for me. I didn't register for her, I signed up to get a job." Jason explained. Roselyn's face was fuming red, gentle laughter escaped my lips when I saw the irritation all over her face. Joel couldn't help it either, his laugh over-powered mine and embarrassed her even further.

"O, so you think this is funny?" The king asked. He seemed to be just as upset as his daughter, but on his right I noticed the queen grinning a bit with watery eyes. When all three of us made eye contact we laughed even more, not caring about what the crowd thought even though we knew there were mixed emotions all over the place.

"He's here to win and focused on the job at hand, there's nothing wrong with that," the queen expressed. "Judging by how seriously he's taking this I just hope he wins, he'll be the perfect man for the job."

"He's just desperate for money, look at him, he clearly needs it," Roselyn bashed. I didn't hesitate to respond this time, I had enough of the hateful words she spewed since we got here.

"When he wins, hopefully you'll finally watch your words and treat us with respect. We're not just peasants, there's a lot more to us than that, he's worth a lot more."

"We'll see about that."

The tension between us grew but I didn't regret a single word I said. The chains around my mouth were finally shattered, I felt so much lighter after building the courage to speak up. I wished I knew what the others were thinking but they all sat there in awkward silence avoiding eye-contact with both Roselyn and I as they stared forward nervously. I focused my mind elsewhere and my ears perked up at the spokesman's attention grasping words.

"There's one last honourable mention that I must make, by the looks of it the crowd already knows who you are. LUKE BLATON! Please, raise your hand and bless us with your presence!"

After he raised his hand I couldn't help but feel intimidated by his presence even though I wasn't going to be the one clashing swords with him. He lifted his lengthy thick spear in the air and the crowd went wild and he annoyingly exposed a proud smile plastered across his face. He was one of the tallest men among them, possibly about six foot six inches. His calves and thigh muscles must've been as hard as a rock and I could only imagine what his stomach would look like underneath his armour. His jet black hair was neatly slicked back with no sign of frizz; of course he had to take care of his appearance to impress the ladies. Their desperate cries of "I love you!" rang out all over the stadium as they hoped for his recognition and acknowledgment. He blew a kiss back at multiple ladies and left them each with a cocky wink.

"In case you didn't know ladies and gentlemen, Luke Blaton is our four time champion of our yearly Last Man Standing Battle Royal! At just the age of twenty-four, his achievements have made him one of the richest men in Mandora. It's about time he earned a noble title and today will be the perfect day to do so!"

If anyone had the biggest target on their back it'd be Luke, but there was also a high possibility that many would avoid him to protect themselves from being knocked out too early in battle. No one wants to be the first loser. I wondered what Jason was thinking, I wondered if he had a strategy planned in his mind. He just stood there with his hand above his hairline to shade himself from the sun. It was about 3:00pm so of course the sun was scorching hot. Luckily for us, we were shaded by the seating area of the battle arena because of the ceilings and thick walls.

"Next time your friend shouldn't give such bias remarks, especially for an event as important as this one," the queen complained. The king folded his arms and grinned, taking the opportunity to remind the queen that he was still in charge.

"Relax, he's only saying what the crowd thinks as well. It's a little too early for you to be giving me orders, the battle hasn't even started, neither has a winner been announced yet so you can't boldly tell me what to do."

Joel hid his face in the palm of his hands hiding his gentle laughter. He clearly enjoyed the consequences of his silly lie that caused a disastrous bet between his parents. I was pretty sure he didn't expect an outcome like that to happen but I hoped for my sake and the queen's, that Jason would come out of this victorious. He knew I was willing to put everything on the line for him by giving up our mother's hand-made necklace. This was his time to prove me right, to prove himself right.

"One more thing before we get started, this is for the brave men before us that are willing to risk it all!" the drunkard continued. "If possible, please refrain from killing anyone. It would be nice to have all contestants make it back home to their families. You are free to surrender and quit anytime you please. The healers will protect and escort you out, but if you choose to fight to the death, that's on you. NOW….. LET THE BATTLE BEGIN!"

I hid myself in Joel's chest as the sky crumbled and cracked as if it was about to fall apart. The loud explosive sounds pained my ears while my body trembled, this must've been the worst time for our enemies to make another appearance.

CHAPTER 30: IS IT WORTH IT TO HIM NOW?

My body trembled in Joel's arms while he chuckled in amusement. "Is this your way of flirting with me? It's cute, but weird....very weird."

I was too disoriented to come up with a suitable response after his cocky remarks. His eyes squinted in confusion upon seeing my petrified face mixed with confusion and anger.

"Wait are you really scared? It's just fireworks."

"Just *Fireworks?*" I struggled to make sense of words I'd never heard before. "So we're not under attack?" I asked, in need of reassurance.

"No one's attacking us, we're fine. Fireworks are what we usually use to start events like these."

"We also use fireworks for celebration," the queen explained. I wiped away whatever tears were evident on my face and took a deep breath. I can't believe I saw some sparks in the sky and freaked out. It was pretty, but the noise was very discomforting.

"Of course, she'd freak out, a peasant that lived in the bush probably never got the chance to experience something like this," Roselyn laughed. At this point she just looked ugly to me no matter how beautiful others perceived her to be.

"It's okay Amaris, I had the same reaction when I was introduced to fireworks at eighteen. Roselyn always talks down on peasants but forgot her mother was once poor too...."

"It doesn't matter." The king interrupted his wife before she could complete her statement but knowing this part of the queen's history caused me to feel much at ease. I was glad that she was generous enough to share a hint of her past to a complete stranger like me.

"She wouldn't have reacted this way if she wasn't in places she should not have been today. I heard you came back to the castle in a bloody mess with my son beside you. Have you not embarrassed us enough?" he scolded. Luckily for me I had no reason to respond when the crowd let out a loud outburst signifying that something big had happened and we missed it. Twelve men laid on the battlefield unconscious as Luke stood before them with his weapon covered in blood and wore a satisfactory smile that he just couldn't hide.

Twelve were unconscious but there were twice as many men that struggled to get back on their feet. I cringed at the site of them coughing up blood, many even cried and surrendered. As the battle continued healers rushed to the field and escorted the injured that surrendered and collected the bodies of those that were left unconscious and took care of them immediately.

"How can one man defeat more than thirty men in less than two minutes?" I observed him in awe mixed with worry. Logan planted a seat beside me and sat comfortably without an invitation.

"It's not impossible, you witnessed when I took care of roughly eighty men in a few seconds almost an hour ago." He wore the proudest smile on his face making it impossible not to laugh. He didn't express his pride in a toxic manner, his confidence was much easier to tolerate and his cocky expressions were nothing but amusing.

"Ha-ha, I guess you're right."

The crowd went wild every minute as Luke took down about fifteen men each time without breaking a sweat. No one else on the battlefield caused as much havoc as he did, which made me wonder…...what the hell was Jason doing? I knew my brother's potential and I was confident in his skills but I was disappointed to see him just lying there surrounded by a large barrier of ice he created for his protection. Even Pia made an effort to fight and display her abilities, I was surprised to see her make it past five minutes but the men paid her no mind.

I guessed no one wanted to face the backlash of hurting a young woman, especially one that may become the prince's wife one day. She stood in a corner directing her energy into the ground and the earth around her rose as she created walls for further protection. The ground shook slightly as boulders rose from the dirt causing a lot of men to lose balance and stumble to the floor. Even Luke faltered, but Jason still laid there in his barrier unbothered.

When she raised her hand in the air, the boulders followed her direction and elevated above the heads of hundreds of men. She waited for a few seconds with some heavy breaths. Some of the men stopped what they were doing and braced themselves for the impact while others continued fighting. The stones fell from the sky with the same force as her arm when she finally summoned up the strength to slam her fist violently to the ground. Eight boulders slammed into Jason's barrier and shattered upon impact without leaving a scratch. After confirming the safety of my brother, I leaned forward and clapped in excitement. Pia's abilities were far superior than what I expected of her. She took down at least one hundred men in that moment. While many were left unconscious by her attacks, the badly injured surrendered and were escorted to safety.

"Why are you clapping? Your brother hasn't done anything but hide behind his shield of ice. My son deserves a man that fights with confidence, not someone that stays hidden while our men risk their lives at war," the king complained. I was under the impression that I concealed my excitement and blended in well with the rest of spectators but I was wrong. The royal family had a very chill reaction for every outstanding thing that happened so far, making me feel as though I was too easily impressed. I was disappointed by my brother's performance as well but I couldn't talk down on him to others.

"I'm clapping because of Pia, she's amazing."

"Amazing? There's a clear difference between our standards but she's okay. She has a lot of power but she lacks the strength. Her body won't be able to support her much longer, she'll either faint or be dealt with by another man. Look at her, she's one of the easiest targets to get rid of right now."

The king was right, she knelt to the ground with her hands dug into the earth. At first I thought she was going to do something amazing again, but her arms wobbled as she tried to support her body from collapsing. It'd be pretty embarrassing to faint after displaying that much power to everyone, I was under the impression that she was one of the strongest.

"Even though she may not last very long she still defeated

over a hundred men," I commented, surely the king would be unfair if he overlooked that great achievement.

"Defeating over a thousand weak men isn't as impressive as defeating one strong foe. You'd be surprised by the number of people that can take down almost everyone here with little to no effort. Soon the diamonds among the coal will reveal themselves." Joel responded.

"But it's more impressive than hiding behind a shield of ice," Roselyn interjected. Her statement didn't surprise me. I knew sooner or later she'd eventually throw shade at my brother again. Defending my brother didn't make sense, not when he barely made an effort to show off his capabilities. I wouldn't go as far as to call him a coward but his decision to stay sheltered in his barrier of ice while everyone fought beginning to end was questionable.

"It doesn't matter to me, as long as he's still in the competition I'm fine. I placed a heavy bet on him so as long as he's fine, I'm happy with what I'm seeing," the queen said. It felt great to know that I wasn't alone when it came to supporting my brother. I just wished he didn't take so long to prove himself, it made me so anxious. I placed my hand on my chest and sighed. As my finger-tips touched the ring pendant of my necklace I remembered the promise we made.

"He'll prove himself when the time comes. He already knows what I'm willing to sacrifice so he won't let me down."

"You told him about the bet?" Roselyn stammered. Joel faced me immediately with the most confused look on his face. His left brow arched all the way to his hairline and his eyes were as sharp as ever. Of course he'd be confused, he had made up that bet on the spot a few minutes earlier.

"Jason knows that something much more valuable is on the

line, I didn't tell him about our bet."

"You speak as though it's a secret, I want to know more," the queen requested. I smiled in a shy manner and showed her my necklace. I was only willing to explain because she asked me to.

"My mother made me this necklace with this ring. I received it as a gift a few years ago before she died. We didn't have the money to place bets for this event so I told him I'd use the ring to bet on him if he was sure he'd win. This and a scarf is all I have in remembrance of her."

"You're even more foolish than I thought," the king's callous comments exposed where Roselyn got her personality from. I brushed off his harsh words and told him the good news.

"It's fine, my friend Brandon paid for me to register my bet so I won't be losing anything but Jason doesn't know that." As the words flew out my mouth I remembered the pouch of coins Joel gave me. I dug into my purse and pulled it out. I flinched nervously as the king stared harshly after recognizing who it belonged to.

"That reminds me, this is yours. You can count the money if you want but I didn't spend a dime."

Joel clenched his jaw and his brows furrowed after laying eyes on his pouch of coins in the palm of my hands. He forced a broad sarcastic smile at me and gently placed his right hand above his money.

"This is my gift to you, keep it." he insisted. Although I desperately needed the money a day before, I didn't need it any more, not when we'd be forced to stay and become pampered in the castle. But more importantly, I couldn't bear to look at the pity in his eyes as if he was giving alms to a pauper outside the city gate.

"It's fine, I don't....."

"So you rather accept money from a stranger than accept money from my son?" The king interrupted with a harsh yet subtle tone to reduce unwanted attention. My heart skipped a beat by the miscommunication that took place but I spoke confidently to hide any signs of nervousness that crept within me.

"When his highness gave me that money I had already intended to give it back after my brother wins, but Brandon unexpectedly paid for me so I'm just returning the prince's money. After Jason wins I'm going to give Brandon back his money as well."

"Hmph." The king folded his arms and looked away. He didn't seem too impressed with my answer. It bothered me that we had that conversation with Brandon sitting above us. Luckily we were discrete enough to not distract him from enjoying the event and getting caught up in our conversation.

"I said it's my gift to you, not a loan. The other women graciously accepted my gifts, why do you have to be so difficult?" Joel complained.

"So you gave everyone a gift already?" Disappointment dance amongst my words but I couldn't understand what I really expected from him. "Did you give everyone money? Or did you give them clothes, jewels and shoes?"

"Yes, something like that, but no one else received money only you," he said his last few words with a beaming smile as if it'll make anything better.

"Of course I'm the only one. The others don't look like peasants in need of financial aid. Your gift has pity written all over it, you're quite thoughtful but I don't think I'll need your money after today."

"It's not about pity. You're not a materialistic girl and I don't know you well enough to get you something you'd appreciate. If I got you a necklace you'd probably just leave it resting somewhere and never wear it. Money was a safer option since you would've been able to buy anything you like. There's about eighty seven silver coins in there, that's enough for rent in some areas, I'm sure you would've enjoyed yourself with a minor shopping spree." After his words left his mouth I hated him less.

"Thank you, I accept your gift." Hot air escaped Joel's nostrils after letting out a deep breath. He rolled his eyes and avoided eye-contact by looking straight ahead at the battlefield. I must've really frustrated him at that point.

"Accepting his money has got to be the smartest decision you've made since you got here," Roselyn stated. "Champions don't achieve anything by hiding behind shields while everyone risks their lives." I couldn't recall ever asking for her opinion, the more she spoke the worse my impression of her became. She was just a bratty attention seeking princess that spoke down to others in order to feel superior. I couldn't figure out what Jason's motives were by staying protected in his barrier of ice but I made up an excuse to defend his name.

"Jason only puts his hands on people when necessary," I explained. My words were definitely unconvincing because even I wouldn't believe me.

"Are you saying that in this battle, to win one hundred pounds of silver and become Joel's right hand man isn't necessary enough for him to fight?" Roselyn inquired in a nasty instigating manner. I slapped my forehead and sighed, disappointed in myself for not explaining things better. The royal family's eyes stared harshly at me for a response, even Logan was a bit intrigued.

"I'm saying that since this battle begun, he hasn't found a

reason to fight and showcase his abilities. Of course that opportunity will arise when someone challenging approaches him, but as you can see, no one has been able to lay a finger on him yet. If no one is able to break his barrier and challenge him, what does that say about the quality of the contestants?" This time my statement left them quiet and stuck in their thoughts for a moment. Even though I had no idea about Jason's thought process, that must've been the only logical explanation for his actions. I smiled as my eyes strayed to the battlefield, my brother really never participated in things that didn't seem worth it and I think in that moment I finally understood him.

"I agree." Logan grinned. "We've seen a fraction of what he's capable of at breakfast, he literally made everyone in the room shiver with his abilities. If he wants he can probably get rid of a third of the competition with ease but he looks like someone that focuses on strategy. I don't think he'd fight unless he's forced to."

"I agree, he's probably giving everyone their chance to shine instead of humiliating them in an instant," the queen concurred. "Don't forget that he also shattered your ice barrier with ease just so he could eat."

Logan's face burned red as he babbled words no one could interpret due to all his stuttering. The king hummed harshly and avoided eye-contact with him. I guessed the thought of my brother being too much for his own right hand man to handle troubled him.

"I was just testing his limits. I didn't think there was anyone in the room powerful enough to break the ice. For God's sake, he has the same power as me so of course he'd be able to get rid of a simple block of ice and chains around his mouth, that's a beginner level step," Logan tried his best to provide a reasonable explanation and I believed him. I witnessed a taste of his abilities in the city. He took down over eighty men on his own in less than five seconds while everyone else struggled to survive.

"If I'm being honest, I'm more worried about Jason ever having to fight you than the men he's dealing with on the battlefield. I only saw a fraction of your strength, but you're definitely a monster." I commented. The king smirked and tilted his head slightly to hide his pleased emotions.

"WHAT THE HELL!" The spokesman shouted. "THAT BASTARD IS SLEEPING IN HIS BARRIER OF ICE!" My pores raised as the crowd booed at Jason but my skin boiled by the audacity he had to sleep comfortably in the middle of a battle important as this. His back faced us with his arm tucked under his head for support. Not only were the spectators mad but the contestants were furious. Everyone gathered around him, even the seven remaining men in our category for the crown. I didn't notice that they avoided harming each other until this moment when they all gathered to deal with Jason.

Swords, axes, spears, punches and kicks were forced upon him by everyone as they attempted to drag him out of his barrier and knock him out of the competition. I couldn't see my brother any more, just the horde of men that swarmed around him. Balls of fire, lighting bolts, rocks and wind were all thrown at him but all it did was disturb his beauty sleep.

I covered my eyes in fear of what was about to happen, the sudden turn of events slowly peaked to the most dangerous part. The loud explosion when his ice barrier shattered told me everything I needed to know. The crowd cheered and danced in excitement hoping to see my brother be torn apart but I refused to be a witness.

"Finally," the king grinned. "Do you think it's worth it to him now?" I hid my face in my lap with my hands pressed against my ears. Joel gripped my arm and forced me upwards gently.

"You're not supposed to do that, it's unethical," he whispered. "I know you're scared, but we have experienced healers that can work miracles, he'll be alright after this." His words were genuine and I noticed the concern in his eyes, but it seemed like he misunderstood me once more.

A broad smile peeled across my lips with gentle laughter as my eyes watered, "I'm not worried about him. I'm worried about them."

CHAPTER 31: Smells like Poison

I quickly leaped off my seat and gripped unto the silver railings as tightly as possible leaning forward to let out a pleading cry.

"What the hell is she doing?" Roselyn whined in her mother's ear. There wasn't enough time for me to explain, my main objective was to save lives.

"JASON DON'T KILL ANYONE! REMEMBER THE RULES OF THE….." Blood splattered everywhere, the cries of grown men bawling their lungs out in agony echoed through the stadium. My knees buckled and my arms wobbled tremendously as Jason raised his head to acknowledge me. Every expression on his face changed, his eyes sharpened harshly but he still managed to mouth the words "thank you." But even with our short lived form of communication his stares became harsher each moment till he rolled his eyes and looked away to break contact.

I turned my back towards him and tried not to over-think his alarming actions towards me. The stadium became tranquil, little to no movement until the king squeezed the arms of his seat firmly and leaned forward.

"What the hell just happened?" I couldn't tell if he was upset or impressed but I took my seat beside the prince and panicked in silence.

"True colours show eventually with a bit of pressure," Logan hinted. "I'm just looking forward to see how long he lasts till he reaches his limit."

"I've never been so eager to witness who'd come out victorious in events like these, but this bet I made with the king has me unnecessarily nervous," the queen admitted, she looked at me and smiled but I couldn't move a single bone in my body to respond. I blinked twice awkwardly and shifted my attention to the men on the battle field hoping that no one died as a result of Jason's rage.

"There's no need to be nervous your highness, I think you made a good choice for this bet. Look around, everyone's uneasy, how many people do you think placed their bets on Luke and are silently freaking out because of Jason's threatening appearance? You saw what Luke just did, he broke Jason's barrier and in that same moment Jason blocked his attack but everyone else suffered the casualties. Luke is responsible for seventy percent of the damage that's done but the remaining men suffered at Jason's hand. I think what everyone's most concerned about is the fact that Jason is still standing without a scratch while Luke is bleeding heavily in his left arm." Logan explained with a pointed finger directing her attention to Luke.

I leaned forward to get a closer look, blood trickled down his arm by a piece of ice about the size of my middle finger that pierced into his skin. I wasn't satisfied, I needed a more in depth analysis. How deep was his wound, was the blood in his body still flowing the way it should or was he losing too much blood? I focused my energy on Luke and scanned his physical state with my eyes closed. I didn't need to see him, all I had to do was sense his energy.

He wasn't in pain, his arm just itched so his tolerance for pain must've been really high. Anytime Jason struck me with his ice knives during training my arm always stung. I couldn't analyse him as long as I wanted to, his energy was far more powerful than mine so it drained me. I had no strength remaining to analyse my brother to make sure he was okay, but he seemed perfectly fine. I just wished I would've been able to tell who was more powerful between the two in that moment.

"Why are you sweating so much?" Joel asked, gently patting my forehead with a handkerchief he took out from his pants pocket. "You were fine a minute ago, now you're panting heavily and struggling to sit up." I couldn't look at him. I didn't want to explain what I did even though it wouldn't have affected their match. I preferred to hide my abilities from everyone till I was ready to accept whatever expectations they'd have of me.

"Amaris, would you like a glass of wine?" The queen offered.

"Yes please!" I may have answered too quickly in an excited manner but I craved for anything that would help ease my nerves. From what I've been told, wine makes people happy so it was worth a try, but it also made people do stupid things.

"She shouldn't be drinking. We should avoid all possibilities of her embarrassing us even further." Roselyn advised. "If she's thirsty some water would be....."

"I don't remember asking you anything Roselyn. This is an event where many people get drunk during the celebration. Offering Joel's guest a glass of wine while we all drink is simple hospitality and etiquette."

"This time if she does anything stupid, she'll not only embarrass herself, but us as well," the king included. They continuously talked about me as if I wasn't there and Joel remained silent the entire time. The queen referred to me as Joel's guest, meaning that I'm not a hostage so if at any moment I wanted to leave I should've been able to do so. I preferred to be somewhere else, seated amongst strangers that were not worried about whether I'd be somewhat of a burden to them or not. I got to my feet and as my lips separated to speak Joel stood beside me and placed his arm forward preventing me from moving any further.

"Please have a seat. Whatever you're planning, now isn't the time," he insisted. I remained still with my feet planted on the ground calculating my next move.

"Excuse me?" He didn't look at me, he just stood beside me with his arm blocking my way of escaping the unnecessary tension that was brought upon me.

"I said SIT DOWN!" He spoke harshly with a biting edge to his voice but quiet enough for only me to hear. I took a seat but only to avoid further unwanted attention in case Joel made things worse. I felt defeated. A man spoke harshly towards me and I sat quietly after, following his demands. There wasn't much I could do when I was up against royalty. He walked forward and held unto the silver railings, taking a deep breath. The arena wasn't as noisy as it was before, most people were still in shock by the sudden turn of events.

"Before we continue, I want to be sure that everyone who can no longer compete is escorted out of the arena with the assistance of all healers present! My apologies but I didn't expect that the turn of events would be this drastic. If there are any men that are still conscious and would like to leave the battle-field, please raise your hand and wait for the healers to assist you. We will continue with the event once all the injured are taken care off. It's too much of a hazard to continue with so many men lying around unable to defend themselves." It was nice of him to make that sudden announcement to help those in need, but I saw no need for him to speak to me like that. He could've just said "Excuse me, I have to make an announcement."

"Excuse me Miss, this is for you." I turned my head to the direction of the voice and noticed a maid before me with a tray of wine glasses in her hand. "Please, pick anyone you like." I stared at my options. The drinks were fairly different in colour, a few were a deep red, others were deep purple almost black, and the remaining had a clear but yellowish tint.

"The darker the berry, the sweeter the juice," I muttered. Joel grinned beside me. I was a bit embarrassed when I realized that I wasn't discrete enough to avoid being heard.

"Are you sure you want that one?" He hinted as if I should reconsider but it made me want to choose that specific glass of wine even more.

"I'm sure."

"Okay, have fun." I was curious to what he meant but as I observed the others I realized that only the king and the prince picked the same glass as I did. The queen held unto the red wine while the princess chose the yellowish one.

"Is this drink only for men or something?" I asked. The queen tried to hide her gentle laughter as she sipped away her glass of wine. I must've asked something wrong but I was just curious.

"We don't assign our drinks to gender but the drink you chose is the strongest of the batch," Joel explained.

"The strongest?"

"Yes, it's more concentrated with alcohol than the others, so please sip with caution."

I stirred my glass of wine and placed it under my nose for a quick sniff. Jason always warned me to sniff my drinks when offered, to make sure it was safe. My head flew back instantly and my nose burned, it must've been a reflex response to the smell, but whatever they gave me it was not safe. Before given the opportunity to query more about my drink, Joel and his mother had a boisterous outburst of laughter.

"Do you regret your drink of choice now? I can call for my maids to get you a glass of white wine if you want. It's the weakest one," the queen offered.

"Do they all have the same pungent odour as this one?" I asked to be sure because what difference would it have made if I switched my drink and still didn't like the smell. The smell was similar to poison, almost like methanol but it rhymed with alcohol so maybe they had something in common.

"They all smell alike, this is just the strongest one."

"It's smells like poison," I said my words blatantly without hesitation, but the moment everything escaped my lips I had instant regrets.

"What's wrong? Don't you want to drink any more? You weren't questioning the drinks last night when you were drunk and made a fool of yourself." The king's words struck me to the core, I knew he was upset with all my complaints and I didn't want to bother the queen or Joel either, so far they were kind to me.

Due to the awkward tension I brought upon myself I quickly sipped away half the cup of wine till my face screwed up like a prune. My mouth was full, basically swollen with wine which was arduous to swallow. The longer it took for me to swallow the greater my urges of throwing up became. My chest burned along with my stomach as the wine trickled down my throat.

Before I knew it my eyes were watery but I blinked the tears away.

"Take your time baby girl, if you drink too fast you'll get drunk," Joel stated. I ignored his words but I wasn't comfortable with him calling me baby girl.

"Baby girl? How many females do you refer to as baby girl?"

"Everyone."

"Don't call me that. Those words will be more useful for someone that has the intentions of actually being your future wife," I suggested. His jaw dropped without a vocal reaction. I never expected to leave him speechless. It was the perfect sight to see even if it was for a brief moment. His words could be very misleading, I was pretty sure that anyone being called 'baby girl' would assume that they were his favourite.

His play boy tactics may have worked on everyone else but I was a different breed. I leaned back and observed the royal family as they sipped from their glasses patiently. I probably should not have taken a big gulp but I surrendered to the pressure and drank half a glass of wine. To be honest, I didn't believe that one glass could have me tipsy or drunk, even if it was the strongest in their category offered, but I knew that time would tell eventually. I leaned forward, slightly above the prince's shoulder and whispered in his ear.

"Are you a light weight?" I asked.

"Of course not, some would even say I'm an alcoholic but that's a topic for another day. It takes a lot of alcohol to get me tipsy."

"So would one glass of the strongest wine get you drunk or will it take a few?"

"Maybe about four glasses of wine would get me tipsy, but six will have me drunk." Joel winked. I wasn't sure if he was flirting or just being extra friendly so I ignored his actions with an emotionless face and kept talking.

"Oh that's a relief, I guess I would be fine with drinking only one glass of wine."

"I'm surprised you're still craving alcohol to be honest. Are you not hung over from last night?" I wasn't sure what he meant by 'hung over' but to be safe I brushed it off and gave a response to what I truly felt.

"To be honest, I don't know what that means but I feel fine physically, I'm just a bit nervous and I believe the wine would calm my nerves.

"Time will tell."

CHAPTER 32: I FINALLY HAVE A HUMAN PET

Six men remained on the battle-field, a drastic change in numbers for an event that began with over six hundred contestants. Judging by their appearances and their performance displayed thus far, Luke was by far Jason's biggest threat and I was pretty sure all spectators shared the same thoughts as I did. He was essentially the nation's favourite and biggest achiever within his age group. There were expectations of him that he had to maintain for the sake of his pride, especially when there were thousands of people watching.

I was not at all concerned about the remaining four men, they looked drained and in pain. I couldn't understand why they even bothered to stay. Two of them walked with a limp and they all had blood-soaked clothes from their wounds. Only those that surrendered received medical assistance from the healers so they were already at a disadvantage physically to compete against Jason or Luke. If Luke was born under a coloured moon, he definitely would've been one of the princess's favourite in the selection. Just when that thought played through my mind I finally had an understanding as to why some of the men were still in the arena.

Two of them were at the breakfast table earlier, as members of the selection so of course they'd try their best to be noticed by the princess. Placing top six is impressive, hopefully it won't cost them their lives but in a competition like this no one cares about the losers regardless of how close they came to winning. Only the champion benefits at the end.

My biggest concern was the final showdown between Jason and Luke, it was what everyone had been waiting for and it was finally about to happen. The other men were just irrelevant factors to the equation taking up space in the arena. If they were wise they'd fight amongst each other for the top three spot and avoid any possible contact with Jason and Luke.

By this time I had already sipped away the remaining wine in my glass and was offered a refill by the queen. Of course I accepted her generous offer without shame. She too was on her second glass of wine. I no longer wanted to be sober, not in a crucial moment like this but I didn't want to be drunk either so I took my time and sipped.

The healers were quick when it came to assisting the weak. It's a shame they weren't as good at their job in warlike scenarios. I remembered the site of them being slaughtered earlier in the day when they took too long to heal the injured, leaving their defences wide open. My ears perked up at the sudden announcement made at the opposite end of the arena by that same drunkard. "Ladies and gentleman, It's what we've all been waiting for! LET THE BATTLE CONTINUE!" This time there was no unnecessary explosions following the spokesman's words, just the sound of clashing metal as the remaining men swung their weapons at each other. The crowd became unnecessarily noisy as they chanted Luke's name. Just as I expected, Luke and Jason were left to deal with each other while the other four fought their hardest for third place and dared not enter into the dangerous territory.

Because we were seated up close in the VIP area, I was able to hear a bit of bickering between my brother and Luke after the disturbance of chants finally died down. Everyone must've noticed a conversation happening between the two because neither of them bothered to lay a finger on the other after the announcement was made. Jason's arms were folded and Luke's hands were in his pockets but both of their lips were moving.

"What do you think they're doing? Do you think they're negotiating?" Roselyn queried. I almost choked on my drink, I had a really tough time swallowing but I managed eventually.

"I hope not. They better not be because what would've been the point of this bet," the queen retorted. I couldn't blame her for her concerns. I had too much to lose as well.

"I believe that too much is at stake for Jason to just give up and negotiate with Luke. He'd rather win fairly. He knows that there's too much to gain and too much to lose for him to just throw everything away like that. He has a point to prove and he will do so in the end." I may have said too much but I knew Jason would never negotiate with his opponent at a time like this. His pride was too high and he already knew what was at stake; my necklace, I couldn't lose my necklace.

"You think rather highly of your brother," Roselyn chimed in. "But we'll see what the...."

"SHHHH!!!" I flinched at Joel's sudden outburst. "We'll know what they're saying if we just stop talking and listen!" We strained our ears to interpret what was being said and within seconds their bickering turned into words and their words eventually formed sentences.

"I won't offer you this opportunity again, you have great potential so don't waste it. Would you rather be remembered as the guy that placed fifth or sixth?"

"Take your own advice, if their presence bothers you get rid of them yourself. But congratulations on destroying my barrier, you seemed to be the only one worth fighting. I can always deal with the easy left overs after. Right now I'd rather have my fun with you."

I didn't trust Luke's words, I was convinced that he had plans to play dirty. Or maybe he was so threatened that he wanted to be sure that if Jason defeated him he'd at least place second. Nevertheless, in my opinion his statements stemmed from insecurities, but I could've been over analysing it. Perhaps he was just a haughty man who took great pleasure in himself.

I leaned back frustrated as ever and released a heavy sigh to put myself at ease but of course that didn't work. There was too much talking and no fighting, I wanted this to be over. It was already difficult to deal with my anxiousness throughout this event and now at the most crucial moment they just stood there. "Jason please make this guy shut up and get on with this thing," I muttered. Joel grinned softly and left me with another shady remark.

"You should relax and be happy that nothing has happened yet, you may need another glass of wine when this is over." I ignored him and clapped proudly in excitement as I laid eyes on my brother finally taking action. Sharp icicles formed in his hands and circled around him.

"Are you ready? Because I am, I imagine the celebratory feast would be bountiful with meat and I'm rather hungry right now so let's please end this quickly."

"I've only known this boy for a little over a day and one thing I'm sure about is that he prioritizes his meals over anything," the king commented in gentle laughter. It surprised me that he managed to laugh in a positive manner to anything relating to Jason, he never seemed to like us.

Displeased by Jason's actions, Luke pulled out his spear and stared harshly, confirming that their big battle was about to begin. "I thought you were different, but this cheap tactic with those tiny icicles won't have any effect on me. But I do hope you have fun in your defeat."

"He's rather bold if you ask me," As confident as my words sounded, my hands trembled while I spoke. I sipped my wine till I realized I was halfway through the second glass.

Roselyn stared directly at me without shame, waiting for me to give her the attention she desperately desired. Judging by the way she batted her eyes with pouted lips I already knew who she was routing for. "Your brother is just as cocky but someone will be humbled today." I chose not to respond, there was no reason to when the action was just about to take place.

I squealed while I tried to stay seated watching Jason's sharp icicles build momentum as they circled around him. A minor sand cloud formed and I was no longer able to see a single piece of ice, just a sharp white circle waiting to be unleashed. Luke stood his ground and aggressively slammed his spare to the earth forming a larger tornado surrounding him in dust. I no longer saw his face, just the dust that surrounded him but Jason's feet were dragging in the sand lowly being pushed back.

"Oh no," I gripped Joel's hand tightly and squeezed with all my might not knowing what I did until he responded.

"Agh! That's quite a grip you have."

I pulled away immediately, embarrassed by my own actions. "I'm sorry I didn't mean to…."

"It's okay, I understand how you feel." Even though he reassured me that he wasn't upset, I was too ashamed to look at him as if I had committed such a grave sin. To get rid of the awkward feeling I drank the remaining wine in my glass and requested another.

"May I have another glass please?"

"Sure, I'm on my fourth," the queen smiled. Her face was red and her eyes seemed puffy. I grinned at her appearance and gracefully accepted my third glass of wine.

"Wait for me!" I giggled. Her glass was full, she hadn't taken a sip of her fourth glass yet.

"Ohhh, you think you can keep up with me?"

"Of course I can!" I quickly gulped away my third glass of wine and requested another.

"No please don't, not everyone can keep up with her. It's best if you take your time and take a break, at least another thirty minutes break," Joel advised. I heard him but I didn't listen, a man telling me what to do always went through one ear and came out the other.

"What glass are you on?" I asked.

"I'm on my second."

"Still? If you can't keep up and you're a light weight just say that. I'm perfectly fine, don't worry about me, watch the match."

"A LIGHT WEIGHT!?" Baffled by my response he emptied his cup down his throat and requested another. "I chose to just keep it classy but Roselyn and my father are still on their first glass, if you should be calling anyone a light weight it should be them."

"EXCUSE ME!" The king stammered till he almost shouted. "I-I'm far from anything close to a light weight. I'm just making sure I'm sober to properly handle your mother when she begins to act out of character."

"And you're only capable of doing that by drinking one glass of wine" my words slipped without me thinking. Maybe the wine was already having an effect or perhaps I became too comfortable. My heart raced rapidly, worried that I may have upset the king.

"MAIDS! BRING THE WHOLE TRAY OF WINE!"

As I glanced at him once more his glass was empty. O well, it was only his first glass anyway.

"I won't be taking part in your unruly behaviour, I'm a princess not a barbarian," Roselyn commented, her glass was half full, signifying that she barely drank anything.

"That's good to hear, we don't want you to embarrass us like the last time," Joel grinned. Her jaw dropped but mine did as well after witnessing my brother flying across the battlefield against his will and landing harshly against a wall.

"Jason!" I cried leaping off my seat but Joel grabbed my arm to keep me from doing anything stupid. "What the hell just happened!" I demanded an answer, I was so focused on drinking that I wasn't paying attention. Before me was a heart-breaking sight of my brother coughing up blood.

"Jason's attack had no effect on Luke and Luke sliced him by using his spare to unleash a sharp gust of wind." Logan explained. "His weapon is what makes his attacks deadly because it sharpens his control of the wind. It's like another knife piercing through his skin without making contact with his weapon."

"YES! That's right, kill that son of a bastard!" A spectator screamed. With his firm grip, Joel forced me back to my seat.

"Relax, he's okay. Just look at him, he'll be alright."

I wanted to scream. I wanted to curse the man that insulted my brother but most of all, I wanted to help. Jason got to his feet with the happiest smile I'd ever seen on his face for years. His teeth were red stained with blood but he was happy.

"Here, drink this and relax, you'll be okay," the queen beamed as she offered me another glass swaying gently in her seat. She just couldn't sit still any longer and she giggled at almost everything. My face tingled slightly and my eyes felt heavy, but I gladly accepted another glass and drank cautiously knowing that the drink finally had a minor effect on me. I flinched at the sudden outburst of the crowd jumping to their feet and screaming Luke's name. Another tornado formed around him with his spare held out to soak up enough momentum for another attack.

My heart raced rapidly and all I did was take a few more sips thinking it'd help my nervous feeling, but the moment I laid eyes on my brother I was immediately calmed. He was laughing. He seemed like a maniac to me but it was bloodlust that ran through his veins, he was enjoying himself. His body language lacked fear and that was all the confirmation I needed.

A gust of frost formed around his right arm till it created something that I least expected. He created a spare identical to Luke's weapon but it was at least twelve inches longer.

"You wanna play? Let's play." He charged full speed with a cloud of frost behind his feet accelerating himself, piercing through Luke's barrier of wind till they both clashed. Luke was on his knees dragging through the dirt with his weapon as his only defence till he was slammed against the wall. Gust of wind formed in his hand but Jason had already interpreted his next move and froze his left arm completely. With a useless arm Luke had a lot of fight left in him.

Backed against the wall with Jason's spare near his throat he managed to heavily stump the ground and sent Jason flying in the air with a gush of wind piercing through his chest. Blood splattered on Luke's face and he wiped it away with a devilish grin.

"If you survive, I want you to be my friend." It amazed me how Jason had the energy to respond while he was in mid-air bleeding through his attire.

"Same." This time he didn't fall, in fact he formed an ice slide allowing him to land perfectly on his feet after a mini joy ride in pain.

"Jason is holding back," Logan stated. I faced him immediately, waiting for a further explanation to determine how well he knew my brother.

"What do you mean?" the king interrogated, I sensed worry in his voice. Of course he would be uneasy by Logan's statement after that bet he made.

"Luke's hand is frozen, as someone that manipulates ice he can easily shatter his arm into a thousand pieces if he wanted to."

"Jason would never do that!" I interrupted. "Luke is his opponent but not an enemy."

"His kindness would cost him the match so I'm happy to hear that he's emotionally weak," the king's words struck me. I gulped away the remaining glass of wine to avoid responding and reached out for another glass from the tray that was placed before me. Luke's one of the kingdom's strongest soldiers, he

263

should've been concerned about someone as valuable as Luke losing an arm.

"Yaaa, you're on your fifth glass like me!" the queen squealed. She definitely wasn't sober but I was right behind her, I felt so happy for no reason.

"That's it, this is your last glass," the king commanded.

"You can't tell me what to do until this match is over. I'm not your pet yet so leave me be." The queen's words bothered me. What did she mean by 'yet?' Jason was going to win, he had no choice but to.

"I AM YOUR KING! You have no choice but to obey me. So listen clearly when I say that THIS IS YOUR LAST DRINK!" his voice was so demanding that it scared me.

"Fine, Is there anything else you'd like me to do for you your majesty?" She got to her feet and bowed.

"Please, now is not the time," I was shocked by how quickly the King's mood changed.

"I know my limit, of course I won't overdo it and embarrass you, but you don't trust me." The queen's manipulation was admirable. I hoped to be like her one day. "After Jason wins, I'm going to drink as much as I want and sit before you so that you don't miss a single second that I sip."

"Mom, I'd advise you not to do that."

"It doesn't matter, she can wish and dream as much as she wants but Luke will become Joel's right hand man, NOT Jason," Roselyn announced. The wine must've had an effect on her with the nonsense she spat.

"Would you like to make a bet between us since you're so sure?" I wanted to destroy her in any way possible and this seemed like the perfect opportunity to do so. She gulped away the remaining wine in her glass before responding as if what I said bothered her. Her eyes rolled heavily at me and as her lips separated I prepared myself mentally for whatever her response would be.

"I don't make bets with peasants, there's nothing to gain from it so don't waste my time. You have nothing to offer me."

"If you're scared just say that, it's clear that Jason has the advantage yet you still have a lot to say as if he's going to lose."

"Oh I'm not scared sweet heart, you should be," she pointed to the center of the battlefield where Luke stood with his spare stretched forward.

"You must've forgotten that this is my territory. We're in an open space within the arena, the wind surrounding us is all within my control. You've done well to last this long but it's about time I take what's rightfully mine and become the prince's right hand man." With a sudden thunder cracking explosion, eight tornadoes surrounded the arena with sharp razors at their circumference. I thought it was never possible to hear the wind be split into pieces, but that's exactly what was happening. The other four men were flung to the walls of the stadium with blood ripping through their chest from sharp gusts of wind even though they weren't touched directly by the tornadoes. Jason formed another ice barrier around him but the surface was slowly cracking while he dragged backwards unable to hold a comfortable stance.

"I don't think this battle is going to last longer than three minutes," Roselyn commented. She took another glass of wine from the tray before us and raised it proudly. "Cheers."

I didn't know how everything would play off but I cheered with her to hide my fear.

"You call this your territory? I'm sorry but you must've been mistaken, this territory is mine. In any open area where there's clouds above, it's my territory," Jason explained.

"You sound like an uneducated fool. The barrier surrounding us won't even allow you to come close to the clouds. Admit your defeat now or die trying to win. I'd have you as one of my favourable soldiers to serve the prince. The pay would be a lot better than any salary you've ever earned before that's for sure. So please, surrender." This was the first time Luke seemed genuine, there were no play in his words but I knew Jason would rather die.

The air around us became noticeably cold, frost released from our lips each time we exhaled.

"It's happening again," I muttered. I was so uncomfortably cold that I wanted to leave.

"Why is Jason's power affecting our barrier? We're not supposed to feel or be affected by anything, even I'm uncomfortable and so is the crowd," the king complained with frost escaping his lips and his body shivering.

"The barrier is weakening," Logan explained. "Pretty soon it will be destroyed." And just as the words left his mouth the golden shield surrounding the stadium shattered and thunder rumbled harshly with a bit of lightening streaks at the clouds. The rapid speed of Luke's tornadoes eventually slowed down till they were frozen, clouds in the sky remained still yet swollen with a cast of ice surrounding them.

Snow released from the sky and the temperature continued to drop. It wasn't winter, consequently no one was prepared for such a cold environment but the extent of his abilities astounded me. It was my first time witnessing Jason create snow.

"Joel do something!" the king demanded.

"I won't let the match end here but I can put an end to everyone's stress." A ball of fire exploded in the air, providing everyone with warmth to continue watching the event comfortably without worrying about freezing to death. Each time Luke tried to form a gust of wind in his hand it was instantly frozen. I leaned back with another glass of wine, finally comfortable with the scenario till I realised my head was pounding and moving in circles.

"Damn, I may have drank too much," I placed my glass on the counter and took some deep breaths but that did nothing for me.

"Then why are you still drinking?" Joel asked.

"I think I'm done, but it'd be a shame to waste it."

"Then let me drink the rest for you," without awaiting my response he took my glass and gulped it away then requested a glass of water for me. Sharp icicles at least twelve inches long hovered under the clouds.

"This is your last chance, surrender now or...."

"I WILL NEVER SURRENDER TO A PEASANT!" Luke protested. Jason unleashed everything he had like hail descending from the sky but made sure they all landed in the arena. I covered my ears and hid in Joel's chest as Luke bawled in pain till he eventually went silent with the crowd. Logan got to his feet and clapped proudly but there was no one to back him up. I should've stood with him, but I was too uncomfortable to see a dead man lying on the floor by the hands of my brother. It could've been a bloody mess.

"It's amazing how he managed to pull this off without killing him," Logan praised. "All those sharp icicles but he managed to hit every part of his body except his head and heart without shattering Luke's frozen arm."

Without observing the battle-field and Luke's state, I got to my feet excitedly with the queen right behind me and clapped proudly with tears running down my eyes. He actually did it. My joy was prematurely terminated when one of the four men we ignored ran a spear through Jason's chest. I screamed my brother's name till my voice cracked. He fell to the ground and looked at me dead in the eyes.

"Don't," he mouthed. I was pissed, he was in pain and all I could do was cry. He knew I could help him and he told me not to. I didn't care what he said and I convinced myself that I misinterpreted his words. Just before I made up my mind to take action, I could hear one of the female contestants, Lisa, screaming behind me.

"Yes Leon! You earned it!"

My blood boiled increasingly fast and I took an immediate turn to address her. "Your brother did nothing but played it safe! If anyone deserves to win it's my..." Joel covered my mouth and forced me to my seat.

"Relax, it's not over yet."

Jason held Leon's leg while he stood proudly beside him thinking it was his turn to claim victory but frost crawled from his feet upwards till he turned into a frozen sculpture unable to move. Jason remained on the ground breathing heavy while everyone else were either frozen or unconscious.

"I finally have a human pet!" the queen squealed.

Chapter: 33: Why Did You Lie?

I wasted no time and left immediately as soon as they announced that Jason was the winner. The prince called out to me, begging me to stay but his words failed to register in my brain. There must've been consequences for disobeying royalty among a massive crowd of people. Those actions never go unnoticed but that was the least of my concerns. I witnessed my brother embrace a sword through his chest, it should've been clear that he was my main priority. I wanted him to win but not die.

As drunk as I was, I managed to remember the exact trail Joel lead me through and took the same path on my way out. The moment I made it to the ground floor, the environment overwhelmed me. Too many people were gathered about and this caused me to feel claustrophobic, there was barely any room to move. My brother had already been escorted from the arena by two men in their attempt to treat his wounds so I knew he had to be near. Instead of searching for him I looked for people that could possibly lead me to him.

269

I scanned through the crowd desperately, even though I was surrounded by past participants and their family members, I still searched for a healer; they were my only chance of locating my brother. After three minutes of searching, my eyes beamed at the sight of a green cloak and hoodie before me. My feet followed as I mimicked their every move until I was led to the recovery room where the remaining participants were treated.

Even though more than six hundred men participated there were roughly fifty persons in the room, including Pia. There must've been many healers at work for this big event or maybe they decided to not finish the healing process completely. There were dozens of men walking around with bandages around their wounds, an experienced healer should've been able to get rid of all their pain, but many men were limping and groaning in discomfort. I worried that they were too drained to help my brother, but I was available so I convinced myself that he'd be fine.

The only face I recognized in the room was Pia's. As I glanced over the room a bit longer I noticed a few men from our selection with white bandages covering their wounds. I felt nothing for them, not one second of compassion existed within me. Some were struggling to stay alive after withstanding Luke's attack. My brother was stabbed by one of them, men that would do anything to please the princess. I purposefully ignored that the reason for this competition was to become a permanent noble as the Prince's right hand man. I was convinced that they all would've reacted the same as Leon did if they had that opportunity at the end.

Pia seemed fine. She just laid on a bed calmly while a healer stood beside her in uniform spreading a ray of green light over her body. I didn't notice any wounds but earlier it was observed that she used up all her energy which was the reason she collapsed in the first place.

"Hey Pia how are you feeling?" I tried to be as polite as possible while killing time to wait on my brother but I genuinely cared so it didn't hurt me to speak to her. The moment her eyes met mine they immediately rolled back.

"Why are you here? I guess you're taking this opportunity to gloat in my face about being the prince's favourite."

"Favourite? We barely get along, I'm just here looking for my brother. Have you seen him?"

"You're obviously his favourite. He kept looking at you when we were together until you hid in the bushes. He spoke to all of us already but for some reason he chose you to sit beside him."

"Are you forgetting that I was ranked last?"

"Exactly, that's why it's so hard to believe. You must've had enough time to seduce him and change his mind"

"Seduce!?" I couldn't believe the words that flew out her mouth without hesitation. Why the hell would I seduce someone I disliked, someone that bothered me just by smiling in my direction?

"Please just leave. Your heavy presence makes my blood crawl. I don't do well with whores."

"Excuse me!? I only came here to help you. I can make you feel a lot better faster than any of these healers if you allow me to."

"I don't want your help you're just trying to sabotage me to get the upper hand with the prince."

"No, I promise, I'm here to help but you can't tell anyone that it was me," I probably should've kept the last few words to myself but I had to be sure that my abilities could be kept secret since I didn't want anyone to find out.

"Excuse me mam, not only are you making my patient uncomfortable but you're making me uncomfortable as well," the healer interrupted. I forgot about her presence, she somewhat caught me by surprise.

"I'm sorry but I was just talking to my...friend until my brother arrives." Of course I hesitated to call Pia a friend, our interaction was awkward and far from what I expected.

"She's not my friend she's trying to hurt me!" Her words stung, I was only trying to help but I regretted every moment thus far.

"Please leave or else I'll have security escort you out."

I gasped and just stood there frozen till a familiar voice joined the conversation. "What's happening here?" My heart raced by the authority that came with his tone, I didn't even want to look at him but his sister triggered me once more.

"What does it look like? She's obviously making the patients uncomfortable," Roselyn accused.

"It's true, her presence bothered me. Even the healer asked her to leave but she's still here."

"I'm just waiting on my brother, what's so harmful about speaking to a familiar face while I wait?"

"The issue is that she does not want you here, yet you refuse to leave and even threatened to hurt her," the healer interjected. She left me open-mouthed gasping for air. There's no way they felt comfortable switching my words like that to paint me as a villain.

"She threatened her?" Joel stammered, his brows lowered with startled eyes. His arms were folded and his glare sharpened towards me. His father hovered right above his shoulder making things worse.

"Who threatened who?"

"Amaris tried to hurt me and said don't tell anyone, I don't want her anywhere near me!" She protested with tears running down her face, although she was pretty to the eyes the ugliness of her heart was revealed to me with every word she uttered. Unfortunately no one else could see the true person on the cot.

"I did not threaten you, I offered you my help!"

"Do not raise your voice at her!" Joel demanded. His sudden anger was the last thing I was willing to deal with.

"How can you help her more than I have? I'm a healer that's been trained to treat her wounds. I've been doing this for over thirty years," the healer expressed.

"I can see that, your age shows. What are you, like fifty?" I said fifty to be nice but my real guess would've been sixty but I've seen sixty year-olds look younger than her. The makeup she wore could not hide the wrinkles on her cheeks and under her eyes. I imagined that those must've been due to stress and heavy duty. She gasped, placing her hand on her chest and looked at the king with pleading eyes hoping he'd say something.

"She's forty five and she's one of the best healers in the land," Joel explained.

"Well that explains a lot," at that moment I no longer cared to think before I spoke. My head was pounding and it was a nuisance to even stand, I just wanted to see my brother to make sure he's okay.

"After my brother gave you an undeserving privilege to sit beside him in such a big event you became rather cocky and have the nerve to speak back to members of the royal family," Roselyn snapped. "Now you insult the people we've trained to protect our citizens and provide them healing and comfort. If you're ever in a position where you need help I hope you never seek it from a healer."

"A healer is the last person I'd ever ask to help me. They might as well waste their energy on someone else." I meant everything I said. I couldn't believe that in any universe there'd be a time I'd seek help from a healer.

"You're drunk, you need to leave," Joel suggested. "You insulted the royal family, and our officers, you disrespected me among thousands of people when I called out to you to stay. What's even worse is that you threatened a potential future wife of mine. Everyone warned me about you but I tried to give you a chance to prove that you were more than a peasant with no manners. But you've proved me wrong time and time again in just one day. At this moment it's upsetting to even be in your presence, please leave before I make the guards escort you out."

My heart sunk to my feet and my eyes twitched while I tried to compress my emotions. What made it worse was that nasty smile Pia tried to hide with fake tears running down her eyes and the princess's grin of satisfaction. I wanted nothing to do with these people. I only wished to see my brother. I bit my tongue three times before responding trying my best not to add fuel to the fire.

"MAKE ROOM! WE NEED AT LEAST 6 HEALERS HERE!" someone announced. My heart raced as I sensed the presence of my brother, his energy was the lowest it's ever been in years. I was severely frustrated seeing him carried on a thin mattress by guards and not healers. Luke was right behind him, unconscious with the assistance of healers but not my brother. They rushed them both to the opposite corner of the room and I followed with those annoying royals behind me demanding that I leave.

"I AM NOT LEAVING UNTIL I'M SURE THAT MY BROTHER IS OKAY!" I shouted. The room became silent and all eyes were on us, waiting to see what their next move would be after my blatant disrespect in such a crowded area. Roselyn rushed forward and my face stung after she connected the palm of her hand to my face with as much force as she possibly could. In my flight or fight moment I clenched my fists and bit my lips to avoid calling her out her name.

I was already beside Jason so there was no backing down now. I turned my back towards them and focused only on Jason because I knew my time was limited. His skin was pale and I barely sensed any energy left in him. My knees weakened as I stumbled to the floor beside him squeezing his cold hand begging him to speak.

"Jason I'm here now, let me help you."

"Before you do anything answer me one thing," He spoke softly, barely able to turn his head and look at me.

"What is it?"

"Why did you lie to me?"

It pained me to see that the first thing he'd ask in his weakest moment was my reason for lying. I had no idea what he was referring to but his anger towards me was the only thing fuelling his mind to stay conscious, maybe even alive.

"I do not want your help until you tell me the truth." Six healers surrounded us followed by two guards grabbing my arms in an attempt to force me to leave.

"WAIT!" the king intervened. "Give her a moment with her brother before you take her away." The healers wasted no time and got to work immediately with six of them providing their green rays of light all over his body. His breaths became heavier by the second, but it was the first sign of improvement that I longingly searched for.

"Why did you lie about where you were going? What was

your reason for leaving the castle?"

"Jason I..." My heart raced rapidly while I struggled to find the right words, I knew no matter how I presented the truth to him he'd be even more upset. It was the last thing I wanted in this situation.

"Just give me your honest answer, you know I lack patience."

My eyes watered as I finally allowed the words to leave my lips. "I was searching for a potential job."

He leaned forward forcing himself to sit upwards but the moment his eyes met mine he coughed up blood in a struggle to speak.

"Sir please lay down, you're not strong enough yet," a male healer advised.

"No, I'll rest when I'm done." He stretched his arm outwards, defying his words, then stared harshly at me. I braced myself for whatever he was about to say. I tried to remind myself that he was in pain and would only speak out of anger. "Amaris sooner or later you'll be the death of me. You're nothing but an anchor tied to my feet when I'm already drowning in water. Our mother is dead because of you, and soon I'll be next...."

My lungs stopped working, I struggled to breathe. I knew he meant everything he said, even if it was out of anger. He suppressed those feelings for years but he finally cracked. I made him crack.

"We finally have a secured roof over our head with servants and three meals a day which we don't even deserve, we got lucky because we just happened to be born under a coloured moon and you choose to waste it all. You put yourself in danger to find a job even though we'd be compensated monthly just for staying here. You have got to be the dumbest person I've ever met. You're like a virus that destroys everyone around you. Many people are dead because of you including our mother. How many times do I have to save you before your stupid actions kill me?"

"Jason I...."

"I'M NOT DONE!" he shouted. More blood splattered on his chest with a deadly cough.

"Jason that's enough," The king pleaded. "Please, we just need you to rest for now."

"I said I'm not done."

"Wow, these peasants really have an issue with respecting authority," Roselyn stated. That girl never failed to piss me off but there was nothing I could do in that moment.

"It's fine I would've reacted the same way if she was my sister and caused me that much pain," Joel's words stung deep, stomping on the remaining pieces of my heart that were already shattered.

"You've been nothing but a burden to everyone since you were born. In this moment it's embarrassing to even call you my sister. I don't want you anywhere near me so just leave. The healers will do their job and that's all I need."

"Jason please..."

"I SAID LEAVE!"

My body shivered as I got to my feet. I took a deep breath and processed my words to make sure I'd leave with no regrets. I opened my mouth to speak but held my tongue and began walking with my head held high. I knew if I bothered to say anything with him beside me he'd just cut me off again. Judging by the shocked expressions on everyone in the room, there seemed to be two dominant emotions, shock and pity. It was clear that they all witnessed that dreadful scene between my brother and I. I kept walking until I reached the door then faced my brother one last time, making sure he along with everyone else heard me.

"IF I'M EVER IN A LIFE OR DEATH SITUATION AGAIN JUST LEAVE ME TO DIE! The anchor at your feet no longer exists and has finally sunk to the bottom of the ocean leaving you free. We have nothing to do with each other again!"

He weakly tilted his head towards me with the most hideous smile. "Thank you"

CHAPTER 34: I Had No One

I stormed all the way to my room with a fountain of tears running down my face while everyone stared. I promised myself it'd be the last time that anyone would ever see me in my weakest and most vulnerable state. I swung the door to our room wide open and slammed it shut. Our room was emptier than usual, we didn't come with a lot of things but for some reason there was more space. All of Jason's belongings were gone. It seemed that he had already decided that he wanted nothing to do with me before we even had that distasteful conversation.

I flung myself on the bed and buried my face in the pillows and screamed as much as possible to let all my frustrations out but it did nothing to ease my pain. I was also drowsy from my alcohol intake and I looked forward to sleep. It was a temporary escape from the pain. My eyelids were heavy and watered at the attempt to stay open. I eventually gave in after a few minutes providing my body with sleep that it desperately craved.

If my heart had the ability to jump out my chest it would've done so the moment that Susan stormed through my door in excitement.

"Amaris why are you asleep!" She grabbed my sheets and flung them aside leaving me exposed to the coldness of the night. "It's almost eight! You need to get out of bed."

I blinked twice before rubbing my eyes to figure out what was so important but nothing came to mind. "I'd rather stay in bed." There was nothing I craved more than sleep. My head was pounding and if I stared at something for too long I instantly got dizzy.

"So you're not attending the celebration to congratulate your brother? It's expected that all selected members attend, a seat is already reserved for you."

"It's expected but not a command." I stretched my legs and placed my bare feet on the ground. The coldness of the floor caused me to flinch a little since it caught me off-guard. While I struggled to adapt to the temperature of the floor I remembered how Jason would always complain that he felt too warm in temperatures like this.

"I don't want to go," I insisted. Her face melted to a frown before pouting her lips as she stared harshly at me. Surely she could not have been that naive to believe I'll attend a celebration that was all about him after he publicly humiliated me. I questioned whether she even knew what had happened between us a few hours ago. I couldn't help but think everyone in the castle loved to gossip.

"Susan have you any idea what I've been through since the battle was over? Why would I attend a celebration in a room full of people praising my brother, after what happened?"

She stared at me with the most emotionless expression she'd ever worn on her face. Clearly she wasn't impressed with my excuse. "That's exactly why you must go! Don't let everyone believe that the situation broke you. You need to show up and prove that you're not bothered. Who cares that the princess slapped you? Who cares about your brother disowning you? Not you and neither do I." She got so worked up that I thought she was about to start preaching. As motivating as she tried to be, I had to put an end to it immediately to avoid more unrealistic thoughts from entering her mind.

"Susan I'll look like a clown if I show up, someone that has no shame and lacks self-respect. People will find more reason to gossip about me."

"Well give them something to talk about! If you are to be the future queen of Mandora you need to prove that you can overcome situations like this."

Suddenly time froze and I knew exactly what her motive was. Usually I'd be irritated but given the position I was in I couldn't help but laugh. "Susan I have nothing to prove, I have no interest in becoming the future queen. Secondly, I'd hate to be in the presence of my brother right now and I hope you could at least try to understand."

"I understand, but the moment you stop caring about what others think, you'd transform into a graceful intimidating person treated with respect."

I knew there was a possibility of me becoming an intimidating person but saying I'd be graceful were bonus points that I didn't deserve. Luckily for me, there was a sudden knocking at my door which I unexpectedly felt grateful for since it distracted us from that agonizing conversation.

"I'll get the door for you my lady."

I would've approached the door myself but my antisocial mood hindered me. A short elderly man made his way through the door and bowed

"My lady. Congratulations, this is your reward for winning the gamble. Only two persons placed bets on Jason and won a hefty amount of money," he explained. Jason was an underdog, no one in the kingdom knew about him, only the villagers we had altercations with.

"Two people? Who's the other person that believed in my brother?"

"The prince, you would've gotten more but we had to split the award evenly and then give ten percent to the kingdom."

"The kingdom or the royal family?" I questioned him like it was an interview but those were questions I craved answers to. The other questions I had, he wouldn't have had the answers to so I left the rest to myself to think about.

"It's the same thing my lady." He dropped a wooden chest stuffed with silver and a bit of gold at his feet and left immediately, gently closing the door with unnecessary attitude. I turned to Susan for her opinion since I might've missed something

"Did I say something wrong?" She folded her arms and stared at me harshly with an arched brow nervously tapping her feet.

"Why would you ask that? The kingdom or the royal family? Are you serious? What does it matter to you anyway?"

"I was just curious about whether the money actually goes back to the kingdom for better development or if they keep all the riches to themselves without working for it."

"What does it matter? It's like taxes, we all give back to the kingdom no matter how much money we make."

"Ten percent is a lot. Don't you think you're being robbed?"

"Judging by the amount of money you won, you have more than enough to buy land, build a mansion and hire workers.

Or is that not enough for you? Would you like to receive five percent more or something?"

I struggled to understand why she got so defensive. I only asked a simple question. "I'm only asking to understand how things really work in this kingdom. I'm not greedy; I don't even plan to keep the money."

Susan's eyes expanded like an owl, she was lost for words and her face screamed that she needed answers. "I'm giving everything to Jason."

"ARE YOU CRAZY!?" Her unexpected protest had me wondering for a second whether I really was crazy. Maybe it was pride, maybe I was being petty, but I didn't want anything that made it seem like I only gained because of him.

"I get that you're upset but don't let your pride cause you to do something as stupid as this my lady...."

"Don't call me my lady." That phrase irked me, I wasn't anything close to being a noble, at least it didn't feel that way.

"My apologies. Are you sure you want to give everything to Jason? You got in trouble for searching for a job, now you have money that can last you at least ten years and you're willing to throw all that away?"

"Did I work for the money? Jason did everything on his own, all I did was place a bet. The prince owes me money so I don't need this."

"THE PRINCE OWES YOU MONEY!?" Her sudden excitement crawled my blood since I didn't expect her to act that way.

"Lower your voice!" I whispered harshly, no one was near but she caught me off-guard. "The prince made a bet with me. He said if Jason won he'd give me ten pounds"

"T-ten pounds of silver!? That's worth four months of my

pay," her lips trembled and her breaths became heavier trying not to raise her voice. "Wait so what would've happened if you lost?"

"That's the least of my concerns. Right now I feel played with." I didn't expect to be so open about my emotions but I needed answers. "Why would he make a bet with me and make it seem like he expected Jason to lose after he gambled that Jason would win?"

"The prince is a tricky man. The more you try to understand him the more confused you'd be. Don't think about it too much, just brush it off and move on."

I couldn't just brush it off. I sat there thinking quietly for a while. Why would he do something like that? It didn't upset me, but I just wanted to understand him. What was his motive?

"He's playing a game." I was sure of it. I said it out loud hoping that Susan would give a reasonable response.

"Ummm if you say so. I just think he's a tricky man that's still discovering himself." Her response wasn't a satisfactory answer, but I stood my ground and believed my opinion was correct.

"How long have you been working here as a maid?" I asked. I needed some clarity about how much she really knew. Maybe she only discovered just as much as I had to the point where we were both playing a guessing game.

"I've been training to be a maid for three months, after you came they assigned me to you."

"Okay… That's interesting." I wasn't sure that three months was enough to understand the way the prince thinks. I thought that maybe she said the prince was tricky because she couldn't understand him, but I've been here for less than two days and I was already jumping to conclusions as if he was my best friend.

"What's that supposed to mean?" Susan's face screwed up like a prune as if I said something wrong but I ignored it and kept talking to explain myself.

"Three months isn't that much to fully understand someone especially if you don't interact with him often. But you're right I do believe he's a tricky person, I just don't like the idea of being played with."

"Awww you must really be interested in the prince since you're so concerned about understanding the type of person he is," She grinned, almost as if she was blushing and proceeded to speak the most ridiculous things I've ever heard. "I think you should apologize for upsetting him and his family to get back on good terms with him. Jason would soon be one of their favourites since he displayed himself as one of the strongest men in the kingdom. It's time for you to show off how valuable you are too."

I was too stunned to speak, she really expected me to prance around the prince and scream 'pick me'. "Huh!?" My brain malfunctioned the moment her lips stretched into another smile as she clasped her hands in excitement. "After you apologize I can give you some tips on how to flirt."

My skin boiled and my eyes twitched until I started laughing. "I don't plan on staying here for long. I'm not comfortable here and I have no interest in competing for a man. I'll save all the money I earn on my stay here and then move on to live a better life."

Her eyes sharpened harshly with her excitement and joy leaving her body. "So you're only here to make money and leave?" She seemed to be on the road to judgment but I had no issues explaining myself or justifying my mindset.

"Of course, if I'm forced to stay here until the prince rejects me I might as well look at the bright side and settle with the money they're compensating me until they choose to get rid of me."

"You should at least make an effort to get to know the prince and see if there's a chance you two can actually have a connection."

"I don't care to have a connection with him. It's too stressful to even try. I just want to earn the money and leave this place as soon as possible."

Her pale cheeks burned red. "If you leave this place I won't have a job since there won't be anyone available to serve. There are rumors going around that the prince is going to reject a few girls tomorrow based on his first impressions."

My heart raced in excitement and my sudden burst of energy made it difficult to hide my enthusiasm about the rumors. I didn't want to seem inconsiderate about her potentially not having a job but I was hopeful about the idea of finally being able to escape a cage where I was hated by many. "With the prince's money I can find somewhere for us to live together and get back on our feet. Maybe we can even start a business together."

"Why are you so selfish? Can't you at least consider staying for a while? It's not like I'm asking you to marry him."

"No but you're asking me to try to like him just for you to stay in the castle for a longer period of time. Why should I sacrifice my happiness for you in the end?" The tension in the room gradually increased to the point where we spoke aggressively to each other.

"Well maybe you don't have to like him but you should at least try to be a tolerable person that people can like. I heard about the conversation with your brother and how you agitated the royal family by lacking respect for them in public. Maybe if you'd stop being so self-centred people may actually have an opportunity to like you." My jaw dropped and I stuttered, struggling to get my mouth to speak what my brain was thinking.

"Well maybe you should stop being such a leech by depending on me for employment and actually make an effort of your own."

"I'm going to the celebration to support your brother and comfort him from the distress you caused him. At this point anyone that deals with you for too long will need therapy. I can't imagine living with someone like you for so long. I feel so sorry for Jason but at least he finally found a way to escape you." She stormed out my room and slammed my door, hard enough for the ceiling to shake a little.

The heavy pounding of my heart fuelled by anger ached my chest. I sat in silence for five minutes trying to make sense of what just happened. As I reviewed my experiences at the castle, Susan was added to my list as the fifth reason to leave this place. After Jason, she was my biggest reason for feeling so distraught. I felt foolish for thinking she might've been the only person I could trust in this place since I considered her a friend. The sad reality was that I had no one.

I know we agreed to split the money in half but I want you to have everything. I don't need anything from you and neither will I accept anything that you assisted with. I'll be fine without you so congratulations on your big achievement and becoming rich in a day all on your own.

I gave my written letter to the guard at my door and requested that he take the winnings to Jason. I didn't stay up for too long. I had no reason to endure the pain of losing my brother when sleep was an option to hibernate from my problems till morning break.

CHAPTER 35: I CAN'T BREATHE

I couldn't breathe. I took deep breaths but my lungs weren't satisfied and neither was my heart. I held unto my chest helplessly trying to figure out what was causing me so much discomfort. At first I thought I was ambushed because of the piercing pain in my chest. I could've sworn I was stabbed with a fat needle near my heart but there were no signs of injury.

I ran through Jason's room and opened the windows. I couldn't breathe but for some reason I craved the smell of fresh air, thinking it would solve the problem. I stuck my head through the windows and took deep breaths, staring at the sky. This time the moon was full and an army of stars flooded the sky.

I was breathing again, I was calm but I was so drawn to the moon that I could've stayed there for at least an hour. I no longer needed sleep. A sudden burst of energy left me restless and the music from the celebration at the ball was unnecessarily loud. I still had no intentions of going but I didn't want to stay in my room either. I figured a trip to the garden would be nice to sit in the middle of nature and stare at the stars. I was still very much tipsy but a drink while I admire the sky sounded ideal.

"My lady! Are you there?" The voice of a middle aged man left me staggered followed by the heavy knocking at my door. His voice was familiar. "My lady, if you're there I need to speak to you, it's urgent."

"You may come in." It didn't make sense to reject him, I was already bored and he said it was urgent. The moment the door swung open I knew I was about to be annoyed. The same man that informed us about the event came back with the chest in his hands half full and placed it beside my door.

"My lady," he bowed. "Your brother asked me to return the winnings to you with half the amount since you two initially had an agreement to split the money. He also stated that you'd need it the most after tonight."

"After tonight?" His final statement perplexed me as if it was a threat, but then I remembered Susan mentioning something about the prince sending a few girls home tomorrow.

"Yes after tonight, which brings me to the urgent matter at hand. I do remember informing you that there's an event tonight which you were expected to attend. The royal family is displeased by your absence and demands that you make an appearance."

My cheeks were swollen and hot. It took me about two seconds before I gave up and laughed. He stood there with a wrinkled forehead trying to understand what was so funny. I was pissed but amused at the same time but I guess the anger wasn't as apparent as my amusement.

"So are you saying that I have no choice? Isn't the celebration about Jason? I'm sure you know what happened between my brother and I this afternoon. I'm not going."

"If you refuse to go I'm instructed to bring you by force."

This time, my forehead wrinkled. I had a very long day, I didn't want more trouble but I also disliked the idea of walking into a den of lions facing further humiliation from everyone gossiping about me. "Fine."

"If it makes you feel any better, this isn't about your brother. The celebration is currently put on hold."

"On hold? Why?"

"You ask too many questions. Has anyone ever told you that before?" He didn't grant me a chance to answer. "You don't have much time left in this place, even a blind man can see that no one likes you. When someone of authority gives you a command you do as they say. The least you can do is make your last moments here less of a nuisance for everyone. You have five minutes to get dressed, if you're not ready in five I'll drag you out myself and...."

"I'm ready." My hair was a mess after rolling around in my sleep and my red dress was still on since I didn't bother to change before I slept.

"You're going like that?"

I had no reason to enhance my appearance for a bunch of people that hated me. Their opinions of me wouldn't change no matter what I did so it didn't make sense to put effort into pleasing the crowd. My chest tightened again but I ignored it and brushed passed his shoulder.

"Let's go."

The pain increased gradually but I had no idea what the main cause was. I took deep breaths and followed the sound of music from the ball to take my mind off things. I was calm until my guard grabbed me by my arm roughly pulling me closer to his side.

"What are you doing?"

"Just making sure you don't try to escape."

"I'm going willingly so there's no reason for you to be that hostile towards me." He didn't budge but I knew if I tried to pull away he'd get my intentions all messed up thinking I'd try to escape. The journey felt much longer than it should've only because I was uncomfortable and upset. It was only a three minute walk but there was no reason for him to treat me like a criminal. He must've enjoyed every moment of it; treating the most hated individual in the castle with such hostility definitely ignited a spark to his ego.

The moment the door swung open a wind of class, elegance and scents of an elite presence greeted my face. The bright lights and sparkly dresses with complicated yet beautiful designs danced around my eyes almost as if I was stuck in a trance. I quickly gathered my mind together and forced myself to adjust. For once the environment wasn't centred around gold, silver and copper. The colour red dominated the space and served as their theme for the evening. Both the drapes and tablecloths were crimson, but they naturally added some gold with the ropes and patterns.

The lively chatter in the room died slowly but the scornful stares increased rapidly to the point where even the musicians stopped playing. I was clearly not welcomed but yet I was forced to make an appearance. My arm felt numb, reminding me that my guard still held me roughly against my will. The discomfort in my chest was still present but it was the easiest thing to ignore at the moment.

"Now that you're here, please join everyone else on stage," the silence was broken and Logan directed me with his arms leading to the stage where all selected members stood. I was definitely underdressed, no makeup, messy hair and a dress with wrinkles after rolling around in my sleep. Jason was at the far end of the stage to my left at the front so of course I went in the opposite direction. My heavy steps echoed through the room as I climbed the three steps before me cautiously to avoid tripping. Whatever was about to happen I didn't look forward to it, not one bit.

There wasn't much space. Whoever came up with the idea of having forty eight people clumped together for a stupid speech must not have thought things through. I purposefully squeezed through everyone in my path not caring about how uncomfortable I made them feel and placed myself to the very back next to Pia. I didn't notice her until she rolled her eyes at me and muttered whatever crap she said under her breath. She shifted away two spaces to the left with folded arms but I was grateful for the extra space she granted me with more air to breathe.

I took deep breaths, not to calm down but to survive. Breathing became increasingly difficult but I assumed I was claustrophobic even though I never had that issue before. The space was cramped but I was willing to struggle for ten minutes max. I heard light footsteps but I couldn't see the face of the individual until he stood at the front centre of the stage.

"Goodnight everyone, my apologies for the temporary hold of the celebration. We would've been done with this minor intermission by now, but as you can see we had a minor setback," Joel tilted his head at me with a sharpened glare maintaining eye-contact for at least three seconds. I stared back without hesitating, waiting for him to get on with his speech.

"I understand that some of you are aware of the new threat

we're facing against a very powerful enemy. Because of this, Roselyn and I have decided to cut the list of our potential candidates in half…." Everyone gasped and murmuring rumbled through the crowds. I must've had the brightest smile on my face while everyone panicked silently. After letting out a long sigh Joel continued.

"But some of you already knew that." He paused facing us again with a displeased look lasting roughly three seconds before he addressed the audience again. "Since that information has already been leaked, we've decided to make this decision tonight, publicly instead of tomorrow." My jaw dropped instantly, it's one thing to be rejected and see it coming, but this was happening publicly. I wasn't nervous, I was patient, finally granted an opportunity to leave that toxic environment. It was clear to everyone that I secured the spot of their least favourite so I must've been the person that they looked forward to leaving the most.

I observed the looks on everyone else that faced public elimination but deep down I somehow felt sorry for them. I was embarrassed enough during my stay to understand that sick feeling in your stomach that you can't get rid of. What I looked forward to the most was the end of the night where a new journey awaited me once the magic words left Joel's tongue. Roselyn stood at his side with a list of names held slightly under her chest.

"When I call your names please step forward."

CHAPTER 36: ANYTHING FOR MOTHER

Worried expressions plastered the faces of almost everyone on stage as well as the audience. I glanced over my shoulder to peep at Jason's reaction but he was chilling, in fact he seemed bored. He didn't have a reason to be invested with the results after securing a permanent job. He had already accomplished his long term goal much sooner than we both expected. I knew he had extraordinary talent but didn't expect him to be placed in a position to showcase his potential that early.

"Jason Yearwood," his name was the first to roll off the princess' tongue, followed by Joel's announcement of the first girl.

"Pia Lanson."

She made sure to wear a dull smile as she brushed passed me purposefully grazing my shoulder. I stumbled a bit from our unexpected collision but I made sure not to fall, but maybe I should've. The thought ran through my mind but it wasn't worth it. The chances of anyone caring about me if I fell to the floor and cried wolf seemed too unrealistic to take that risk. No one knew for sure who'd be staying; names could've been called to be eliminated from the selection or chosen to stay a bit longer.

I shrugged a little, the discomfort in my chest increasingly graduated to an immense amount of pain. I didn't cry out due to my familiarity with pain but I definitely fidgeted continuously. It no longer felt like a needle was piercing through my chest, this time I could've sworn it was a sword targeting near my heart. My eyes watered but I dared not blink to make it seem like I was crying but I really wanted to. I wasn't bleeding, there were no signs of injury, yet this unbearable pain continued to torment me.

Aside from pain, a vast amount of unmanageable energy mustered within me. I was losing my mind. At this point I was convinced that someone was messing with me and I refused to be a pawn in their circus any longer.

"To hell with this shit." I pushed passed everyone before me and tripped on one of the contestant's dress falling right off the stage. Of course the audience laughed, I've been nothing but a joke to everyone since I got here but I kept making it worse for myself.

"WHAT THE HELL IS WRONG WITH YOU!?" Joel shouted. That must've been the second time he raised his voice at me so aggressively but I had no reason to care. I didn't even look at him, I struggled to get on my feet and noticed a few bloody droplets directly under my nose. My face didn't hit the ground I fell hands and knees first to the floor. I couldn't breathe. I violently coughed but covered my mouth still trying to demonstrate that I at least had a bit of ethics left in me. Blood stained my tongue and the palms of my hands were red. My insides burned like the pits of hell but it kept getting worse.

I didn't understand how it was possible to be boiling with energy while my body felt weak and brittle. Even as all this was happening my brain kept telling me to go outside. Fresh air was what I craved the most but it didn't make sense. Why would fresh air heal me? And would I be forced to stay outside for the rest of my life to survive? If so, I figured that I might as well just die, but the urge to survive saturated my blood. I convinced myself to contemplate about death another day and focus on the main mission ahead; to survive.

I lacked the strength to walk so I crawled. As crowded as the room was, it was easy to crawl my way through since they all scattered anytime I was near. Their reaction was no surprise to me, I looked like I was poisoned or struck with a deadly disease that they feared could be contagious.

The piercing voice of the king demanding for the healers to make an appearance increased my worries. They couldn't help, they wouldn't even know what's happening to me, even I had no clue. I experienced the pain before but it wasn't this drastic, I just wished I knew what caused it. The only thing that I was knowledgeable about was how to stop the pain, but it wasn't enough. The more I thought about it the more hopeless I felt. Less than an hour ago I couldn't breathe but fresh air helped me, "So why am I in pain again if I fixed the problem not so long ago?"

I fought with my thoughts, speaking out loud wasn't an option since it'd only cause another bloody mess and possibly stain my clothes, or even speed up my process to death.

"T-there's at least twenty licensed healers in here... ..somebody help her now!" Joel stuttered through his words, battling with the side effects of shock but he sounded just as demanding as his father. I couldn't allow the healers to hold me back, the balcony was finally in my line of sight with the glass doors already opened. Although it was a good distance away, a smile peeled across my lips as a gentle kiss of outside breeze flustered my cheeks. I took deep breaths, trying to absorb as much fresh air as possible as if it was the cure. I felt much lighter, but the pain was still there.

"Finally!" Joel exhaled. His instant relief worried me. The echoes of heavy footsteps becoming louder by the second confirmed it. The healers were coming. My toes tingled and adrenaline instantly flowed through my veins as a perfect reminder that I still had some strength left in me. The balcony was my only shot at survival. I crawled to my feet, determined that even if I was forced to utilize the last ounce of my strength to make it, I would.

My footsteps were heavy, but I still managed to make it past the crowd. Fresh air became more attainable since I stood only six feet away from the glass doors to enter the balcony. I ignored the voices that called out to me along with the echoes of swiftly approaching footsteps. My strength increased gradually each time I got closer until I was eventually able to run. I took full advantage of the opportunity and ran as fast as I could until I fell to my knees and held unto the silver railings above the cold concrete walls.

I was blessed with a warm sensation of healing as fresh air flowed through my lungs while I took heavy breaths. The blood stains on my dress disappeared, almost as if my body absorbed it all back. "Finally, I made it," I panted, not enough oxygen was restored for me to breathe comfortably.

I flinched by the unexpected touch of a man tripping on

nothing as his body clashed with mine. I couldn't see his face, just his golden blonde hairs that rested under my neck. His face was on my chest. I laid there without moving a muscle, trying not to panic by the inappropriate sight of a man laying above me. I diverted my attention to the sky, for a simple distraction. It wasn't long before his heavy weight left my body with an audience of healers surrounding me.

I was fine. The pain had already left seconds after I stepped foot on the balcony, I didn't need their help. Variations of confused faces stared at me harshly, revealing the scornful looks in their eyes. I laid there silently enduring the hideous view of everyone judging me once again for something they couldn't understand. They murmured among themselves in confusion trying to figure out the best way to handle the situation. I lost interest and just gazed at the sky. I couldn't go back inside, not after everything that happened. I had no proof that I was actually dying. It only felt that way until I stepped outside. It was only a matter of time before they discovered I was fine and try to force me back inside.

I found myself buried in my thoughts gazing at the sky until the noises around me extinguished themselves. The sky shone brighter each second as the moon and its allies of stars lured me in. It enchanted me, nothing else in the world mattered, nothing could've compared to the peace it gave me after what seemed like endless turmoil.

"Closer, I need to be closer," I reached for the sky but the heavens denied me. I didn't know what I was hoping for but I desperately needed an escape. "You lured me in, why reject me now?" My eyes watered without my permission and the bickering of those surrounding me became more apparent. A bright ray of green light shun above me interrupting my moment with the sky.

"My king she's fine." I recognized her voice instantly but confirmed her identity when our eyes met once again. That foolish middle aged woman stood right above me performing her useless abilities on me. The other healers stood behind her in a horizontally straight line as if she was their leader. I didn't care what her position was; I just wanted her to leave my sight. My ears twitched at the multiple swift footsteps approaching.

"What do you mean she's fine!?" The footsteps came to a sudden stop but I noticed the additional shadows of men to my left. Judging by the voice, I already knew that the king was one of them.

"I believe it's a prank from a heartbroken drunkard seeking attention. Look at her, she's fine. There's no traces of blood or any signs of poison."

My eyes twitched uncontrollably while my body fought against my mind to keep still. I didn't notice my arm was still reaching for the sky till she roughly pulled me to my feet. I kept my head low to avoid eye-contact. I wasn't ready to speak. I was still processing my thoughts.

"She even muttered something about rejection, she did all this for show," she nagged. No one could convince me that she didn't have it against me since we first crossed paths.

My lips separated to speak but Jason beat me to it. "Her pride is too high to publicly humiliate herself for a man." My eyelids rose as I turned my neck upwards to see the look on my brother's face after he defended me. Even as I stood before him he refused to look at me maintaining that signature emotionless look as he stared right passed me.

"My son isn't just any man. He's the crowned prince of Mandora, the next heir to the throne. Don't you ever disrespect him like that again." As sternly as he spoke to Jason he kept his eyes on me scanning me from head to toe. "Nothing she does surprises me, she's been nothing but a nuisance since she got here."

His harsh words had no effect on me. I had become accustomed and immune to his scalding remarks about me. At this point his words were just noise that never registered long enough in my brain to have any kind of injurious effect. Joel gently tapped his father's shoulder to break the tension between us.

"Father please, she was obviously in pain...."

"WHAT PAIN!?" I flinched by the King's sudden outburst and took a few steps back. "Look at her! She's moving just fine, there's no blood and Eloise already stated that nothing was wrong with her. What more proof do you need?"

I never would've thought that sly nasty middle aged woman would carry a name as elegant as Eloise.

"Amaris this is your time to explain what just happened." My heart sunk by the concerned look on Jason's face, he was no longer able to hide his emotions. He actually cared, or was maybe just curious. After our last conversation, I preferred that he didn't care at all.

"I- I don't know what to say....." I couldn't give an explanation when I didn't understand what was happening either. Jason let out a heavy sigh and the frost that escaped his lips tickled my nose. I watched anxiously as he bowed before the king, worried about what his next words would be.

"My king, however you decide to deal with this matter I won't object. May I please go back inside? I can't take much more of this."

I couldn't take much more of it either, in fact I chose not to.

"I DIDN'T DO THIS ON PURPOSE!" I raised my voice. There was already an audience so I figured I might as well let everyone hear me. "I WAS LITERALLY DYING!"

"DO NOT RAISE YOUR VOICE AT ME LITTLE GIRL!" The king roared to assert dominance but that wasn't enough to intimidate me after escaping death. His muscle tensed as he took a few steps forward, I must've really struck a nerve but I stood my ground.

"This is obviously my last night here, when the celebration is over you'll punish me for being disrespectful then kick me out the castle. Whatever trouble I caused won't be relevant after a week since I'll make sure you all never see me again."

"It's good that you have a clear idea of what the future should look like," He left me with a satisfactory smile then turned his back on me. "Everyone return to your places, the intermission was long enough," He glanced over his shoulder with a contemptuous gaze. "Except you. Stay here, away from everyone. I don't want you causing any more problems tonight. I'll deal with you when this is over."

His final words were music to my ears, a perfect gift I gladly accepted without complaints. I smiled as I watched them leave, allowing me to have the balcony all to myself. I gently passed my hands over the surface of the balcony's walls while I enjoyed the view. I had a terrible fear of heights but I was comfortable enough to walk to the edge since the walls reached my neck. The likelihood of me falling to my death from the third floor was almost impossible but then I wondered, would that be enough to kill me?

"Closer"

The world froze for a few seconds. I refused to move a muscle and listened attentively. Reality didn't feel like anything real.

All I wanted was peace, but random voices in my head had different plans.

"That's the wind," I convinced myself with good reasoning that I wasn't going mad.

"I SAID COME CLOSER!!" This voice was much deeper and demanding than the last. I spun around in circles helplessly searching for the owner behind the mysterious voice but found nothing but chairs and tables with reserved notices for high ranking nobles. The tiny hairs on my arms stood at attention, giving me the semblance of a reptile. The lights were too bright to provide shadows for anyone to hide.

"Look up!"

The instructions confirmed that it wasn't just the wind speaking. This voice was different, very high pitched and excited like a little child under the age of seven. I raised my head with nothing to lose, temporarily blinded by bright light streaming from the sky. My pupils remained opened, refusing to blink. The intensity could've blinded anyone that stared at it for too long but it didn't sting, it felt warm. My view sharpened on its owner revealing the source of light while slowly drawing me into another trance. The moon had my undivided attention once again.

"Closer!" This time I heard two voices sing together in harmony. Ownership of my body was stolen. I became a slave doing exactly what they said. I firmly planted my hands on the wall and bent my elbows to support my body while I pressed heavily forcing my feet off the ground. My arms wobbled as a proper demonstration of the strength I lacked but I was still a slave determined to serve my masters. I mustered the strength to drag my right leg over the wall and my left leg followed.

"Stand up." As ridiculous as their instructions were, my body

moved on its own with my eyes still fixed to the moon. Although I lost control of my body, my thoughts were still mine and my fear of heights activated. I thought I was done for when I felt the wind caress my cheeks but my body remained still and balanced while I suffered through a silent panic attack.

"It's time."

My lips quivered. The pores on my neck raised and my legs trembled, no longer able to keep still. Endless childhood memories flashed through my mind with teary eyes. "Mom?" I finally sobbed. My mother's voice spoke to me, I was sure if it. Two words, only two words. Whatever it meant I didn't care, I just longed to hear her voice at least once more, determined to do whatever she required of me.

"Amaris!" The piercing cry of my brother calling out my name echoed in the wind. High pitched screams of spectators in the ballroom left my ears as quickly as they entered. Nothing in the world mattered enough to distract me from my mother.

"REMOVE HER FROM THERE AT ONCE!" The king's roar was demanding enough for all soldiers in the vicinity to take action.

"WAIT!" Joel's tone outmatched his father's, fuelled by fear. "I'll go. If we approach her too aggressively she'll…. JASON WAIT!"

His steps were much more distinct than the rest, much faster, too fast. I didn't have much time. Joel followed him with the same speed begging him to slow down. Roselyn began her shady complaints and the queen begged them to be careful. I kept my loyalty to the moon reminiscing on my mother's words willing to obey the next request.

"Relax."

It was her, she spoke to me again. She must've sensed my

sudden panic about the guards trying to separate us. But was it really her? The sudden tug of a man roughly grabbing my arm boiled my blood.

"Amaris!" He disowned me as his sister but couldn't leave me be. I silently snapped with a sharpened glare over my shoulder. He gasped till he choked, falling backwards into Joel's arms.

"Jason what's wrong? Did she do something!?" He slid his arms under Jason's armpits lifting his weight till he got to his feet. Jason revamped his dumbfounded face into a sharp menacing gaze.

"Your eyes, they're blue"

"Huh?" Joel's eyes travelled from my chest to my eyes, expanding till his jaw dropped. "They're sapphire blue...."

"Ignore them, focus on me." I turned my head like a trained puppet obeying its master. Anything for mother.

"You'll be okay, just breathe. We don't have much time."

Branches bellowed harsh whispers with the wind as animals gathered their cries to the sky. The cries of new born babies and toddlers screaming their lungs out pierced my ears. My body burned in solacing heat as trapped energy rumbled within me breaking through all barriers. Thick liquid escaped my nostrils and the smell of blood stained my sense of smell. I was bleeding again. My chest ached like a heart resting in the palm of someone's hand as they squeezed. I was fine with the sudden burst of infinite energy making me restless until immeasurable power slipped in.

I feared the possibility of destruction if I lost control but my abilities were never meant to harm anyone. I felt as though I was suppressing a sneeze from an allergic reaction. The invisible tension of boulders resting over my shoulders increased gradually each second. I couldn't breathe. I coughed relentlessly, desperate to force a passage way of oxygen into my lungs. In return I created the easiest passage way for blood escaping my throat. I couldn't resist the chaos much longer, my strength was fading.

"Relax. Stop resisting and let go...... It's time."

I couldn't resist any more even if I wanted to, power leaked through me till it poured endlessly like a shock wave of warmth devouring the land. My body remained as a broken vessel pouring till it emptied, until I was empty.

"Amaris!"

CHAPTER 37: Resurrected Demon.

I slowly opened my eyes and blinked repeatedly till brightness no longer irritated my eyes. Blonde hairs dangled above my brows with a distinct scent of cologne greeting my nostrils. I'd recognized that scent anywhere. As my vision sharpened I made sure to get a proper look at him this time. His heavy gasp left his jaw wide opened allowing me to figure out whether he brushed his teeth or not. He did. His glasses slowly slipped off his face until it fell on the bridge of my nose.

"M-My Lady! Y- YOU'RE AWAKE!" His excited screams pierced my ear drums while he remained a few inches away from my face. After realizing what he did he fell to his knees stuttering his apologies. "I- I'm so sorry. I-I was checking to see if you were still breathing but when you opened your eyes it scared me. Y-you resurrected like a demon. I was so happy I couldn't control my excitement. And I'm sorry about bumping into you on the balcony, I should've….."

"You've apologized enough, there's no need for another apology. I never really cared for formalities so you can stand up." I tried not to be too harsh but he just wouldn't stop talking. He muttered non-stop while he scrambled to his feet revealing that he was slightly less than six feet tall. After dusting himself off, he faced me courageously but his cheeks burned red with quivering lips.

"H-How can you speak so clearly? It's only been a minute since you've regained consciousness." His eyes sharpened before me as he observed in silence contemplating his next move. I shared the same disoriented look, completely befuddled by his presence. Without warning, he abruptly turned and sprinted to the door. "I need to inform the king that you're awake!" He slammed it on his way out finally granting me the silence I craved since he began talking, but only for a few seconds.

"Quick! Inform Lord Yearwood that his sister is awake!" He whispered harshly at the door with the same panicky energy but incorporated a demanding tone this time with his words.

"She's awake? You're keeping her here in his room right?"

"Y-yes, till we fully examine her to make sure she'll be fine. L-let's go!" Footsteps echoed in two directions until they faded away. *Lord Yearwood?* It caught me off guard to hear my last name called in such a formal manner. I wondered how he felt about citizens bowing before him or clearing a path for him when he passed by. I didn't waste time pondering his new lavish lifestyle for too long. There were many other things I worried about.

My entire body was sore. Attempts to sit upright felt like trying to move a boulder off my back. I groaned in pain with each adjustment made until I was comfortably in a position to observe my surroundings. Flashbacks of the previous night's events played through my mind as I searched for a clearer understanding of my current situation. I covered my mouth with my hand while my jaw remained opened frozen in shock. I remembered feeling as though my body was tearing apart with immense energy ripping through my chest.

"What were those voices in my head? How am I breathing fine again when I'm not outside?" I muttered countless questions to myself but had no answers. I feared the interrogation I was destined to receive when the king found me. THE KING! I remembered his vow to deal with me when everything was over and trembled nervously.

"I need to start packing." My legs wobbled like two flimsy noodles with every step. Maintaining a steady balance was the most difficult thing to do. I continuously stumbled, simply because my legs were too weak to stand on their own, but I managed to brace myself against a wall with whatever strength I had remaining in my arms. I counted twelve photos of Jason and I scattered across the walls. Just us two, our family didn't have the funds to afford a photographer, but the Piersons did. Judging by the rough torn edges of each photo, he made sure to discard the complicated details of our past with the Piersons. We looked happy, well dressed in expensive attire we couldn't afford but our smiles were genuine.

I endured too much pain over the past two days to feel anything positive while I stared blankly at the photos on the wall. Jason had already expressed his true feelings towards me; happy photos of the past couldn't have changed anything. I felt pain, a lot of physical pain; my muscles were sore, my body weak, but what tormented me the most was my stomach. Aside from being hungry, the never ending cramps constantly switched locations in my stomach.

"Oh shit….My period."

Becoming aware of my situation made everything worse. Pain travelled from my stomach, to my back then punishing me with the final blow of cramps in my butt hole all at once. My back dragged against the wall accepting defeat as I crawled into a circle with my arms wrapped around my stomach. I experienced pain of being stabbed multiple times, but nothing was worse than this, simply because I'm forced to endure the pain much longer. My body heals itself much faster than the average human but there was no healing menstrual cycle cramps. My body always viewed it as something that simply needed to happen. Ginger tea was usually my saviour but I had no access to it.

"Where is she!?"

I blinked twice, realizing that I had fallen asleep on the floor with the bed-sheets covering half my body. I remained still, silently listening to the voices in the room. Their presence felt heavy, I was pretty sure there were at least three people but the bedsheets hid my presence for a while.

"I-I'm not sure, she was here five minutes ago, we even had a brief conversation your majesty..."

"I can believe all that, but what I don't understand is why she's not here!"

"Is it that you left my sister alone unsupervised while you ran across the halls screaming that she's finally awake?"

"How's Amaris? Is she doing okay?"

My ears flickered by a woman's voice finally entering the room providing me with the perfect opportunity for help. I realized I was much weaker than I felt five minutes ago, my arm was heavy, refusing to move more than two inches.

"I'm here." It shocked me that I had more than enough strength to carry a conversation but the effort left me exhausted.

There was a brief moment of silence followed by swift footsteps swarming my way. My eyes were half open but somehow the royal family, Jason and that geeky healer made it through my line of sight. Jason stooped before me, probably about fifteen inches away but this time with a face of expressions I could read. His eyes exposed a mixture of worry and anger, I still couldn't figure out what was going through his head.

"Why are you on the floor?"

"I need to speak to the queen. Alone." I panted. Breathing wasn't an issue, air flowed through my lungs easily but I couldn't bear my cramps much longer. Everyone exploded in a minor uproar, except the queen, her cheeks flustered red and she covered her mouth with the palm of her hand.

"Amaris I know you don't want to speak to us right now but you need to be reasonable." Jason couldn't even look at me when he said those words, all the more reason to ignore them all. Whatever Roselyn said had already entered my ears and left without my brain taking note of it. Her voice was literally background noise. The king responded just as any king fuelled by pride would.

"I am the king, you cannot dismiss me. You cannot dismiss anyone here actually, except Eliot the healer." He took his attention off me for a second and faced Eliot. "I expect you to stay."

I began cold sweating around my forehead and my eyes were still half open but I just had to push through. "Please your majesty," I pleaded with the queen. The clacking sound of her heels echoed with each step as she approached me slowly. My eyes opened to its fullest potential after the queen entered my personal space and sat beside me on the floor.

"What are you doing!?" As demanding as the king sounded

she ignored him and leaned over my shoulder.

"Tell me what's wrong."

I wasted no time and whispered my situation in her ear. With a brief gasp of shock she got to her feet faster than she sat down. "Everyone please give us ten minutes, I promise it won't take longer than that."

"Mom what!?" Joel blurted. I almost forgot his presence since he barely spoke.

"Everyone out! I won the bet against your father didn't I? And please, send for two maids and a cup of ginger tea." With those words there was silence for a few seconds with a bit of agitated murmuring from the king.

"Oooh, ginger tea. Yeah you don't have to tell me twice, I'll be back when you say it's okay." Jason gave in. He knew exactly what was happening the moment ginger tea was mentioned.

"I'll be right behind you," Joel said on his way out. I assumed he figured it out since he didn't put up a fight to stay. Roselyn followed behind them quietly while Eliot ran out announcing that ginger tea was needed.

"Am I missing something here?" the king asked. His forehead was a wrinkled mess while his arched brow indicated that he had no idea.

"Please, it's only ten minutes." The queen negotiated. I remained quiet. A debate between the king and queen wasn't something I think anyone would want to involve themselves in. His muscles tightened after folding his arms expressing his dissatisfaction.

"Is ginger tea code for something? I will not leave."

"I said ten minutes!" She raised her voice, much more determined than he was. The atmosphere slowly turned into a staring contest, I stared at the powerful couple while they stared intensely into each other's eyes to see who'd break first. It was just us three, hierarchy and authority no longer mattered in their husband and wife argument. I watched in awe as the queen stood her ground to defend me. I knew I'd be punished later for whatever happened last night but she made me feel safe.

"Fine." The king finally gave in leaving us with a dramatic exit by slamming the door.

"Don't worry about him, you'll be fine. Let's get you cleaned up."

CHAPTER 38: Leave?

Fifteen minutes, that's how long it took to get me cleaned up with a cup of ginger tea in my hand. It would've been ten if I hadn't stained Jason's bed sheets with blood, I was almost embarrassed but I suffered too much pain to care. Luckily for me his blanket hid the stains during their first encounter with me after they discovered I was awake. Surprisingly, the queen assisted the maids with changing the bed sheets working much faster than they did.

I knew she wasn't born into royalty so she already had the experience but I didn't expect her to be that good at it. My physical issues were solved, allowing a path for the conversations I tried to avoid the moment I opened my eyes.

"There's no need to worry, she just needs to rest and eat. The fact that she had enough strength to talk and crawl out of bed already shows vast improvement."

"Is she well enough to have a conversation now or does she need more rest?" The king directed his gaze at me making sure that we locked eyes. His eyes were cold. The longer that I stared the more intimidated I felt, so I broke eye contact by rotating my neck for a brief stretch.

"YES! She can definitely speak your majesty," Eliot confirmed.

"Good, then leave us. She's already occupied with her ginger tea, she can eat something when we're done."

As Eliot was on his way out his sulking expression matched mine. I couldn't understand why he'd want to stay but I had many reasons to not look forward to speaking with any of them, except maybe the queen. I sipped my tea while they surrounded me quietly; Joel, Jason and Roselyn to my left, the queen and Logan to my right. The king remained exactly where he was, directly in front of me, gently guiding his fingertips over the bed frame near my feet. The silence was loud but I knew its temporary bliss would end as soon as Eliot closed the door on his way out.

To take control of the conversation for the least devastating results, I knew I had to speak first so I grabbed hold of that opportunity as soon as Eliot left

"I'm sorry for all the trouble I've caused, especially last night. I promise I'll pack my things and leave before the day is over, you'll never have to worry about me again. I'm also willing to…"

"Last night?" The king interrupted with furrowed brows and squinted eyes. "Nothing happened last night. You were fast asleep in here."

My brain stopped processing information after the king's statement left me confused. I knew I wasn't crazy. The last thing I remembered was Jason's celebration and standing on stage waiting to be sent home. I remembered talking to the moon, I must've looked like a freak but I surely couldn't forget coughing blood. But what I couldn't remember was how I got in this bed.

"Huh?" I needed answers. The more I thought about it the more nothing made sense.

"Of course she'll think the celebration was last night, she just woke up. I'm surprised she even remembered it," Joel chimed in. His neck tilted till our eyes met, staring a little longer than I expected him to, until his eyes squinted with the resemblance of his father. "What do you remember?"

"Yes let's start there!" The excitement in the king's voice worried me, he was eager to talk about it the moment I opened my eyes.

"Take your time, it's okay if you don't remember everything right now. You were unconscious for two days so don't feel too pressured," the queen interjected. Her kind words almost made me let my guard down but I knew the king was out to get me so I had to be as strategic as possible.

"But still tell us everything you remember with as much details as possible," Jason insisted. Logan and Roselyn remained quiet but all eyes were fixed on me with intimidating stares as if they were all waiting for me to say something wrong. The tension in the room was thick enough to be sliced in half with a knife but I couldn't remain quiet forever.

"Would you like me to start from the celebration or before?" I noticed Logan grinning in the corner after I asked my question. Secretive glances were shared among the men as if they had already discussed this topic.

"I knew it," Logan muttered under his breath. "Start with before." My heart was racing all I could do was tell the truth and hope for the best.

"I cried myself to sleep after the competition was over…." It pained me to mention that part but I needed to gain a bit of sympathy for a lesser punishment. I took a quick glance of their faces to read the room before I continued. They all looked guilty, avoiding eye contact with me as if they felt sorry. I accomplished my goal so I talked freely. "I don't remember what time I woke up but I couldn't breathe and my chest was hurting. I thought I was going to die and felt trapped inside so I ran to the windows in Jason's room. After a few breaths of fresh air I was fine, then the guard at my door told me that you demanded my presence." I paused and looked at the king again, this time he nodded his head, intrigued and waiting on me to continue. That sympathetic appearance of his didn't last five seconds.

"Continue."

"On my way there it felt like a needle was piercing through my chest but I ignored it and kept moving. When I made it on the stage the pain increased but I sucked it up until I couldn't breathe. That's when I tried to leave and fell off the stage. I think someone was controlling me. I heard voices in my head. I don't even know what caused me to cough blood but I suffered a pain I've never felt before. When I made it to the balcony I was breathing fine again and the blood on my clothes disappeared." I paused for a moment, a little embarrassed by my words. I sounded ridiculous. "I know I sound crazy but please believe me."

"We believe you," Joel assured me.

"Continue." The king spoke so plainly making me wish I knew what was going through his mind.

"I even heard the voice of my mother, but she's dead so it couldn't be her. Everything the voice told me to do I did. That's why I climbed the wall, someone or something was controlling me. Power that wasn't mine rumbled inside me, I felt like I was dying the longer I fought to keep it in…."

"That explains why it took you so long to heal," Jason mentioned, following with a heavy sigh.

"I'm so sorry for ruining such an important event." I wasn't sorry, but I hoped an apology would make the king reconsider his intended punishment for me, whatever it was.

"So that's it?" The king asked? I didn't know what else to say, he seemed displeased as if I was hiding something. They weren't the only ones seeking answers; now was my opportunity to get some clarity for myself.

"Did I fall off the balcony? Is that why I took so long to wake up?" Their heavy sighs and gentle frustrated taps to their foreheads confirmed that I was dealing with something much more serious than I expected.

"So you don't remember floating in the sky?" Joel asked.

"In the sky? The moon told me to come closer but I didn't fly, I climbed the wall." My pores raised by the king's swift approach towards me.

"So you connected with the moon?"

I needed time to think, hints were given but not enough to grant me understanding of what really happened. "What's going on?" I didn't enjoy playing the guessing game when everyone around me were witnesses to what happened. "I know I'm in trouble so can someone just tell what happened and what's the consequence for my actions? I'll gladly accept any punishment, then I'll pack my things and leave."

"Amaris your eyes were blue and so was the moon while you floated in the sky," Jason explained. I avoided eye contact with everyone and just stared at the blank wall before me. "Amaris I know you're scared but you're the only person I know that's capable of performing such a miracle."

"I'm not capable of doing anything great, don't forget I'm only a burden!" I snapped, but only out of fear. I didn't want to be seen as a miracle worker, people would expect too much from me. I'd never be able to do anything freely.

"I knew she was gonna be petty," Roselyn spat. The queen sighed whilst rubbing her forehead. Logan dropped himself onto one of Jason's red sofas while Joel's lips separated to speak but failed to release the words after his father beat him to it.

"Amaris!" The king raised his voice, "Now is not the time for your immature behaviour." I found it rather insulting that he thought this was all a game for me, I was terrified. A conversation about punishment for all the trouble I've caused would've been much better.

"Everyone please relax, she's in a state of shock right now. It's too soon to even have this conversation." The queen chimed in. I always admired her peace making qualities. Without her the kingdom probably would've crumbled. She was the glue that held everyone together.

"I get what you're saying but we're running out of time," Logan mentioned, including himself in the conversation. As comfortable as the sofa was he couldn't just sit back as the King's right hand and say nothing on the matter. "The Piersons left us with another letter and we're at a great disadvantage. War has already begun, this is the right time."

"Can we please forget what happened that night?" I pleaded. "I just want to pack my things and leave."

"LEAVE!?" The king questioned before bursting into laughter along with Logan.

"It was obvious that I was going to be sent home when the selection was cut in half. There's no reason for me to still be here so of course I'm ready to leave."

"Amaris you were on my list to stay," Joel admitted. The queen blushed and covered her mouth. I wished I knew what was going through her mind.

"Now I'm concerned about your taste in women," the king stated. I felt insulted but it wasn't worth responding to.

"I chose to keep her a bit longer for information. As Logan stated, we're at war with the Piersons and she has a past with them. I'm not going to risk losing whatever information she has."

"So does that mean I can't leave?" I asked.

"Welcome to the second stage of the selection."

About the Author

Afiya Clarke was born September 4th 2001. Since the age of 9 she fell in love with creating her own worlds with just pencil and paper. She attended Maracas SDA primary school then moved on to St. Joseph college at the age of 12. Even though she was a science student in high-school, she moved on to achieve a degree in HR at the University of the Southern Caribbean and graduated in 2023 at the age of 21. Over the years she never stopped writing, in fact she had a few stories of her own that she rejected to publish. In March 2024, she wrote a script and hosted a play called Rescue Me at UWI LRC Auditorium. She continues to write in hopes of becoming a full time-author one day.

Follow me on tiktok @Afiyawrites and Instagram @afiya._writes if you wish to witness behind the scenes of my characters' journey.

Made in the USA
Columbia, SC
27 January 2025

52512922R00198